There is in every true woman's heart a spark of heavenly fire, which lies dormant in the broad daylight of prosperity but which kindles up and beams and blazes in the dark night of adversity.

—WASHINGTON IRVING

Chapter One

The Presidio of San Francisco
July 1900

Beth Hammond walked briskly along the outer wall of the Presidio of San Francisco toward the Lombard Gate. It was only a quarter to six in the morning, but she hurried as she was due to begin her shift at six a.m. She was one of twelve contract nurses employed by the US Army to care for its wounded and sick soldiers.

It was a twenty-minute walk from her home at Divisadero and Washington Streets to the Presidio, the army's largest western fort, and Beth used that time to wake up and prepare herself for the day. To her left, she could see the Pacific Ocean and the Golden Gate, the entrance to San Francisco's famous harbor. Across the strait, the fog hung over the Marin hills and flowed near the surface of the ocean. It would be noontime before it faded away. Beth didn't mind the fog because it would always remind her of the night she'd finally confessed her past to Kerry in Golden Gate Park and their journey together had truly begun.

At the still-under-construction hospital, the overnight staff was preparing to leave as the day shift arrived. Chief Nurse Marjorie Reynolds would already be at work, distributing work assignments for the day and no doubt interrogating the night shift as to the status of the sickest patients. Beth thought fondly of Marjorie and her exacting ways. Thank goodness she was up to snuff and she and Marjorie got along quite well. They also had more in common than just nursing.

Beth arrived at the infectious ward, where she had asked for and was granted assignment, another advantage of being trusted and liked by Marjorie. She received the posting she wanted and what she considered herself best suited for. She put her shawl away, straightened her white cap, and went off in search of Marjorie.

A number of boys were occupying the beds. The Philippines war was still going on, and the soldiers who'd been wounded or who had taken sick were sent back to the Presidio to recover. Beth had served in Manila on the hospital ship *Golden Gate* the previous year and knew from experience that the vast majority of the hospital's occupants were suffering from some tropical disease rather than war wounds. Although she didn't welcome their suffering, she preferred to care for the sick soldiers rather than the wounded ones. Ever since completing her nurse's training, Beth had been fascinated by infectious disease. In fact, she had become so expert at spotting the symptoms and understanding the treatments of cholera, typhoid, malaria, yellow fever, and the various parasitic infections common in the Far East, her friend and mentor, Dr. Addison Grant, had encouraged her to consider becoming a doctor. His suggestion intrigued her, but she didn't feel she was qualified and the prospect was daunting. She had only a high-school education and a nursing certificate. Besides, her other close friend and mentor, Marjorie, was dead set against it.

Beth was of two minds about the idea. Though she was intelligent and capable, the prospect was so far out of her experience, it terrified her. With the distraction of work and day-to-day life, she scarcely had time to contemplate it. The only other person with whom she was close, her sweetheart Kerry, was actually no help at all. Kerry only said, "You should do what will please you, what will make you happy."

Ah, Kerry, her mischievous, handsome, wonderful Kerry. Beth called her "sweetheart" because that was what she was. They were in love. Beth had come to recognize the true nature of their relationship the previous year, though it wasn't something she'd expected to have. She had no desire to marry or to have a family, and she never questioned that fact. She hadn't known what she truly desired until Kerry came along and showed her. It was a revelation; it was a miracle. Beth didn't really understand it. But she'd concluded it

A SPARK OF HEAVENLY FIRE

By the Author

Awake Unto Me

Forsaking All Others

A Spark of Heavenly Fire

A Spark of
Heavenly Fire

by
Kathleen Knowles

2014

A SPARK OF HEAVENLY FIRE

© 2014 By Kathleen Knowles. All Rights Reserved.

ISBN 13: 978-1-62639-212-0

This Trade Paperback Original Is Published By
Bold Strokes Books, Inc.
P.O. Box 249
Valley Falls, NY 12185

First Edition: November 2014

Credits
Editor: Shelley Thrasher
Production Design: Susan Ramundo
Cover Design By Gabrielle Pendergrast

Acknowledgments

Thank you to Bold Strokes Books, Radclyffe, and the entire production team, and especially, thanks to my editor, Shelley Thrasher, for teaching me to write better, smoother sentences and catching my dumb factual mistakes.

As always, I got loving support from my spouse, Jeanette; my sister, Karin; and my friend, Kent.

Dedication

To Jeanette,
Without whom nothing would be possible

wasn't important to understand why she wanted her life and her future tied to a young woman her own age who was masculine in appearance but so very female in her emotions. Her pulse raced as she thought of Kerry. Her reaction was inexplicable, but there it was.

She spotted Marjorie at the far end of the ward, standing with another nurse by the bed of one of the soldiers. Beth could tell by her gestures that she was displeased, though she couldn't hear what was being said. The nurse looked dismayed as Marjorie spoke to her in the low voice she practiced when in the ward. Marjorie could convey bottomless fury in a whisper. Beth felt sorry for the nurse, who'd surely made some simple but ridiculous error.

At last, Marjorie strode over to Beth, who was checking their supplies and considering whether she needed to go to the quartermaster to replenish anything. Beth was vigilant about such things because Marjorie hated to be caught shorthanded, especially of something vital.

"Good morning, Nurse," Marjorie said. She was formal during work but would relax during their social times.

"Good morning, Chief. Would you like for me to do anything special today?"

"Yes. Please watch Andrews as she charts. I found some gaps in the records and told her to apply herself more thoroughly to recording the patients' vital signs in an accurate fashion. I find her work haphazard."

"Yes, ma'am." Beth kept her voice level and hid her anxiety. It made other nurses uneasy when Marjorie instructed her to check them, but she did it because Marjorie asked.

"And Nurse?" Marjorie spoke as Beth was about to leave. Beth turned around and waited.

"I'd like you to take dinner break with me. Twelve thirty outside in the pavilion."

"Yes. Gladly."

❖

Beth and Marjorie prepared themselves a simple meal of coffee, soup, and bread and carried it outside. All the nurses were responsible for cooking and serving the meals to the patients so the hospital had a kitchen. The staff paid a small sum to partake of the food supplies. What could Marjorie want to talk about? When she asked for company like this, she usually had some confidence to impart.

Like Beth, Marjorie was partnered with another woman. Another nurse, in fact, who was currently working at the French Hospital. That had been one of the primary reasons she and Beth had become close friends. Beth had discovered that Marjorie and Florence were lovers when they'd all been on duty in the Philippines, and that discovery had pointed Beth toward her epiphany about Kerry. They hadn't discussed it exactly, but Marjorie had been present one day when Kerry came to visit Beth at the hospital, and without saying much, Beth was able to let Marjorie know she was aware of their similarity. Marjorie had responded by taking Beth into her confidence and they'd become intimate friends.

They were seated on the outdoor pavilion when Marjorie asked, "I was curious if you intend to stay here at the Presidio General Hospital? I know our employment isn't entirely stable, but our contracts will most likely be renewed next month. I expect that at some point we will be made permanent. One of my classmates, who's close to Dr. McGee, says the doctor has assembled a committee to lobby Congress to create a permanent army nurse corps. It may be some time before that happens, but I'm sure it will come to pass."

"I fully intend to continue working here for the present. I'm not sure of the future."

"Surely you're not still entertaining the idea of trying to become a doctor?"

Beth's face heated. She and Marjorie had discussed this topic a few months previously, and Marjorie's reaction hadn't encouraged Beth to bring up the subject again. They'd become closer because of their private lives, and their working relationship was harmonious, yet Beth hadn't broached the idea again mainly because she and Kerry needed to find new lodging, which had distracted her. Why had Marjorie brought it up? She didn't want to argue.

"I haven't decided anything. I've been busy." Beth hadn't confided in Marjorie about the recent traumatic events in her life. It was enough that Marjorie was in on her secret about Kerry.

"Well, you hadn't spoken of it again, but I wanted to be sure you'd abandoned the idea." She spoke in a chill, dismissive tone.

Beth didn't feel Marjorie had any right to dictate to her. Incensed, this time she spoke her mind. "Marjorie, you disdain this idea, but I'm not certain where your hostility comes from. It's not unheard of for women to be doctors, and it does seem to me that, given the proper training, women would make very good ones. Why do you cling to convention so tightly when you're unconventional?"

Marjorie lifted her chin a bit and her gray-blue eyes darkened, as did her expression. She clearly understood what Beth was referring to.

"My connection to Florence isn't in the same category at all. It's my private business. No one in the world but you and Kerry know about it, and it must always remain so. You can't choose to be discreet about being a doctor."

Beth pondered Marjorie's self-delusion. It was unfortunate, but given Marjorie's nature, Beth would probably never convince her otherwise, but she didn't have to agree.

"Women are changing, and yes, some can become doctors as well. Dr. Grant told me that some women run an entire clinic for women and children right here in the city! If I were to choose to make that my life's work, I hope you would see it positively and applaud me for it. As a true friend." Sad, Beth hoped her sincerity would somehow reach Marjorie.

"Elizabeth, I don't want to see you hurt or castigated by society. That's what would happen. I'm sure of it." Marjorie, who'd been stiff, relaxed, and she looked concerned as she patted Beth's hand, an unusual gesture for her.

"You can't be sure of that, Marjorie. Though if I choose this path, I'd want your blessing, even if I can't have your full approval."

"I couldn't tell you I could stand with you in such a decision. It's entirely unwise. I'd never forgive myself if I allowed you to pursue something that would harm you. If you don't understand this, then it's best we keep our relationship on a strictly professional level." Now she sounded and appeared wounded.

Beth was stunned and tried to get Marjorie to look at her. "I suppose so. I won't try to persuade you otherwise, but I'll miss our talks." Beth wasn't surprised at how sad she felt. Being able to share with Marjorie had comforted her. What a shame.

"I'm sorry this has come between us. I so wish it could be different."

"I do too." Marjorie wouldn't meet her gaze but sat looking down at a spot on the pavilion floor. Without another word, they gathered their eating utensils and returned to the kitchen, cleaned up, and started caring for patients again.

❖

When Beth returned home in the early evening, the house was empty and quiet. Kerry wouldn't be home until midnight or later, and their landlady Mrs. Thompson was clearly out somewhere. Beth picked up the mail from the floor under the door slot. Shuffling through it, she was surprised to find a letter from Addison Grant and opened it eagerly.

Addison, Kerry's guardian, had been a friend of her father and had taken her in after his death. He was also one of Beth's instructors during her nurse's training and the reason she and Kerry had met. She was quite fond of him, and they hadn't seen each other since the previous year when his wife Laura had forced him to ask them to find other housing. Kerry had been very upset and had become estranged from Addison in spite of Beth's attempts to get her to forgive him. Kerry was more than a little stubborn, Beth thought fondly. She read the letter.

My dear Beth,

I hope this note finds you well. Please share its contents with Kerry. I wanted to ask you both over for supper a week hence. I have something important to impart. Please assure Kerry that Laura will not be present. You may respond by telephone if you like. The City and County Hospital has newly installed a telephone at the main entrance, and you may reach me that way. I trust the Presidio General Hospital has followed suit. I look forward to hearing from you.

My goodness. First, Beth would either have to leave a note for Kerry to awaken her, or she would have to wake up Kerry at five in the morning. She cursed their work schedules and decided it was best to leave the choice up to Kerry.

The next morning, when Beth awoke, she found a note telling her to awaken Kerry.

She looked at her for just a moment. She was peaceful in sleep, innocent looking and sweet. The conscious Kerry was anything but innocent, but she was still sweet and loving. She patted her shoulder a few times and whispered her name until she stirred and turned over. When she finally opened her dark eyes, she grinned. Her short, springy brown hair was disordered

"Bethy."

"I'm sorry to wake you, my love, but I have to ask you something."

Kerry stretched and groaned. "It must be important."

"It is. I wish the Palace had a telephone so I could call you." The Palace Hotel had one telephone in the front lobby, which kitchen staff was forbidden to use.

"I'm awake. Is everything well?" She looked concerned.

"Yes, of course. Addison invited us to supper next week."

Kerry flopped back on the pillow and sighed deeply, apparently experiencing an internal conflict. Finally she said, "If you wish to see him, Beth, go ahead. But I'll be at work."

Beth frowned and pursed her lips. "Chef would let you have one evening off if you ask him. We haven't seen Addison for months." She sounded cross but couldn't help it.

"We're very busy just now."

The Palace Hotel restaurant was *always* busy, and Kerry was making an excuse.

"Very well. I'm sorry I had to awaken you. Please go back to sleep. I'll set the alarm." Beth reached for the big clock that sat on her bedside table.

"Beth, don't be angry." Kerry grabbed her arm.

Beth could never truly be angry at her. She wound the clock. "I'm not angry. Just disappointed."

She set the alarm clock down, smoothed Kerry's hair back from her forehead, kissed her, and got out of bed. Kerry watched her as she put on the heavy white cotton nurse's uniform she wore every day.

❖

They sat together, just the two of them at the dining-room table. Everything looked much the same, yet somehow the house had an unlived-in feel. A dull-appearing woman in a drab gray dress served their supper. Addison was chipper and greeted her with his usual warmth, but he had a distracted air as though he wasn't quite sure of something.

After the strange, silent woman finished serving, she disappeared and Addison looked closely at Beth. "You seem well. Life must be agreeable in your new home with Kerry?"

"Yes, very much so. We have a pleasant room in a home owned by a widow. It's on Divisadero Street, conveniently between our places of employment." Beth took a sip of water.

"We're saving to buy our own house." She felt shy saying it out loud, but Addison was a friend.

He raised his eyebrows. "I'm sorry Kerry couldn't join us."

"She had to be at work this evening." There was a pause.

Beth was chagrined by her small but significant lie, and before she could think she said, "After these several months, she's still unhappy and angry with you."

"I understand. I'm sorry for that. Things are different now, though, and I wanted to tell you Laura has gone back her parents for good. I hope."

That was what made the house feel so unlived in. Beth was curious, though it was none of her business. Addison was merely stating a fact. But almost as though he could read her mind, he said, "She and I concluded we could no longer live as man and wife. Divorce is out of the question. She was quite clear about that. I don't know what she's telling family and friends back in Missouri, but it doesn't concern me. I'm content here by myself. Mrs. Evans cooks and keeps things tidy. That's all I need."

Beth was shocked. How much of his nonchalance was real or feigned? Men always needed women's care, and it couldn't be easy for him to have to fend for himself. On the other hand, Laura was such a nasty and domineering woman, it was perhaps better this way.

"Beth, I wanted especially to find out what you're thinking about medical school."

"Uh. I'm not sure. Still. It seems so daunting."

"Yes, I know. But what concerns you the most?"

"I don't know, really. For one thing, I haven't gone to college. Cost, for another. I'd need to leave my nursing position. And the, um, the problem of being a woman. You remember Marjorie Reynolds, don't you? She thinks it's a terrible idea. She says women are nurses and men are doctors, and that's the way of the world."

"Let's take these things one at a time. Tell me what you think, and then we'll examine these various obstacles."

"I'm not sure. I'm flattered that you consider me intelligent, but I've never thought about that. I'm happy being a nurse. At times, especially with doctors other than you, I feel deeply how little they appreciate us and how they dismiss our abilities. Occasionally, I have to bite my tongue when one makes a mistake. I haven't seen one cause the patient irreparable harm yet, but…"

Addison nodded seriously. "Oh, the things I could tell you. Bah. But you're far more capable than most men I know. Look at it like this. As a nurse, you're wasting your talents. As a doctor, you'll care for patients, but you'll use your head as well as your heart. I'm convinced women are even better suited to be doctors than men. They're empathetic, sensitive, gentle. That combined with intellect is a magnificent marriage."

"I truly appreciate your confidence. Perhaps I could learn to share it, but what about the other things I mentioned?"

"Medical school isn't that costly. You can pay for it on time or receive a loan. Don't let finance stop you. I can help prepare you for the examinations. I know exactly what they'll expect. You'll need to study for a long time, and study hard, but you're capable. As for Nurse Reynolds, she's a fine nurse and manager and a hard worker, but she lacks imagination. Some doctors would say that's why she's a good nurse, but not I. Please don't let your respect for her prevent you from following your heart."

"You're right. I have to find my own way. I'll continue to think on it and speak with Kerry. But what of you? How is the City and County Hospital?

"Ah, like it always is. The San Francisco city fathers don't see fit to spend sufficient money to care for its ailing citizens. But I can't complain. We don't have a shortage of patients." He laughed and took a bite of food, then looked thoughtful as he chewed. "I've been asked to consult on a fascinating case, one that could have far-reaching consequences. The Department of Public Health asked me to attend an autopsy and examine tissue from a Chinese man who died in the hospital a few days ago. They suspect the plague. Rather the public-health officer, Dr. Kinyoun, suspects it. He told me there have been a couple of cases already, but the powerful political forces in Chinatown, as well as the city itself, vehemently deny such a possibility. I examined some tissue samples and found *Yersinnia pestis* bacteria. You remember we had a few cases of bubonic plague in Manila."

"Yes, it was alarming, but when we isolated them, some folks recovered and it didn't spread."

"Certainly. It's not one hundred percent fatal, and it's not passed from person to person. It requires the bite of a flea who acquires it from the infected rat. Dr. Kinyoun and I had a long discussion. He thanked me for my service and swore me to secrecy. I doubt if that will be the last case."

"Do you think it'll reach into the general San Francisco population? How many cases have been reported? Does Dr. Kinyoun know of any connection between the people?" Beth was eager to learn more. It was just this sort of problem she and Addison had worked on together in the Philippines.

"I don't know, since I merely confirmed this one fatality, but you see, Beth. This is what I mean when I say you're born to be a doctor. You could apply your abilities to this very type of problem. The spread of infectious disease, especially within a large city, is one of the most important areas of study right now. In regard to public health, the British have shown us the way. Not everyone believes in the germ theory yet, but all those who have their heads on straight do. You can be part of something bigger. It's fine for you to nurse the sick soldiers at the Presidio, but you could be and do so much more!"

Addison's passion made Beth see herself in the hospital wards with him, solving the mysteries of diseases they both didn't yet know of, contributing to science and to the public good. When Addison talked about it, it seemed irresistible, even possible.

"Addison, I see your points, and when I talk to you I believe I could do anything. I need to think about what you said, and consult Kerry, of course."

Addison waved his hand but he was glowing. "Of course. It's not a decision to take lightly and will involve great sacrifice for you and for Kerry, but I'm confident it's the right path. I'll help any way I can. Sorry. I've distracted you so much, you've stopped eating. Come, finish your supper before it gets cold, and then we'll have coffee in the parlor. I believe Mrs. Evans has made compote for dessert." His expression indicated the compote might not be too delectable.

Beth laughed and took a forkful of mashed parsnip. It wasn't as tasty as Kerry's version of the dish but was edible. Addison could somehow eat while he talked, and she didn't notice or sense any lack of manners. He beamed at her and sipped his wine. They discussed hospital gossip and various pieces of medical trivia until Addison drove her back to Mrs. Thompson's house.

❖

"Hey, Kerry, you daydreaming?"

Hearing Davey's voice brought Kerry suddenly out of her reverie. She blinked and pulled her mind back into the present, into the hot, noisy kitchen of the Palace Hotel restaurant and away from what had been a combination of memory and fantasy in which she and Beth were swimming in the Sutro Baths.

"I hear you, Davey. Say it again?"

"I was trying to tell you to fire two salmon and two trout. I got worried when you didn't yell back like usual." Kerry was a griller and Davey was the sous chef. She had to shout back orders to him so he'd know she'd heard and understood amid the controlled chaos of dinner service. It was Saturday night, which usually meant a full house and nonstop activity. Kerry generally enjoyed the challenge of keeping up and didn't fear work or Davey, not that he was a bad sous chef.

They were friends who'd conspired together to rid the kitchen of the previous sous chef, who all the cooks hated. Compared to him, Davey was a prince, although one with no education and bad grammar. Kerry didn't mind that. He was a good, honest man and as kind to her as he could be. He'd been the first cook in the kitchen to stop the cruel harassment she'd been subjected to when she began to work as a dishwasher some six years previously.

"Two salmon, two trout!" she shouted, and dribbled oil and threw spices on all the pieces of fish before slapping them on her grill. She stepped back as the oil hissed and spat in the fire. Her hands and forearms were dotted with tiny burn scars from the fire spits. Along with the knife cuts, they were badges of honor that showed she was a real cook. She loved all of it: the burns, the shouts, the aching in her feet after standing seven hours straight. Most of the time, she was able to avoid even having to stop to go to the outhouse. She was determined to never appear weak, to never falter, and she never did.

The smallest mistake would cause Chef Henri to toss her out of the kitchen in an instant. He didn't tolerate many errors at all from the men, and she was convinced that one on her part would be her downfall. It hadn't happened yet, and she was determined to keep it that way. But she would have to pay attention and not get caught napping again

It was a hard thing, though, the long days and even weeks going by without ever speaking to Beth, let alone anything else, anything physical. They were each allowed only one day a week off, and it was almost never the same day. Kerry had to work as much as possible to make money. This was what had sent her briefly out of reality.

Their favorite thing to do together was to ride out to the beach and rent bathing suits and play in the waters of the Sutro Baths. They would swim and frolic together, buy some food at one of the vendors along the hillside, and then return home, pleasantly tired but aroused. They'd fall into bed, make love, and then go to sleep sated and content.

It was long past time for them to do any of those things, Kerry thought as she deftly scooped up each filet with her spatula and turned it over to finish its cooking. In the meantime, another order came in and she started two more pieces of fish cooking. She tapped each with her finger to test its doneness and, satisfied, flipped all of them onto plates, added the proper garnish, and slammed her hand down on the bell that signaled order done. The waiter swept them away.

Yes, it was necessary to engineer a day off together, and soon. As she watched her fish cook, she resolved to inveigle the day off out of Davey as soon as she heard from Beth which day it could be. She'd promise him a double shift, a luncheon and a dinner service, if necessary. She needed time with the woman she loved, and she'd get it, by God.

Chapter Two

It took two more weeks and several notes back and forth, but it had finally happened. It was Saturday night, and Kerry returned home from the dinner shift and crawled into bed next to Beth, who was sound asleep.

Kerry thought about waking her up; it would be so good to touch her. It was like this sometime, because Kerry would be wide awake from her constant state of alertness while cooking on a busy night. She'd stare longingly at Beth but never be so cruel as to awaken her. Beth's days were as long and as grueling as hers, although in a different manner.

Kerry gazed at Beth. It was almost good enough to be able to lie next to her and marvel at her beauty, to know she belonged to Kerry and loved her fervently. She often had to shake her head with wonder.

They'd been friends at first, with Kerry hiding her secret passion, which had ignited on their very first meeting. She'd had to hide and suffer in silence and unrequited love for a full year. Then when Beth had finally confessed her love for Kerry and they were poised to become lovers, Beth's past had emerged to disrupt their present. They'd had some trouble sorting it all, and then Addison's wife Laura had discovered and subsequently banished them from Addison's home.

Kerry shook her head, not wanting to remember that part. She watched in the moonlight as Beth turned over, sighed, and seemed to slide more deeply into sleep.

She was so lovely. Kerry liked to trace her finger over Beth's eyebrows and down her slightly curved nose, and over her well-shaped lips and sweet cleft chin. The chin would jut forward if Beth was displeased, but fortunately Kerry didn't often displease her. No, she could please Beth as no one else could and render her a mass of moaning, quivering need. Kerry grinned in the dark, thinking of all the ways she could please Beth.

Well, that would be tomorrow, and tonight she needed to sleep in order to enjoy their day. She burrowed under the covers, comforted by Beth's warmth and nearness, and fell asleep.

❖

Out of habit Beth woke early, just after dawn. She looked at Kerry for a moment before stealing out of bed and into her dressing gown and slippers. She smiled, thinking about the day ahead and wanting to wake Kerry up, but she didn't.

She went down to the kitchen to see if Mrs. Thompson was about and had made any coffee, but the parlor and kitchen were empty. Mrs. Thompson must have gone out early. Beth was happy to have the early morning quiet time to herself. She lit the wood-burning stove and put the coffee pot on to boil. Kerry rarely let her do any cooking at home, not that she cared. Kerry's cooking was so much more proficient than hers. Beth was required only to prepare food that was simple and nutritious, suitable for invalids. She did, however, like to make coffee and sat down to wait for it to boil.

She looked out the window at the overcast sky and hoped it would be sunny for their outing. In the summer the ocean could be blanketed with fog or it could be crystal clear. When it was foggy it was cold, and Beth didn't care for bathing on foggy days, though Kerry didn't mind.

The coffee finally boiled and she poured a cup, savoring the freshness and warmth and then the "wake up" feeling, as she thought of it. She mused about her conversation with Addison a couple of weeks previously and her encounter with Marjorie. It troubled her to have the two people she most respected give her directly opposite advice. Well, she'd have to make up her own mind.

She wanted to discuss the situation thoroughly with Kerry, who other than her would be the most affected. And they would have a whole day in which to do so, and to enjoy themselves as well. Sometimes Beth still found it hard to give herself over to pleasure. Her childhood had been an endless quest to please her parents, but Kerry showed her joy and pleasure. She shivered a bit, thinking of the various forms pleasure could take.

The kitchen windows brightened a bit, and Beth saw a scrap of blue sky. She checked Mrs. Thompson's grandfather clock in the parlor. Eight thirty. That was late enough. She poured a cup of coffee and took it upstairs, then touched Kerry's shoulder and put the cup under her nose. Kerry opened her eyes, sniffed the coffee, and looked at her. She appeared sleepy, but her face still conveyed love and gratitude.

Beth kissed her. "Good morning, my love."

"Good morning, Bethy. My, that smells good." She took a sip and raised her eyebrows as she gazed at Beth over the rim of the coffee cup. "It's our day off!"

"Yes, it is. We're going to have a lovely time. I know it. The sun is coming out."

"Yes, I'll make sure we have a grand day."

Kerry's expression made Beth laugh. Kerry's ideas of fun always panned out. "Get up then, lazy bones, and let's be off."

"Two more sips of coffee, please."

❖

They sat on the train as it wound its way around the northern border of the city. The trip took a while, since they had to go downtown to catch the train first. It'd be easier with a carriage to drive themselves, Beth thought. If she were a doctor, they'd have to have one. What a conundrum. She'd have to make a decision about that entire situation, soon.

She wore a capacious shawl, both to keep warm in San Francisco's chilly ocean air and so she and Kerry could hold hands underneath it as they sat on the train. When they did this, Beth would squeeze Kerry's hand and Kerry would smile at her. Sometimes Beth would want to faint from love and gratitude, and sometimes she felt warm and tingly.

Today, though, instead of just happy togetherness, they needed to speak seriously.

"Kerry, dearest?" Kerry turned from gazing out the window at the passing scenery and looked back at her gravely. Alert and sensitive, Kerry would pick up the tone of her voice.

"Yes, love?"

"These recent weeks I've begun to think again on the question of whether I should study to become a doctor, go to medical school."

"Yes? What have you decided?"

"That's the trouble, I can't."

As Beth described Marjorie's and Addison's conflicting opinions, Kerry listened without interruption.

"That's all very well for each of them to say, but what about you?"

"That's the question, isn't it? I don't know. We would both have to sacrifice a lot. I might have to stop working, at least for a time, so I could study to pass the entrance exams, and then we'd have to find a way to pay for it. Oh, just a thousand things."

"Beth, that's not what I asked. I asked what *you* think. What do you want?"

"I would like to try to become a doctor. Addison says it would be good for me. I would be able to use my brain and would also make a higher wage. We could buy that house we've talked about."

"But?"

"But I don't know. I'm frightened."

"Bethy, you're practically the bravest person I've ever met. Nothing scares you." Kerry sounded so convinced that Beth was amused.

"Oh, you think so. You're not very impartial."

"I know what I know. But listen to me. You don't always do what other people think you should do. You told me about how you decided to take nurse's training when your ma and pa thought you ought to stay with them and run their store."

"Yes, that was a difficult decision, but it was the right one." Beth thought of her parents and their narrow, stultifying lives, their rigid conformity and their betrayal. She shook her head and looked out the window. Kerry patted her shoulder and Beth turned toward her

"My love, no matter what you do, I'm with you. You'll make the right choice. You always do. Look. You chose me!" Kerry beamed.

Beth gave her a little shove, but she was amused and charmed. "I'm not sure if choice entered into it. But here we are. Let's leave off this serious talk. We're on holiday."

"Yes. Look. I think I see the Seal Rocks. We're almost there!" Kerry pointed out the window and Beth followed her direction. They turned and grinned at one another.

The train pulled up at the top of hill, where a jumbled collection of food stands and souvenir shops stood. They alit from the train with the rest of the throng. It was Sunday, and many people were out for amusement. As they walked down the slope toward the Sutro Baths, they could see the Cliff House Hotel, perched on the cliff above the sea. Since it was near noon the sun was high in the sky and the waves glittered as they crashed on the rocks named for the many marine creatures who perched there. The Sutro Baths were to their right and down in a bowl made from the cliffs. The building's huge windows reflected both the sun and the ocean.

They paused to take in the sight.

"Let's walk down a bit and see how many people are out at Ocean Beach," Kerry said.

"Oh, yes. Isn't it a wonder people bathe in the Sutro Baths when the ocean itself is right here?"

Kerry laughed. "Yes it is, but I think Mayor Sutro was on to something. It's much warmer inside his baths, even the cold-water pool. And there's the warm pool and no wind."

They strolled past the Cliff House Hotel and around the curve of Point Lobos Avenue, and spread out below them was Ocean Beach, with hundreds of people flying kites, picnicking, and playing badminton. They turned to look again at one another. In this moment of perfect, undiluted happiness Beth saw her own feelings reflected back in Kerry's face.

Inside the Sutro Baths, they made their way to a changing room and removed their street clothes to don a couple of the worn-out, chlorine-stained bathing costumes that bathers were required to rent and wear. The suits were distasteful, but one could do nothing about it, and it saved having to buy and bring one's own suit. They locked up their belongings and pinned the key to Kerry's bathing suit strap, took their towels, and made their way upstairs to the pools.

The Sutro Baths were so large, a thousand people at a time could easily enjoy them and not feel crowded. A series of small and large pools, separated by walkways and gates, was spread out in the enormous, cavernous, glass-enclosed interior. Over the sound of the people yelling and splashing, they could hear the crash of waves outside and the hum of the giant steam boilers underneath the baths that heated the salt water in one of the pools to a pleasant temperature.

Kerry and Beth had their own routine. They went to the biggest cold pool first—the one with the deep water. That way they could avoid the raft of rowdy children.

As they stood on the pool's edge, shivering a bit from the cold rinse they'd gone through for sanitation, they turned to look at one another. Kerry took Beth's hand. "Ready? One, two, three!" They jumped into the pool.

Beth had taken a deep breath, but she always had a tiny moment of panic as the chilly water closed over her head. Kerry's firm hold on her hand anchored her, though, and her fear passed quickly. They plunged down from the momentum of their jump and then floated upward. As their heads broke the surface, Beth enjoyed the look in Kerry's eyes, which shone with exhilaration and joy. She shook the water out of her face and spit a little.

"Let's swim!" Kerry shouted and was off. Beth followed right behind her. Kerry had taught Beth to swim the year before, and though she wasn't quite as good in the water as Kerry, she was close. They raced to the other side of the pool and turned around and swam back, then repeated this a couple more times until Beth called out that she wanted to stop.

Hanging onto the pool's edge, panting and smiling at one another, Beth said, "When may I get another lesson?"

"Oh? You don't think you're good enough yet?" Kerry's brown eyes glittered. This was one of their jokes. For reasons other than instruction, Beth liked to beg a swimming lesson from Kerry even though she was quite proficient in the water.

"No. I want you to show me again."

"All right then, let's go."

They went to another shallow pool and there, in waist-high water, Kerry could stand and support Beth as she "practiced" her strokes. It was an acceptable way to embrace publicly. In Kerry's arms, Beth felt safe and loved. She also liked remembering their first few visits together and their early swimming lessons. She'd been so naive then she hadn't understood the complicated emotions Kerry's embrace caused. She knew well enough now and turned her dreamy smile on Kerry, who looked down at her with the same expression.

"I don't know how I ever learned to swim. The way you used to hold me and look at me like that, I could barely concentrate."

"Ah, you didn't have the least idea what was going through my mind. You were safe enough."

"Am I no longer safe? Beth laughed.

"In one way, you certainly are. If you mean are you capable of handling yourself in water and swimming without fear, then yes."

Beth turned over on her back and stared up at Kerry, languidly moving her limbs in a backstroke motion. Her upper torso came up out of the water, and Kerry could get an unobstructed look at the wet bathing suit clinging to her breasts. Beth watched Kerry's dark eyes darken further as she inhaled sharply. At that moment Beth knew precisely what she was thinking.

"Should we get warm or would you like to play a little?" Beth asked, smiling as she watched her beloved struggle to keep a straight face.

"I...um...would like to make some jumps if you wouldn't mind waiting to go to the warm pool."

Beth nodded. "That'd be fine. I adore watching you play." Kerry was a sight to behold as she dove off the highest diving platforms and swung out over the pools on ropes or rings. She was the only young woman who'd do so. Only young boys seemed to play the same. Beth loved watching her enjoy herself so thoroughly.

She sat on the side of the pool, wrapped in one of the Sutro Baths' tattered towels, and applauded each daring feat Kerry took on. They finally sat in the warm salty water for a half hour or so, letting their heads lean back as the steam wafted around them and they became drowsy.

"Are you ready to leave, my dear?" Beth asked.

Kerry's eyes were closed and she didn't answer right away. She opened her eyes, gazed at Beth for a long moment, and said, "Yes, I believe I am."

In the tiny dank cubicle where they struggled out of their wet suits, Beth sensed Kerry looking at her. She was no longer ashamed but aroused when they could be together like this. She was tired, but in the pleasant, sensual fashion that seemed to happen only when they'd been bathing. The cement floor was cold on her feet, though, and she wanted to be dressed and done with being wet. Kerry stroked her back, and her hand stole around to her breast, her palm brushing her nipple lightly. Beth shivered, but not from cold.

"No. Kerry, dearest, not here. We mustn't…" She faltered, then moaned as Kerry kissed her shoulder blade.

"Ah, but love, you're so beautiful right now. The cold water does things to your body that it would take a saint to resist you. I'm no saint." Kerry gently squeezed Beth's breast. "But this isn't the time or the place." She moved a strand of Beth's wet hair away from her face and kissed her neck one last time.

❖

It was late afternoon before they arrived at their house, and to Kerry's dismay, Mrs. Thompson was home and bustling about the kitchen. She was a widow of indeterminate age with colorless hair, an indifferent figure, but a kind if distant manner that suited Kerry and Beth quite well. She wasn't intrusive, but the three of them enjoyed a pleasant domestic conviviality, often sharing supper when at home. Kerry was always willing to cook, which pleased Mrs. Thompson, who wasn't very good in the kitchen. In return, she reduced their rent by a small amount.

Today, Kerry would have rather they retrieved a bit of bread and cheese and some fruit and retired to their room for the remainder of the day. But it wasn't to be. Beth started chatting with Mrs. Thompson and Kerry took over the food preparation.

All through the meal, as they spoke of their daily lives, Beth's work, the Palace restaurant, and Mrs. Thompson's anecdotes about their neighbors and local merchants, Kerry would catch Beth's eye across the table and stare so intently she was sure Beth would melt from the heat of her gaze. Beth would smile knowingly and then turn her hazel eyes politely back to Mrs. Thompson. Another hour passed as Beth helped Mrs. Thompson clean the kitchen. Kerry pretended to read in the parlor and feigned enjoyment at her respite from cooking. She was in a fever to get Beth to bed, but Beth was too polite to rush their social time with Mrs. Thompson. If Mrs. Thompson understood the nature of their relationship, and Kerry could scarcely credit that she didn't, she never gave any indication.

At last, to Kerry's great relief, Mrs. Thompson and Beth returned to the parlor and sat down, Mrs. Thompson in the armchair and Beth next to Kerry on the divan.

Kerry imagined the war between propriety and need going on in Beth's mind. She was sitting on the edge of the sofa as though poised to spring into action. Her normally pale coloring clearly showed a slight flush.

Mrs. Thompson asked, "Would you mind giving us a little tune on the piano?"

Beth blinked, but she nodded and, with a 'what can I do?' look to Kerry, went and sat on the piano bench. She shuffled the sheet music, chose something, opened the cover, and began to play. Kerry recognized the piece. It was one of their favorites because of the title, *Liebesraum, The Dream of Love.* Once when they were alone, Beth had played it and they had made love a bit awkwardly but joyfully on the piano bench. Beth had sat on Kerry's lap with her legs open and her arms wrapped her around Kerry's neck. Kerry nearly gasped aloud at the memory. She couldn't take another moment of delay and rose, stretching and yawning elaborately.

"The swim we took today tired me. I'm going to go lie down." She caught Beth's eye and Beth blushed even redder. She would follow as soon as she could politely take her leave of Mrs. Thompson.

In the dusk, Kerry lay in bed. She hadn't put on a nightgown, and every pore in her skin sensed the sheet around her. She thought of Beth's body and touching it in the dark. She trembled and the muscles in her legs tensed. It seemed forever until she saw Beth come in the room, carrying a lamp, its dim orange flame casting shadows as she moved. Kerry had drawn the curtains to ensure the room was quite dark, with only a sliver of moonlight from where the curtains didn't quite meet.

"Are you asleep?" Beth sat on the bed and whispered as though someone could hear.

"Not at all." Kerry pulled Beth's free hand under the quilt to her warm flesh, and Beth drew a sharp breath.

In a few moments, Beth crept into bed beside her. She was naked as well and smelled faintly of the chlorinated water from the pools at the Sutro Baths. Kerry embraced her, thinking of them in the water swimming. Lovemaking and swimming seemed the same in some way to her. Her caresses warmed them, and Beth's breath quickened as they moved together.

Kerry threw the covers aside and raised the lamp. In the glow of the gas flame, Beth looked otherworldly. Her hair was down and spread over the pillow. Under Kerry's and the lamp's gaze, she stretched out, displaying her body. She raised her arms and Kerry put the lamp aside and fell into them, kissing her everywhere she could reach, moving her hands restlessly from Beth's hair to her knees. Beth cried out and put her legs around Kerry's torso, trying to get closer. Kerry kissed her mouth, then her cheeks and her temples, and whispered, "Now?"

"Yes, please." The edge of need in Beth's voice cut straight to Kerry's heart. At moments like this, she found no difference between the body and the heart, either hers or Beth's. They were joined and inseparable. Kerry searched and found the warm, slick core of her desire. Beth's fingers dug into her arms but she scarcely noticed the pain. She watched and listened, and in a few moments, Beth clapped a hand over her mouth to muffle her screams. She writhed, her legs coming together so forcefully Kerry's wrist was caught, but she didn't flinch. Finally, Beth fell back on the pillow, panting. She relaxed her grip to a tender embrace. Kerry kissed her gently.

The previous year when they first became lovers, Beth had asked her, "What is that? What is that storm that happens to me and to you too?"

Kerry had shaken her head. "I only know what Sally called it. A coarse word that probably all the whores used."

"Tell me."

Kerry had said, "You don't want me to. You don't like Sally." Beth was very jealous of Sally, who had been Kerry's sweetheart when she was young.

But Beth wouldn't be put off. "That's true but tell me anyway."

It was impossible to resist Beth when she made up her mind so she gave in. "She called it 'coming.'"

Beth had been quiet for a long time, then finally said, "That makes sense to me."

Now Beth turned to her side and ran her hand over Kerry's shoulder to her waist. She didn't say anything but moved closer and pulled Kerry into her arms. The sensation of their bodies so close together made Beth's already racing heart beat faster. Kerry made little sounds of pleasure. She was on fire and wanted from Beth what she'd just given her. Beth, who was once so tentative, now was certain and firm with her touch.

It was as though she could feel every touch she gave Kerry in her own body. It was always like that, always the same but always a little different somehow. In the dark together they would find light and ecstasy, then peace and so much love and trust.

CHAPTER THREE

The young soldier in the bed under the window in the corner wasn't recovering quickly. If anything, he seemed to be getting worse. He'd come in three days previously, complaining of headache and sore neck, nausea and fatigue. The attending army surgeon, Captain Moore, diagnosed mumps and ordered cold alcohol baths to get his fever down and belladonna to help with his pain. Beth had dutifully followed orders, but the soldier's fever hadn't gone down, and he began to vomit blood.

She didn't like Captain Moore very much. Cavalier and lazy, he was an older man probably close to the end of his army term. He no longer liked his work and it showed. Like many of the old army doctors, he didn't care for women nurses and made that clear to Beth in every way except actually saying so.

As always, she hid her annoyance and concentrated on her patients. The civilian doctors like Addison no longer worked with the army. The crisis at the beginning of the Philippines war was over, and they made do with their staff surgeons. It was unfortunate, however, that the best surgeons were overseas and the dregs were assigned to the Presidio General Hospital. Beth overheard Captain Moore tell another officer he was "sick of malingerers and mama's boys with head colds." She presumed he meant soldiers like Corporal Ramsay, but she thought Ramsay was seriously ill.

It was late afternoon, and Beth summoned Captain Moore because Ramsay's fever was spiking and his neck was becoming discolored. He wasn't ill with the mumps but could possibly have bubonic plague. She recalled her conversation with Addison a few weeks previously and her experience with the plague in Manila. But she wasn't a doctor so she needed Captain Moore to give the orders to move Ramsay into isolation and begin more heroic treatment. She wracked her brain wondering how to discuss it with him. He obviously was still convinced it was mumps or he would have done something. Beth thought for only a moment, then had another nurse summon Captain Moore.

When he arrived on the ward, he was grumpy and spoke tersely. "What is it, Nurse? I'm about to leave for the day. Make it quick."

"Captain, sir. I'm sorry to detain you but I'm worried about Ramsay. He's getting sicker. I just took his temp and it's one hundred and four. He's vomiting blood off and on. I've saved some sputum for you. And I looked closely at his neck. See, his lymph nodes are hugely swollen and turning—"

"What? Are you a physician now? The man has the mumps. He's going to recover."

"He may have the plague, sir. See where his neck is swollen. He—"

"Nurse, be silent. You're not supposed to speculate. You're here to carry out my orders. Nothing more. The plague! What nonsense. There's no plague in San Francisco. I heard they may have trouble with the Chinamen, but I don't see where this man is Chinese."

"Yes, Doctor. But a couple of men from his unit came to visit. I heard them say something about going on leave and visiting, eh, women and gambling in Chinatown. They didn't know I was listening. He could've—"

"Enough. I suppose you believe that germ nonsense as well."

Beth closed her mouth, stunned. Captain Moore had to be one of those who still thought disease came from bad water or dirty food. Addison had explained to their nursing-school class in detail why Dr. Pasteur's and Dr. Koch's studies proved the existence of microorganisms that caused disease. Beth believed Addison.

"Doctor, however he may have acquired it, I'm positive he has the plague. He may die, but if we can get some Yersin serum to him, he could recover. You could call Dr. Grant at the City and County Hospital. He told me—"

"Bah. You're talking nonsense, Nurse. Which is what you are. I'm the doctor. Don't forget that. I'm astonished at you even speaking up. I'm reporting you to Chief Reynolds."

Beth pressed her lips together. She didn't want Marjorie to dress her down again. They were already stilted around each other, and this would only damage their relationship further.

"Doctor, forgive me. I spoke out of turn. I must be mistaken."

"Hmph. Very well. I'll see you first thing in the morning."

Beth went back to watch over Ramsay for a time before she left for home in the early evening, full of dread.

❖

The next morning, Ramsay's bed was empty and stripped. Beth found the night steward and questioned him.

"Dead, miss. We took him down to the morgue just an hour ago."

Beth thought for a moment. Then she went to Marjorie, who was the only one who could convince the head surgeon, Colonel Stewart, to let them use the one available telephone in his office.

Marjorie was skeptical but finally agreed to let Beth use the telephone to speak to Addison. She asked Colonel Stewart to give them privacy, and though his brows furrowed, he gave in.

Beth was overflowing with anxiety that she might be too late, excitement at her discovery, and fear she was wrong. The doctors' constant reiteration of their superiority hovered in the back of her mind, nearly paralyzing her. But she took a breath and gave the phone operator Addison's name and location. It seemed to take hours for the hospital to locate him. They didn't have many telephone devices, Beth was sure.

At last, she heard him say, "Addison Grant, here." He sounded displeased to be interrupted.

"Dr. Grant, it's Nurse Hammond at the Presidio." His manner changed instantly.

"Beth, my dear, what a surprise. Is something wrong? Are you ill? Has something happened to Kerry?"

'No, no. Nothing is wrong. All's well with us, but I believe one of our soldiers died of the plague."

Addison was silent for so long, Beth feared the telephone connection had broken.

"What makes you think so?"

She described Ramsay's symptoms and the course of his sickness. She added that Captain Moore had diagnosed mumps.

Addison blew out an exasperated breath. "Arrogant fool. It sounds like the real thing. Only one thing wrong. How in the world did he get it?"

"I heard his comrades talk about how he would go to Chinatown and gamble and, er, visit women there."

"That's enough, we have to examine him. Where's the body?"

"In the morgue. They're planning to embalm him tomorrow and ship him to Oregon to his family."

"Then you must act quickly before that happens. Can you get a piece of one the buboes and bring it to me?" Addison meant the black, swollen lymph nodes so characteristic of the plague. Beth glanced at Marjorie, who regarded her with narrowed glance and compressed lips.

"I'll try."

"It's essential we get a tissue sample to take to Dr. Kinyoun, the federal health officer on Angel Island. You must be discreet though. You can't raise suspicion. The best place to take one is in his groin. Can you do that? It's unlikely anyone would notice."

"I'll have to do it tonight, when the morgue is unattended." Beth was more nervous than ever with Marjorie listening to every word.

"Very well then. I'll get word to Kinyoun. He's the only one who can make a definitive diagnosis. Try to keep it cool so the flesh doesn't putrify."

"I'll do my best, Doctor."

"I have every confidence in you. You've never failed me."

She was pleased at his fervent declaration. It gave her courage to go on.

"Let us say nine p.m. then. Be sure to dress warmly. We'll be taking a boat ride in the Bay."

Beth turned to face Marjorie then. "You must help me find a container and some ice."

"Nurse, I don't think—"

"Nurse Reynolds, Dr. Grant requires my assistance. I must see to his request." Beth lifted her chin and held Marjorie's gaze.

Marjorie seemed ready to say something else, but she said only, "Since it is Dr. Grant, we'll accommodate him. I have little confidence in Captain Moore's judgment. But, Nurse, let us be clear. It's only because of Dr. Grant's request that I am allowing this irregularity."

Beth was grateful that Marjorie respected Addison so much. "Marjorie, I'm in your debt. Thank you."

❖

Beth didn't return home at six as usual but stayed around busying herself with odd tasks. After lights-out was called on the ward, Beth made her pilgrimage to the morgue. It was quite dark, but she could make out the outlines of the bodies by the light she carried. Which one was Ramsay? She would have to find him. It took three tries. Beth was not unused to the sight of corpses, but in this dark and dank room, it was more unnerving than she would have thought. She had brought a scalpel from the surgery and rolled the canvas cover back. The morgue was chill to preserve the bodies, and that and her own apprehension made her shiver.

Ramsay would be in rigor, and his body wouldn't be easy to manipulate. She set the lamp on his stomach. It wasn't difficult to lift his penis and testicles aside, but the swelling was located between his legs, and she had to force them apart. The absurdity of this errand made her grimace. She wished for some assistance but of course had none. She finally found some large metal tongs to keep his anatomy pushed aside and pried his legs apart, cut an inch-square tissue from the swollen lymph node, and put it in the can with some ice. She was wearing rubber gloves, as Addison had ordered her. She covered the can and washed the gloves in the sink.

After she left the hospital she walked east to the Lombard Gate, and Addison was there waiting in his carriage.

"You were successful?" He flipped the reins to get the horses moving, and they took the road around the northern tip of San Francisco along the Bay toward the Ferry Building.

"I was. But it wasn't easy to cut the tissue. I hope I've gotten enough."

"We'll find out. I cabled Dr. Kinyoun we were coming, and he'll be waiting for us at Angel Island.

Addison whipped the horses up and they flew downtown to the Ferry Building. Beth covered the can with its diseased tissue with her shawl, as though she was carrying some sort of contraband. In a way she was.

At that late hour, the ferryboat was nearly empty. As they steamed past Alcatraz Island, its prison loomed white in the darkness. The sight made Beth shiver from dread because Alcatraz housed only the most desperate prisoners. She walked to the rear deck where she could see the lights of the city, a far more attractive sight.

Addison joined her at the rail. "How does it feel then? To play a part in an enterprise such as this? Whatever did you tell Marjorie?" He was laughing, but underneath, he was very serious.

"It's exciting. Fascinating, and I suppose it's a little unnerving and very cloak-and-dagger. I told Marjorie that Dr. Grant required my assistance and that I must do my best to comply. That's how I secured her cooperation in spite of the irregularity of my request. That and the fact that she thinks Captain Moore is an incompetent." Beth raised her eyebrows, wondering how Addison would take her daringly frank denigration of a doctor.

He only laughed and shook his head. "That's almost certainly true. It's best to approach the situation such as this with a woman like Nurse Reynolds as a request for assistance. But I'm more interested in your thoughts."

He was looking at her and Beth struggled to form her words. "To be part of something like this, to look beyond the usual, the workaday routine. You remember the war?"

"I do."

"It's something like that but different. The war was never routine but it was horrible. It was only us trying to bring some order to chaos. We were constantly endeavoring to keep up. You've asked me to help solve a medical mystery. That's much more compelling."

"Yes. It's vitally important that we do this. I'm grateful you were able, but your resolve has never failed."

"Thank you, Addison. I truly want to know if I was right about the diagnosis."

"Well. We'll speak more of it later. We're arriving. I think Kinyoun will be waiting for us."

They walked down the gangplank to the dock. Addison waved at someone, and a tall, sandy-haired man waved back. He and Addison shook hands, and Addison said, "Here's Nurse Hammond, whom I spoke to you about."

"How do you do, young lady?"

"Fine, thank you, Doctor. I'm honored to meet you."

He led them over to an automobile. Beth was astounded but kept quiet and listened to Addison and Dr. Kinyoun converse about the plague cases and what could possibly be evidence of another one. They drove up to a hill to a large building that overlooked the dock.

When she told him, he nodded. "That is certainly suggestive. His venture into Chinatown is significant. This would make the fourth case. I've tried to make the city officials understand the potential gravity of the situation, but they're more concerned with trade and with offending the Chinatown leaders than with public health. I fear my attempts at persuasion are futile. It will take many more deaths."

Addison said, "But what would be the consequences if it turns out this is a case of the plague that has felled an ordinary citizen, that is to say, a Caucasian?"

"Ah, that could be the turning point. But first, let us see. I'll have to confirm with a test in some animals."

He led them into a dark wooden structure. The signs, in English and Chinese characters, pointed various ways to indicate to newcomers to the United States where they must go and what they must do.

"I wasn't aware this place existed," Beth said.

Dr. Kinyoun ushered them into a large open room in the rear of the building. "This is the federal quarantine station for the entire west coast of the country, the equivalent of the one in Ellis Island outside of New York City."

"The immigrants must come here first then?" she asked.

"Yes. This is the first stop and for some the last. We cannot allow foreign diseases to enter the country."

Addison raised an eyebrow. "But you fear they're already here?"

"Yes. I *know* the plague is here. I just have to convince others of that reality."

His laboratory smelled of animals. Beth could see the monkeys and the rats in cages around the room. The monkeys set up a fearful noise as they stepped inside. Even the rats became restless. Beth was certain they must sense their fate was somehow tied to the humans.

Addison and Beth watched as Dr. Kinyoun lit lamps about the room. His laboratory had some electric lamps that emitted a harsh and inhospitable light. It made the laboratory even more sinister, but the federal government's modern conveniences impressed Beth. Dr. Kinyoun was clearly a very important official.

Dr. Kinyoun put on gloves and dropped the piece of diseased tissue into a tray. He quickly cut off a small piece and then mashed it with some water in a glass dish. As he worked, he asked Beth and Addison questions. Addison allowed Beth to answer, only adding certain extra details or his opinion when it was needed. Dr. Kinyoun made Beth describe, in detail, the progress of Ramsay's illness and asked what made her so certain it was bubonic plague. When she said that Captain Moore thought Ramsay had the mumps, Dr. Kinyoun's burst of laughter surprised her.

"Hah. A classic mistake. What a fool! You, Nurse, have far more acumen." His praise warmed her.

He took a glass slide and, with an eyedropper, dripped a tiny globule of the water and tissue on it, covered it with a small square sliver of glass, and sat at a microscope. Beth had seen such instruments in the Presidio labs and wondered what it would be like to look through them. She realized she was going to get her chance.

Dr. Kinyoun whirled the knobs of the microscope and minutely adjusted the position of the glass slide.

"Ah. Yes. I believe I have it. Grant, look at this." He stood up to allow Addison to peer into the scope.

"Hmm." Addison's mutter meant he was thinking.

"Doctor?" Addison stood up and looked at Dr. Kinyoun. "I've formed my opinion, but in deference to your greater expertise, I yield."

"It is the plague. It's unmistakable." Kinyoun looked grim. "Young lady, have a look."

A thrill went through her, and she sat and put her eye to the tube. She could see nothing at first, then heard Addison say, "Turn those knobs at the side and find something to focus on. It will become clear to you. All of us have slightly different vision, but the microscope may be adjusted."

Beth followed his directions, and when she squeezed her left eye shut, she could see better. The microscope had a light underneath that showed through the slide. She saw amongst the bits of tissue, the curled, tubular-like creatures, the plague bacteria.

Dr, Kinyoun shook hands with Addison and then with Beth. "I must confirm with inoculation of a monkey or two, but I'm certain. This changes everything. Please keep this discovery to yourselves, but I am in your debt. Miss Hammond, is it? I must congratulate you especially on your sharp eye and good memory."

"Dr. Grant taught me, sir, and he and I worked with plague patients in the Philippines. It was no great stretch—"

"Tut. Don't demean yourself."

They went to Dr. Kinyoun's office for a drink, and Beth let herself take a sip of the whiskey but no more. She didn't need the artificial joy of the drink. The excitement of her accomplishment was far more gratifying.

This was the reason to become a doctor. She could solve problems and make diagnoses, and if she was right, then another doctor would have more reason to listen to her. She wouldn't be at the beck and call of the doctors but would be their peer. Her assessments of patients would matter. She could direct their treatment and heal them in a way she couldn't as a nurse.

Chapter Four

A few weeks later, Addison heard from Dr. Kinyoun by telephone. "I confirmed the diagnosis and tried to get permission for an autopsy, but I wasn't able to. In any case, the local health officials are far more intent on assuring the local population that this scourge will be limited to Chinatown. Or that it doesn't exist at all. It depends on whom you ask and who's got the mayor's ear at any moment. Ah well, Grant. You did your best. Give my kindest regards to your protégé, Miss Hammond. If anything else happens, I'll inform you, and I hope if you run into any more suspicious cases at the city hospital, you'll take the necessary steps."

Addison assured him he would and hung up the phone. It was sometimes hard to accept that the word of doctors actually meant very little amid so many competing interests. It was frustrating but inevitable. Meantime, the sick and poor of San Francisco were crowding his wards and he had never-ending work to do.

He heard a knock on the door of his tiny office and shouted, "Come!"

The door opened. Outside stood the chief of staff of the hospital, and next to him, a woman. "Grant. I wanted you to be the first to welcome our new doctor. Dr. Strauss, meet Dr. Addison Grant."

Addison hid his surprise at the gender of his new colleague. It wasn't as though he was unaware that women doctors existed. Two women had been in his class at the Medical Department of the University of California. The women and children's clinic run by women doctors at St. Luke's Hospital was just a few blocks away from the City and County Hospital. It hadn't occurred to him, though, that one would be joining the staff of *his* hospital.

The chief continued. "Esther Strauss, recently of Bellevue in New York City, I would like to introduce Addison Grant, infectious-disease specialist. Dr. Strauss will be assisting in your department."

"How do you do?" It was unfortunate the chief hadn't warned him ahead of time.

"Very well, Doctor. I'm pleased to meet you. I'm quite happy to come to the West, and I've heard so much about this hospital and the city it serves."

Addison took in the looks of the woman. She had black curly hair and black, penetrating eyes. She was of medium height and build but stood quite erect, which gave her the illusion of more height. He believed that was on purpose. No group of doctors or men anywhere would readily accept a woman among them, so she had to project great confidence and forthrightness. She certainly carried herself as though she was self-confident

"I'll leave you two to become acquainted. We'll meet again for dinner at one."

With that, Addison was left facing Dr. Strauss or Esther or… he was unsure what degree of familiarity was appropriate. None, he decided. "So. Dr. Strauss. Have a seat and tell me more."

"Dr. Grant, if we are to work closely together, I think when we are off the ward, we could address each other by our first names, if you are amenable. May I call you Addison?"

"Yes, of course, Esther. I would be honored." He remembered his same words the previous year to Beth. Beth. This might be his opportunity to finally help her make up her mind. If she could meet another woman who was also a doctor, the example would be more persuasive than his words. They hadn't spoken since the night of their trip to Angel Island to see Dr. Kinyoun. He pulled his attention back to the woman before him.

"…Women's Medical College of Pennsylvania. Then two years in the Royal Free Hospital in London, after which I returned to New York to take a post at Bellevue in 1897."

"Ah yes. To be sure. And what is your particular interest, Doctor?"

"Tropical fevers. That is why I've come to the West. I don't fancy living in the southern states, where the weather is oppressive." Her dark eyes danced and Addison was charmed. They spent another hour talking, then went to visit the wards under Dr. Grant's care. Addison decided he would have to wait until they were better acquainted to make his request concerning Beth.

❖

"It is our only chance to be together in a great many weeks, and I wish to make use of it."

Beth and Kerry were having breakfast and wondering what they should do and how to spend their Sunday. Mrs. Thompson had by coincidence been called away to attend a cousin's illness down the peninsula and was expected to be gone for several days. Kerry was of the mind that they should stay home and make use of the empty house and their unexpected privacy, and Beth was having difficulty convincing her to take a trip to Golden Gate Park for a picnic.

Beth had been waiting for this day so they could have a serious discussion about her going to medical school. She feared if they remained at home, they would do very little talking. She wanted to go to the park, which had been the site of their first meetings together and where they'd had at least two significant and deeply serious conversations. When Beth returned from the Philippines she had declared her love there and induced Kerry to be honest about her feelings. And during the crisis about Beth's past she had chosen Golden Gate Park to open her heart to Kerry. It was only fitting for this next momentous discussion to take place there. Beth wasn't superstitious, but she had a deep sense of the rightness of things and wanted this moment to be just so. But Kerry was unconvinced and at times could be difficult to persuade.

"The park is there forever, Bethy. We can go any time we wish. Today I want you in my arms in our bed or on the couch, wherever our fancy may take us, but here at home. All day. It's foggy out, and the park will be foggy as well. It'll be windy and—"

"Kerry, dearest. I understand, but I have something we must talk about, and I want to talk in the park."

"Oh." Kerry's face fell, then brightened. "But maybe if we wait until the afternoon—"

"No, love. I don't want to wait. I want to go now. We'll take some food and have a little picnic and then, I promise you, we'll come home."

"Very well. You know I can't refuse you anything." She wasn't angry and had capitulated gracefully.

"I very much appreciate that. Let's hurry, for we'll have to walk several blocks to get there, even if we take the cable car."

They arrived finally at the eastern end of Golden Gate Park, spread the blanket they'd brought, and took out the simple food Kerry had prepared: bread, cheese, fruit, and lemonade. Where they sat on the soft grass before the Conservatory of Flowers wasn't crowded with holidaymakers yet, since it was still overcast. As the day warmed, more folks would arrive. On the grand promenade, only a few people drove carriages or bicycled.

"Do you remember asking me if I wanted to try bicycling?" Beth asked.

Kerry laughed. "I do, but you thought you would fall and be injured."

"I didn't really think that, but I wanted to know what you'd say next. Do you remember what that was?"

Kerry looked into her eyes, her own brown ones glinting mischievously. "I said I'd pick you up and carry you off to Addison for care."

'I think you'd have taken any excuse to be able to touch me, even that."

"I would have, but I don't need to manufacture reasons any more."

"No, you don't. Now. What I want...no, what I *need* to speak with you about is extremely important to both of us."

Kerry grew somber and nodded that she was listening closely.

"Kerry. You remember I told you about my adventure with Addison and going to Angel Island to see Dr. Kinyoun?"

"Yes."

"Well, that experience convinced me that I want to become a doctor."

Kerry was very quiet and merely looked at her, saying without words that she wanted Beth to go on.

"It would mean great sacrifice for us both. I may be able to continue my employment for the year I need to study to pass the entrance exams, but after that, if I manage to gain admittance, I couldn't continue to work as a nurse."

"How will we pay the fees? I'm sure they'll charge you."

"Oh, yes, it'll cost money, but we can make arrangements. I hope you may be able to help with your savings?"

Kerry said nothing but looked off into the sky. She was very sensitive and secretive about the money she saved. At first, Beth had been hurt but came to accept that as part of Kerry's background and hadn't pursued the matter.

"Oh, Kerry, dearest. I don't want to ask that, but if you would, I'd pay you back."

Kerry took Beth's hands into hers and looked into her face. "Do you want this? Is this what you want most in the world?"

"It is." And Beth couldn't help but start to cry a little.

"Then you must have it. There's nothing else to it. For you, my Beth. Anything. I want you to always have what you want. We'll find a way. I promise you." They embraced chastely while sitting on their blanket together, but that embrace promised more later.

❖

Kerry lay awake long after Beth had fallen into a deep sleep. They'd made love from the late afternoon until late at night. Beth had to arise as usual at five a.m. to return to the hospital. Kerry wasn't needed at the restaurant until noon so she wasn't concerned with losing sleep. She couldn't sleep anyway.

She had promised the previous year, after Beth had given herself to her, that nothing would ever trouble Beth and that Kerry would provide whatever she needed. She wanted to be a doctor. Then Kerry would work to ensure that happened. But how could she do that and still continue the plan to which Kerry also had pledged herself: to acquire enough money for them to buy their own home? How could she make these two dreams both come true?

She didn't see a clear path, but there had to be some way. Beth had to get what she wanted. Kerry would find money for both of their desires, but she would have to discover how to make enough. She didn't want Beth to worry about that. Kerry didn't know what it would take to become a doctor. Addison had been in school for several years, to college first, then medical school. Would Beth have to do the same? Her head was aching from trying to figure it all out. She would do whatever she needed to. She would find a way. For Beth.

❖

"Marjorie. Let's have our dinner break together. I want to tell you something."

Marjorie said nothing but nodded as though resigned. An hour and half later they were back out on the pavilion, sipping soup.

Beth said, without preamble, "I'm going to medical school. I want to be a doctor. I want to be able to do more than I can do now. I'm determined. I want your blessing."

Marjorie looked away, pain in her expression. "It's not that I don't think you're able—"

"Then what is it?" Beth couldn't keep the impatience out of her voice.

"You won't find the men welcoming," Marjorie said at last

"I don't care what they think. Why should that matter to me?" Beth was incensed that Marjorie seemed to always focus on what could go wrong or what other people might think instead of why this would be good for Beth. If she didn't know better, Beth would have thought it was jealousy.

"It does matter a great deal. You'll need to be able to get ahead. It's going to be too difficult. You're not one to be subservient, and I fear you'll create ill will among the very people whose good will you'll need most. It's just so out of the norm and not what people expect. Women doctors are just too strange."

Beth had finally had had enough of Marjorie's strangely negative attitude and believed it was time for some plain talk. She tapped her fingers as she tried to frame her words. "I find it odd that you're so concerned with what is normal or expected when your lover is another woman. Don't you think people would find *that* unexpected or odd?"

Marjorie paled and looked away. She was stung, that was clear, and Beth was sorry. "I don't understand. I truly don't. I don't want to hurt you, but your reasoning is mistaken. You won't admit that this is good for me to do, and you won't offer your wholehearted support. You just look for excuses to give me for why I shouldn't. Why shouldn't I, if I can?"

"Elizabeth. I can't explain it to you. I'm sorry I can't."

"Well, then. That's the end of it. We won't speak of it any more." Beth gathered her eating utensils and walked back inside, angry and sad but still determined. She was off to Addison's that evening to begin the course of study he was planning to help prepare her for the entrance exams.

He'd warned her. "You'll need at least a year, and you truly must study the whole time, Beth. You don't possess a baccalaureate education, and Mission High School isn't accredited with the university, so you must take and pass more examinations. Your extensive reading will be very helpful. You've supplemented your English classes with your own interest in literature. But we must ensure that your Latin, physics, chemistry, mathematics, and botany are all up to snuff." He was trying to convince her to resign from the Presidio General Hospital, but she was reluctant to do that

"I'll study when I can and how I can. I must still fulfill my duties at the hospital. We need what little money I earn there if I have to stop working in a year to attend to my studies full-time."

"But you can't possibly prepare in your spare time. There's too much to learn."

"I can and I will! I must. There's no other way."

She had defeated Addison. He'd said he hoped Beth could channel some of her determination into learning. He didn't doubt her intelligence but remarked that teaching her all she needed to learn, that she was missing because she hadn't gone to college, was daunting.

He'd promised to make the best of it. She would have to be ready by August of the coming year, when examinations would be held for students wishing to enter in the fall of 1901.

❖

Kerry walked through the Grand Concourse of the Palace Hotel. She'd become so used to its opulence it scarcely registered in her consciousness. But inside the lobby, she saw the finely dressed customers going about their day. She was on her way to find her childhood friend, Teddy Black, who worked as a bellboy. They met and spoke only rarely since they worked in such different parts of the hotel. The kitchen staff by custom didn't mix with the hotel staff. But it was different with her and Teddy since they'd known each other their whole lives.

Kerry was frustrated. She'd told Davey she'd be happy to work extra hours, but he'd said he couldn't help. Too many cooks to choose from.

"I can't play favorites," he'd said. "I'd be in hot water with Chef. His nephew from New Orleans is here to learn the ropes. I've Shelton and Howard and Mick to think of. And you know they're only just able to bear you being in the kitchen as it is. If I give you any breaks, they're bound to see and start thinking you're my girl." He'd rolled his eyes.

Kerry didn't mind what he said because it was true. The kitchen was cutthroat, and they all had to watch their backs, even Davey. For a sous chef, he was a good man, but she was still on her own. The constant turnover of cooks meant that every time a new cook started, he would torment her. Davey did his best to help, but it was usually up to her to teach the newcomer he couldn't bully her.

So she was off to talk with Teddy regarding her money troubles. The bellboys always had some sort of scheme. It was just the way they were. Like her, Teddy was from the Barbary Coast, and plotting to make money was second nature to him. Kerry had chosen honest labor as a cook, but that wouldn't be enough now that Beth was planning to attend medical school. She wasn't sure what she could do.

She found Teddy in the messy luggage room where the bellboys waited to be summoned. He gave her a cigarette. He smoked constantly, and when they met, she tended to smoke with him. She liked the sensation of smoke in her lungs and the rush the first draw gave her, but since Beth disliked it, she never smoked at home.

"Ho, Kerry. What news?"

He was, for once, alone. When the other bellboys were about, he had to constantly keep them from haranguing Kerry. Davey had cowed the cooks into silence, but the bellboys were as bad as ever.

"Ah, you know. The kitchen is hot and it stinks. We labor to serve the swells, you by carrying their bags and me by making their suppers. I suppose it's a living."

"That it is, more or less. How's the great chef?"

"The same." Everyone in the hotel knew the French chef, Chef Henri, who ran the restaurant.

"How's Miss Beth?"

"That's why I came to huddle with you, Teddy. It's Beth."

"Somethin' wrong? She ill?" Teddy looked alarmed

'Nope, nothing like that. She wants to go to school to be a doctor."

"Don't that beat all. She wants to be a lady doctor?"

"Yep, and she'll be one if I have anything to say about it. We need money though. That schooling don't come free."

"I reckon not. Jeepers, Kerry. How much is it?"

"Don't rightly know, but it don't matter 'cause I don't have the money. Well, I got some, but we have to save too. If she goes to school, she can't work. I wanted to ask you if you got something on you can get me in on?"

"Naw. Nothin that'd suit you. Rodney's got a couple girls he brings in every so often, quiet-like."

"Stop. I don't want to hear it." The ladies of the night who frequented the Palace were usually well dressed and behaved like ordinary women. The hotel wouldn't want its reputation sullied. She didn't like hearing about whores, and Teddy rarely said anything because she'd told him long before to be quiet about it.

He didn't mean any harm. Kerry's mother, her first sweetheart, Sally, and her closest friend from childhood, Minnie, had all been prostitutes, but it was Minnie that haunted her the most. Kerry never forgave Sally for setting Minnie to work the moment she turned thirteen.

❖

A couple of days later, when Addison arrived at the hospital, he was startled to find Esther waiting in his office. She smiled brightly. "I read through all the rest of the charts last night and hoped you would be so kind as to take me through the ward so I can examine each patient."

"Eh?" Addison wasn't quite awake yet and wasn't ready to begin his rounds until he'd had some coffee and perhaps a little shop talk to loosen up. Esther appeared to expect him to begin work at that very moment. He was unhappy, but he didn't want appear laggardly in front of any new doctor, let alone a woman, so he took a breath and said, "By all means. Please allow me to remove my hat and coat and prepare to meet patients." He put just enough of an edge in his voice to let her see she couldn't rush him.

She remained standing, charts clutched to her chest. She didn't tap her foot, but she might as well have as she waited for Addison to put on his white coat and gather his notebook and stethoscope. For the next several hours, they visited each bed and Esther performed a thorough and, to Addison's mind, wholly unnecessary examination. By the time they reached the third patient, he decided to speak. "I think you'll find my notes comprehensive."

She beamed at him, disarmingly. "I'm quite sure of your thoroughness, Doctor, but I prefer to make my own examination. You understand." She said no more but addressed herself completely to the patients and with each one seemed to be able to elicit far more information in a few minutes than he would have thought possible.

They reached the last patient in the men's ward, who was secluded at the end of the row. Addison had received numerous complaints from his nurses that Mr. Blackwell was impossible. They said he was surly, uncooperative, and downright disgusting at times. He was certainly able to get up to go the toilet, but he insisted upon bedpans, something that the nurses couldn't comprehend. But he'd be so rude and abusive they'd give in and allow him whatever he wanted.

What would Mr. Blackwell make of a lady doctor, since he was barely able to abide his female nurses and was only marginally civil to Addison.

"Who're you?' Blackwell asked Dr. Strauss.

She appeared calm, but her smile contained a bit of a challenge.

"I'm Dr. Strauss. How are you today?"

"I ain't any better than I was yesterday, thanks to the quacks in this place."

"Ah? Your chart says your fever's gone and you've been able to eat solid food." She put the chart down and, before he could protest, picked up his wrist to check his pulse.

"You a doctor?"

She held up a finger to indicate he must wait a moment, then let his arm drop and wrote a note.

Blackwell's eyes were round and alarmed as he gazed at Esther. "You can't be no doctor. You're female. I want him!" He pointed at Addison.

Addison shrugged and stayed back.

"Mr. Blackwell. By my reckoning, you're ready for discharge."

"No, I ain't. I got pain here and..." He pointed toward his abdomen.

"Ah?" Esther raised an eyebrow and put her stethoscope into her ears, ripped down Blackwell's bed cover, and opened his nightshirt at the same time. He turned bright red and attempted to push her hand away,

"No. Stop!"

Esther lowered the stethoscope and said, "Very well. If you will not let me examine you, then I will go by the notes written here."

He pouted and then finally said, "Don't go poking around any more than you have to."

She listened to his heart and felt over his abdomen. "Seems like you've recovered. I'll write orders for you to take home with you."

They went on and Addison said, "It seems you've got a way with patients. You can divine just what they require."

"This surprises you?" The question appeared to annoy Esther.

"Not at all." Addison cocked his eyebrow and indicated the bed of the next patient.

Esther gave him a much less charming smile in return and they went on.

Later, as Addison drove home, he didn't rush but let his horses take their own pace, thinking about the new and unusual doctor. She was a puzzle—sweet to the patients when they needed and tart if they required that, like the hapless Blackwell. He grinned. She wasn't to be trifled with, that was certain.

Addison sat in his study at home, staring at the books in his bookcases. He was as overwhelmed as he was sure Beth would be when he explained the particulars of how they'd organize her studies. He took up a pen and began to list subjects, then the books he had on hand and the ones he'd have to find elsewhere. He tried to concentrate, but the face and voice of Esther Strauss kept intruding. He shook his head as though that would help. They'd start with Latin, Addison decided. That would help make the other subjects such as biology and chemistry seem less challenging since they used Latin so often.

He retrieved all his old textbooks and piled them on his desk. Then he returned to his lists but it was impossible. Esther's voice was in his head, in his ear. Her rather sharp laugh and the clipped and nasal consonants of the Northeast had grated on him at first, but in spite of that, when he heard her voice, he looked forward to seeing her.

Earlier, after they went to see all the current patients, they had sat with their case files and charts to discuss the various treatments. It was as if he were speaking to any other physician in one way but completely different in another way. Addison was only too aware that she was a woman but endeavored not to be. They weren't in a drawing room, he'd told himself sternly. He wasn't making idle chitchat. They were doctors, and he was charged with quickly catching her up with the status of all the patients and the routine of the City and County Hospital.

She was quiet at first, taking in all the sights, sounds, and facts without comment. She asked to take the charts home with her, and he'd agreed. The next day when they continued their discussions, he was astounded at all she'd absorbed just in one evening. It was uncanny. And with the patients, she became an entire other person. When in medical discussion with him, she was dispassionate, succinct, unemotional. On the ward, she sat down to speak to a young man who was suffering from tuberculosis, and she was like an angel. Addison had rarely seen a nurse be so gentle and caring.

Quite the opposite, he recalled. Many had no time for niceties because they had such numerous duties. He thought of Marjorie Reynolds, for instance. She wasn't precisely a battle-ax, but she was certainly tough and no-nonsense. Not Dr. Strauss. She sat by the young man and patted his shoulder and reassured him as a mother would. Then she stood up, asked for the chart of the next patient, and, without reading it, correctly recited the patient's symptoms, diagnosis, course of treatment, and prognosis as dispassionately as before. Then she spoke to the patient and the same transformation took place. Addison didn't know how to react. He'd never encountered such a woman,

Addison sat unmoving, staring at his pile of books. He ought to be making study plans for Beth, but he kept thinking about Esther. Maybe the bravado was a façade, and perhaps the doctor wasn't so quite as self-assured as she appeared to be. Why it would matter was something Addison was annoyed with himself for thinking. Her personality was of no consequence to him. They were going to be working together, and that was that and no more.

The realization disappointed him though. Since Laura had left, he hadn't given any thought to women. He never even consciously looked at any of the nurses at the hospital, although some of them were keen to find a doctor husband and made no secret of it. But he wasn't interested. He never used prostitutes, and no respectable woman could possibly accept the attentions of a married man. Not even one whose wife wasn't even in the same city as he, let alone in his house or his heart. And Esther was surely a respectable woman.

But nonetheless, Esther's face and voice lingered in his mind so much so that he found it disquieting. He was happy that he had Beth's tutoring to distract him. He thought again about introducing them, and to accomplish that he would need to exert himself to be pleasant and to cultivate Dr. Strauss.

He hoped she wouldn't get the wrong idea. He'd hate to set up some expectation on her part only to have to cruelly dash it later. That was a sad thought, almost as sad as the one that he sternly told himself to dismiss: he would never again enjoy the touch and love of a woman.

Chapter Five

Beth's head ached. She was sitting outside the hospital, hoping the fresh air would revive her as she ate her lunch and studied Addison's Latin-grammar text. She'd stayed up until almost midnight the night before and then arose as usual at five to come to work at the hospital, and she was exhausted. A huge number of patients had arrived from Manila the previous day, and Marjorie in her typical fashion had kept them running as they settled their new charges. As usual, they were suffering from a variety of tropical diseases.

She and Addison had begun their studies two weeks before. That he was willing to give up two evenings a week to tutor her, combined with her own ambition, drove her, but she was encountering a cold, hard reality. It wasn't going to be easy to combine intense study and work at the hospital. She shook her head and tried to focus, but the letters on the page swam and she dozed off. She'd studied Latin in high school but had detested it so thoroughly she barely remembered a thing.

When Addison had quizzed her on her knowledge of chemistry and mathematics, she'd done well, but not so much when he asked about botany or physics. She would also have to reread many of the required English literary works to be able to write credible essays. The entire scope of the project was so large she became even more tired just thinking about it. She sternly told herself to concentrate on one thing at a time, and at the moment it was Latin, which always made her sleepy and grumpy.

"Nurse Hammond!" Beth jerked awake. Marjorie stood over her, frowning.

"Yes?" Beth rubbed her face and blinked, attempting to wake up. She'd forgotten where she was.

"You are due back on the ward. Overdue, as a matter of fact. It's time to give Nurse Selden relief. Is something the matter? Are you ill?" Marjorie, although clearly irritated, was still concerned, still her friend.

"No, nothing. I'm well. I apologize." As Beth stood up and brushed her skirt into place, the Latin grammar slid to the floor of the pavilion with a thump. She bent and picked it up, and she and Marjorie locked eyes. Marjorie narrowed hers, appeared to be about to say something, then thought better of it and said only, "I'll see you after Nurse Selden returns from her break."

She turned and walked back into the hospital, and Beth followed. After splashing water on her face, she hurried back to the ward. It would be time to serve lunch to the patients. She dreaded the thought of talking to Marjorie later. Marjorie abhorred laziness in her nurses above everything. Mistakes and inattention to detail irritated her, but to Marjorie, sloth was the worst sin. Beth would have to try to explain and wasn't looking forward to it.

With the door of Marjorie's closet-sized office closed, it seemed the walls were even closer. Marjorie tersely invited her to sit and read something on her desk for a moment and before raising her eyes to regard Beth without speaking. Marjorie had round, rimless glasses that seemed to magnify her blue-gray eyes, which, when she was displeased, shone like sapphires.

"Well. What do you have to say for yourself?"

"I've no excuse, Nurse Reynolds. It won't happen again." It wasn't the time for familiarity.

"What precisely caused you to fall asleep?"

Beth thought that an odd question, since sleepiness generally made one fall asleep. Marjorie clearly wanted a more elaborate explanation.

Since Beth had declared that she intended to apply to the University of California Medical Department to pursue a medical degree, Marjorie had been quiet but distant, and Beth hadn't pursued the ordinary interaction of their friendship. She wanted Marjorie to have time to reflect and, she hoped, come to terms with her decision. This incident wouldn't help. Latin verb tenses had caused her to fall asleep this time, but exhaustion was the real culprit.

"I'm sorry, but I haven't been getting sufficient rest at home. I'll remedy that." Just how she was going to do that was another question.

'I see. And what would cause you to neglect something so important?" While they were on duty in the Philippines, Marjorie had kept her eye on all of them, especially in times of heavy duty, and would order a sleepy nurse off the ward to get some rest. Her vigilance about such things had earned her the respect of the other nurses, if not their love.

"I'd rather not discuss that, but I assure you I will take care." Beth honestly thought their friendship should allow Marjorie to give her the benefit of the doubt.

Marjorie looked at her for another moment. "See that you do. That's all." She dropped her head to continue scrutinizing the papers on her desk. Beth was dismissed and said no more, but closed the door softly behind her.

She returned to work. Would it be better to study early in the morning before leaving for work? But she would be burning kerosene in the lamp, and she and Kerry were attempting to economize. It wasn't easy since they had so few corners to cut as it was. They wouldn't even be able to visit the Sutro Baths for the time being, as they couldn't spare the train fare and the admission fee.

Kerry had readily agreed to everything, not making even a peep about their lack of entertainment. They were both nearly always at work or asleep and didn't see much of one another. That was another source of heartache for Beth, but she didn't see any way to remedy it.

"Doctor, may I speak with you?" Esther stood at the threshold of Addison's office.

He usually hated interruptions when he was at his desk, but he welcomed a visit from Esther. He now thought of her as Esther rather than as Dr. Strauss.

A month had passed since she'd first come to work at the hospital. So far, their interaction had stayed on a strictly impersonal level. He was hoping they would relax formality at least enough for him to ask her to meet Beth and become her mentor. When he'd courted his wife, their meetings were so closely chaperoned, they hadn't had a moment alone together until they were married. That had prevented him from having enough experience of Laura to be able to predict what she might become, and if he'd known more about her that would have saved a great deal of trouble for everyone. But no hovering parents controlled his interaction with Esther, and here in San Francisco, people had more freedom. Then he realized that again he was thinking of their relationship in social terms, and he needed to correct that.

The other hospital staff members were standoffish with Esther. He had no idea how that fact affected her, but he wondered if she needed a confidant. Within the hospital hierarchy, she would never be friendly with the nurses. Of all the doctors, he was the only one in his section who was, well, unattached. The other doctors would stay distant since, if their wives found out they were friendly with Esther, that might cause difficulties in their homes. Perhaps he was the only person who could truly be friendly with her. In spite of his misgivings, the thought excited him.

She came into his office and seated herself without ceremony. Addison was amused, thinking that, somehow, the stiff manners of the East Coast hadn't taken hold with Esther. He composed himself to give his full attention to what she might have to say.

"I haven't been here for very long." She seemed to choose her words carefully. "I'm not sure how to proceed with proposing changes in procedure, but I want to sound you out about something."

"By all means." Addison replied with what he hoped was a gracious tone.

"I've seen that our patients come to us in dire straits, quite ill."

"That's the nature of a hospital such as this. I'm sure you've seen the like in London or New York." He was a bit surprised at what he considered a naive observation.

"Yes, that's true, but Bellevue and the Royal Free Hospital are making some strides in prevention. The citizens of San Francisco would benefit from the same offers."

"Pray continue."

"I want to begin a clinic for mothers and children. Teach them basic home care, nutrition, the like."

"Such a clinic already exists, I believe."

"I've made inquiries, and that's not what I propose."

"I see." Why, as a doctor, did she wish to enter the province of what he considered wealthy do-gooders.

"It would not be open everyday, but surely one or two days a week, we could—"

"Esther, it's not that I don't believe this is a worthy endeavor, but the obstacles are numerous."

Her eyes flashed, and her spirit warmed Addison even as he mustered intellectual arguments to counter her proposal.

"I'd hope you'd be an ally."

"I'd like to be, but I'd also like to give you good advice before you go banging your head against a wall."

She closed her mouth, leaned back in her chair, and folded her hands in her lap in an attentive fashion.

"I want to first say that we have so many patients, as you've seen, that we barely have room for the patients, let alone anything else. We have to turn people away."

"If the people were better able to care for themselves, fewer of them would be in the hospital."

"I understand that, but we wouldn't see such a result for many months."

She said nothing more but waited for Addison to continue.

"The hospital wouldn't have the space, nor have the funds, nor spare the staff. I'm sorry to quash your enthusiasm, but these are the facts."

"I see. Thank you for your time, Doctor." With that she stood up as abruptly as she'd sat down, turned on her heel, and left Addison's office.

He was stunned and more than a little annoyed.

❖

Kerry was worried about Beth. Since she'd started studying for the entrance exams for medical school, she'd become tired and distracted. They'd rarely had any disagreements in the course of their relationship, at least not since Beth had told her the story of her childhood abuse at the hands of the family pastor. The weeks leading up to that revelation had been hard because they'd been so at odds and unable to communicate. After they'd begun to work through that dilemma and their life together had begun to become harmonious, Kerry hadn't had a reason for concern.

Beth never complained about *anything* and particularly wouldn't admit she was fatigued. She'd said to Kerry more than once that she wanted to take care of others and didn't wish to be taken care of. That was *her* vision of herself, but she would, if Kerry was subtle about it, allow Kerry to care for her, although she had to be clever so as not to raise Beth's suspicions. Beth, for instance, enjoyed it when Kerry prepared her a bath and washed her back and cooked her favorite foods. Those things were enjoyable *and* didn't interfere with Beth's need to think she could do or handle anything.

Still, Kerry was terrifically protective of Beth. She never wanted her to feel pain or heartache, and she wanted very much for her to have what she wanted: to be a doctor. But the real cost of this endeavor was just becoming apparent.

The day Beth came home with the many large and heavy textbooks Addison was lending her for study, Kerry started to realize just what Beth was undertaking. She'd been so excited, though, and Kerry was loath to dampen her spirit.

"Look, Kerry. Addison's written out a study plan for me. I must start with Latin because of all the scientific terms. Then I must pass examinations in seven subjects, including botany. Why I need to be able to quote Shakespeare is beyond my comprehension, but Addison says I must be ready. I read a great deal as a child, but we didn't study all of the required books in high school so I must read them now. You and I can read the Shakespeare together, can't we? Addison said that was one author you enjoyed when he tutored you."

Kerry agreed, but when would they ever have a moment to enjoy reading anything together? Beth devoted what spare time she had to study, or so she presumed. She wasn't at home in the evenings to see. A few times she'd returned from the restaurant, however, and found Beth at the kitchen table asleep with her head on an open book. She was growing more tired by the day, and Kerry was worried. Beth had told her with her typical firmness that she must find time around work and she would not quit her job, even though Addison thought she must. They had to save money, Beth declared, for there would come a time when she would have to devote all her time to her studies.

Kerry was at a loss. Beth was right about their financial dilemma. But how was she going to possibly learn everything she had to know to pass her entrance examinations in a year of part-time study? She was afraid the effort would take a terrible toll on Beth, who'd never admit she couldn't do it. But she couldn't exert any influence in this situation. A year and a half ago, she'd had to threaten to leave Beth to get her to talk about her past, and she wasn't prepared to repeat it. She had to find some other way.

❖

It was time for Beth's Tuesday meeting with Addison. She walked home from the Presidio and waited there for him to come fetch her. She hadn't wanted to allow this, but it made sense since she was carrying so many books.

Addison insisted that she eat supper with him first so that they could both have a break before they began their studies. Beth was already in his debt for the tutoring and felt even guiltier for allowing him to feed her as well. He wouldn't listen, however, and told her Mrs. Evans was cooking and they couldn't effectively study unless they had sustenance, so she gave in.

After supper, Mrs. Evans cleared the dining-room table, removed the tablecloth, and Addison and Beth spread out the books and papers and pencils. Mrs. Evans brought them coffees and they set to work.

Picking up the Latin-grammar text, he hefted it in his hand, smiling. "When I was a boy and a student at Boston Latin School, they required we perform translation every class. One student would be picked to translate out loud. It was a frightening prospect, but I learned to be prepared. I'll ask you the same, but we need to do this only a few times. Let's start with this one. You'll need to translate both ways, from Latin to English and from English to Latin. They'll also examine you on grammar rules."

Beth took the book out of his hand and read it through. Then, slowly, she began to recite in Latin until, in the third paragraph, she stopped. Her mind had gone blank. Addison sat with his hands folded over his waistcoat, quiet and patient. She looked at him, aghast, knowing she couldn't summon the rest of the Latin translation from her foggy brain.

"I, I don't remember the word for grass," she said.

"Well, take a moment. It'll surely come to you."

Beth stared at the English passage, trying to summon the Latin equivalents, but it was useless. She was full of remorse. Here she was in front of Addison and wanted to reward his efforts to teach her with efforts of her own, and she was failing utterly. "I can't remember, though I know I did the translation."

"Well. Never mind. Show me your written version."

She pulled out a sheet paper and handed it to him. He read it through, then took up a pen and began to mark it. He handed it back to her, seeming disappointed.

"I found four mistakes. Try to be more correct. I want two mistakes at the most. My dear Beth, I'm sympathetic. Latin isn't easy. I suspect learning it at such a young age helped me. This is perhaps the most difficult of all our study subjects, since you enjoy it the least, but it'll be vital to your medical studies, and the examiners will be keen to have you demonstrate expertise in it. So try again with this passage and do an additional one. We'll skip the oral recitation for now, but kindly begin your work. I'll retire to my study and meet with you again presently."

He rose from the dining room table and called out, "Mrs. Evans? Another coffee, please, but in my study. Beth, do you care for anything?"

"No, thank you." If she drank any more coffee she'd never get her hands to stop shaking. This reminded her of the typhoid epidemic they'd endured in Manila where she hadn't slept for three days.

After Addison left, Beth bent over the Latin grammar book and struggled to piece together a correct Latin translation of the new paragraph he'd marked. Her mind began to wander as she paged through the book looking for the correct words and verb tenses. She put her head on the table to rest for an instant. The room was over-warm, and the next thing she knew someone was shaking her awake. It was Addison.

"Beth? Are you all right?"

"I-I. Yes. I'm fine. I must have fallen asleep."

"Yes. I see that. Well, that's all for today. We'll pick up on Thursday. Try to get some rest."

Beth was quiet as Addison drove her home, making desultory remarks about nothing in particular. He was probably upset but didn't want to say so. When she got inside, she was a bit more awake, and as it was only nine thirty, she thought she might as well try to work. She took up her Latin translations as she sat in Mrs. Thompson's kitchen and was gratified that she was able to stay awake until Kerry came home.

"Beth, love. It's after midnight!" Kerry said, after kissing her.

"I know, but I have to get this done so I can read some more tomorrow night to be ready for Addison." Beth didn't like that she sounded ill tempered but was powerless to stop herself.

Kerry's eyebrow shot up. "You have to get some rest though, or you'll be exhausted at work tomorrow."

Beth bit her tongue. Kerry was only concerned for her, but she didn't seem to grasp how important the studying was. "I'm fine. Don't wait up for me."

Kerry stopped and looked at her. "I'm going to sleep. Right this minute."

Beth thought she heard reproach but didn't want to risk any more conversation.

❖

Beth awoke with a start. The light streaming through the kitchen was terribly bright and sharp. She panicked. It had to be very late in the morning. When she raced into the parlor and checked Mrs. Thompson's mantel clock, it read ten thirty. Her stomach turned over as she realized she was more than four hours late to work. When she entered the bedroom to wash her face and comb her hair, Kerry awoke and gaped at her.

"No time to talk. I have to leave immediately" was all Beth could manage to get out.

When she walked into the hospital, the first person she saw was Marjorie, who was bending over a patient, one of her patients. Beth swallowed and squared her shoulders. "Nurse Reynolds?"

Marjorie turned, looked at her, and straightened. When she stood up straight, she was a good two inches taller than Beth, and when she was angry, she was formidable.

"I apologize. I—" Beth said.

"My office, please. Immediately."

"My patients?" Beth couldn't quite keep the tremor from her voice.

"Nurse Simmons is looking after them."

Without another word, Marjorie turned and Beth followed her, her dread building with every step that brought them closer to Marjorie's office.

Marjorie didn't slam the door, but the sound was unnaturally loud in the tiny space.

"Marjorie, I'm so sorry. I overslept."

"You are never late, and that's the only reason I have for not showing you the door this instant."

"I understand." Beth composed her face in a humble and contrite fashion.

"What could possibly have occurred to cause you to behave so irresponsibly?"

Beth was deeply reluctant to admit the real reason, so she paused to think of something plausible to say. "I became overtired and didn't hear my alarm." That was mostly true.

Marjorie scrutinized her for a long moment. "Very well. Don't let it happen again."

Beth went about the rest of her day in a roil of uncertainty, remorse, and fear. If she didn't study, she wouldn't be able to pass the entrance exams. If she did study, she couldn't sleep and was subject to dismal mistakes like being late or, worse, making an error in patient care.

She couldn't reach a conclusion. She was boxed in, without a path or a plan. She didn't want to talk to Kerry because Kerry would be upset. She couldn't talk to Addison because he would only urge her again to leave her employment. She couldn't talk to Marjorie because Marjorie disapproved of what she as doing as it was. She didn't have any recourse and had no idea what direction she should take.

Chapter Six

Esther was waiting for Addison when he arrived at the hospital and asked him to come to her office. He followed her, staring at the back of her head with its mop of dark, wavy hair. Why, he mused, had he never considered dark hair attractive. Laura was blond so he supposed he'd just become used to thinking of her looks as beautiful. Later, when their estrangement began, he no longer thought of her as beautiful in any way. But he told himself to stop looking at Esther's hair because it distracted him.

He took a seat and she sat behind her desk. It was an odd feeling to be in this position, almost as though he were the underling and she were the superior. But that wasn't true. They were equals. If anything, he was more senior because he'd been at the hospital longer than she. Nonetheless, he reminded himself, they were just colleagues.

She didn't waste any time on niceties but said, instead, "I haven't convinced the administration that we should open a clinic, but they have given me permission to initiate a program of vaccination, priority given to women and children, but certainly anyone who appears and requests it. I'd like your help."

Addison, who'd tried to begin such a program before, was suddenly annoyed that she'd secured permission where he hadn't been able to. "Eh. Certainly, and they've allocated funds for this project?"

"Yes, though they're scarcely enough. Will you assist me?"

Was she asking him as a doctor or for some other reason? He chided himself once again for letting his mind wander along the path of social interaction.

As though she were reading his mind, she said, "The chief informed me that you'd made inquiries last year about just such an undertaking, and they told you there was no money for it. I showed them some numbers from a vaccination program at Bellevue. The year after we started vaccinating children for smallpox, the numbers of patients, both adult and child, were vastly reduced. I was also able to show him the cost savings. That, I believe, is why he agreed. And that's why I'm asking you to assist. I could use your expertise." She fell silent, regarding him with her dark eyes.

His irritation melted away and he was momentarily speechless. "Naturally, Doctor. I'd be honored. When can we begin?"

"I've ordered a thousand units of smallpox vaccine. As soon as it arrives, we can start. I thought perhaps we could offer it to the patients who come in for other reasons. Then the news will spread by word of mouth. Those who receive it would be encouraged to bring in their neighbors and other family members."

"It seems you've thought it out well. Keep me informed and I'll make myself available."

"Thank you, Doctor."

And then she smiled so brilliantly Addison was taken aback and stuttered slightly as he realized their conversation was at an end and he should take his leave. "Doctor," he said by way of good-bye. She nodded and he turned to leave.

Kerry found Beth awake and at the kitchen table with her books and a lit lamp when she returned at midnight. She kissed Beth and sat across the table from her, waiting for what she would say. She looked less tired this evening, but her face was still drawn.

"I was several hours late to the hospital this morning," she said with no emotion.

"I know. I was here when you left." Where was this going to lead?

"Marjorie was very displeased. If I can't pull my weight, she won't hesitate to dismiss me. That's how she is."

"Can you speak with her? Explain?"

"That's the problem, don't you see? She doesn't think I should want to be a doctor, and she won't help me achieve my goal."

Kerry was aghast at Beth's anguish. She wanted so much to make things right, to find a solution, solve the problem, but she couldn't.

"Marjorie isn't the most flexible of women," Kerry said. She thought about their visits with Marjorie and Florence and how Marjorie bossed Florence mercilessly. She'd leave Beth if it ever became like that with them.

"That, my love, isn't the half of it. She's notably stubborn."

Kerry didn't dare smile. She thought that Beth could be speaking of herself, but she didn't want to point that out.

She moved her chair over and sat closer to Beth so she could put an arm around her and kiss her again, on the cheek this time. She took a moment to nuzzle into her hair, its texture and smell both comforting and arousing. Beth leaned into her, seeming to seek solace in their closeness.

"Why don't you ask her to put you on night shift? That way, you can study in the wee hours when everything's quiet. It'll give you more time for it."

Beth stared at her, not seeming to comprehend, but then she grinned. "You're ingenious, my love. I was thinking I'd always be on day shift because that's where Marjorie wanted me to be and where I'd be able to do the most work. It didn't occur to me that maybe I should do something different while I study. If I volunteer, she won't refuse me."

Kerry hugged her close. "Wonderful. Now will you come to bed with me?"

"Oh, in a moment. I have to just finish this translation." Kerry shook her head good-naturedly and went upstairs relieved that she'd found a solution to Beth's trouble.

Beth sat looking at the Latin book for a few minutes, but she couldn't concentrate. It was no use. She longed to be cuddled in bed with Kerry and to fall asleep. It was midnight, and five a.m. would come early. She was more hopeful, though, than she'd been in more than a week.

What Kerry had said made a lot of sense. Why hadn't she discussed it with her before? It was an ingrained habit. Her parents had never made it easy to come to them with her concerns. She'd been looking after herself and solving her own problems since she was very young. She was no longer on her own, though. She had someone who cared deeply about her and wanted to help.

She closed her book and piled all her study material on the entry table in the hallway. She would try to take some time the next day. She had so much to learn, so much to do. She wanted to be prepared on Thursday when she met with Addison again. He was kind and patient, but she had to meet his expectations, not to mention show respect for his time and efforts.

She climbed the stairs slowly. Lord, she was tired. She was only twenty, but she felt twice that old. At the end of the climb, however, was a comfortable bed where she could lie down and rest next to Kerry—safe, warm, and loved.

❖

The waiting room was as crowded as usual for a Saturday afternoon. The working folk of San Francisco, if they or one of their children was sick, were more likely to come on a weekend than they were to arrive during the workweek. None of them could afford to lose an hour's worth of pay. Addison didn't blame them, but it made for large crowds and long waits. No one, neither the physicians nor the patients, was very happy to be in clinic on a weekend, but that was reality.

Addison was keyed up on Esther's behalf. She planned to start trying to convince people to vaccinate their children and themselves against smallpox, which could prove problematic. Ordinary folk were highly suspicious of something like a vaccine. They thought they could be made ill. Unfortunately, some would have reactions very like becoming sick with the smallpox. These symptoms would be mild and generally pass away, but some people would become very sick indeed. The San Francisco newspapers, whose main raison d'être was to sell as many newspapers as possible, would sensationalize and exaggerate the stories, spreading misinformation and hysteria.

He turned from the waiting room and strode back to the treatment rooms, where he found Esther laying out syringes in neat rows. She looked up as he entered, seemingly unruffled. Perhaps her experience at Bellevue had given her confidence and she wasn't expecting trouble. He hoped so.

"Greetings. Are you ready?" he asked.

"Yes, I believe so. Please bring back the first case. If you would escort them and make them feel comfortable, that would be very helpful."

"I'd be happy to." Addison was finding it rewarding to be helpful and to play second fiddle to Esther, though he wasn't apt to do that with any other doctor except her. He didn't question himself too closely as to why this was true. They had an important and delicate task to perform, and she needed his assistance.

The desk nurse handed him a chart she'd prepared and motioned to a couple with a young child, a girl, who looked to be around nine. They were shabbily dressed, so no doubt the father was a working man. His hands were grimy about the nails. The mother wore a clean but worn dress, and the little girl looked healthy. That was a positive sign. Addison had seen enough patients who were so malnourished they couldn't fight any infection. The father was sober as well, he noted. All to the good. He nodded to them and smiled in a reassuring fashion as he read through the nurse's notes.

"Come with me, please."

They trailed after him silently. "We ain't going to have to pay, is we?' the man asked.

"No, not at all. Please don't worry."

The man nodded but still looked skeptical.

When they entered the room, Addison handed Esther the chart. "Doctor, this is Mr. and Mrs. Harrison and little Sarah. Sarah has had this rash for several days that is making her itchy and fretful." He said to the father, "This is Doctor Strauss and she'll be examining Sarah." He held his breath. Other than the man's eyes widening slightly, he didn't react. So far so good. He apparently wasn't of Mr. Blackwell's ilk, harboring a prejudice against lady doctors.

Esther looked at the family, then at the chart. "Sarah? I'm Doctor Strauss. Would you be able to sit on this table and let me talk to you a little?"

The youngster looked at her parents uncertainly, but they smiled and nodded. She visibly relaxed and climbed up on the table.

Esther patted her hair gently and stroked her cheek. "You have nice hair. Do people often tell you that?"

Little Sarah nodded, still unable to speak.

Her mother said, "Sarah, baby, show the doctor where else you got that rash."

Her face was covered with reddish-yellow bumps.

Sarah rolled up her sleeve. Her forearm was lumpy and scabby, likely from much scratching, and covered with bright-red welts.

Esther looked over the rash carefully and glanced at Addison. "This is called impetigo. It's quite common in children. She may have picked it up at school. It's not serious, but it *is* contagious."

She turned to her young patient. "Do your schoolmates have this rash?"

Sarah was staring wide-eyed and somewhat worshipfully at Esther. Esther did have a way with patients that was most impressive. "Yes." Sarah looked surprised with herself that she'd spoken up.

"Well. We're going to make it go away with this lovely purple stuff." Esther had taken a bottle of gentian violet out of the cabinet in the corner and showed it to the Harrisons. They were silent but seemed relieved.

"Close your eyes," Esther said, and Sarah obeyed. Esther swabbed the solution over her cheeks and forehead, then her arm. "I'll give you some to take home with you. Apply every morning and it should go away in a week or so. Sarah? Can you stop scratching and let your sores heal?"

Sarah nodded, speechless again.

Addison waited. The treatment was nearly over, and Esther was going to have to make her proposal soon. She'd won the trust of the Harrison family fairly easily.

"Before you go, I'd like to vaccinate Sarah against smallpox."

Mrs. Harrison, who'd been paying attention to Sarah, looked at Esther suddenly. "The what?"

Esther spoke slowly and clearly. "We have a vaccine for smallpox and would like to give it to Sarah while she's here, and to the both of you as well. Dr. Grant will assist me."

There was long moment of silence. Mr. and Mrs. Harrison looked at each other, then at Esther, and then at Addison.

Mr. Harrison said, "We heard that's going to give us the smallpox."

Esther flushed, then took a breath, clearly trying to calm herself. "That isn't true, Mr. Harrison. It's a myth. It's quite the opposite. This vaccine will prevent you from contracting smallpox."

"You don't know that," Mr. Harrison said, with a surprising air of authority.

Addison thought it was time he intervened. "Mr. Harrison, sir. How can I allay your concerns?"

"You can't. I ain't letting you give a disease like the pox to me and my family. I heard them Chinese got it and it's going to be everywhere in San Francisco."

Esther interrupted, and this time, Addison saw she was indignant. "Mr. Harrison, I have come from New York City, where we gave this vaccine to many thousands of people with no harm. It will not give you smallpox, I assure you."

"You ain't no real doctor. You can't be. Why should I listen to you?"

"Mr. Harrison, I'm a real doctor," Addison said, and I can assure you so is Dr. Strauss. We aren't attempting to lie to you or harm you. We don't have any reason to do that. We aren't forcing you to take the vaccine but asking you."

"No. I don't want it, and not my wife or my child either."

Esther seemed about to say more, but she didn't. She looked at Addison as though willing him to speak the magic words that would change the man's mind.

"I'm sorry you feel that way. Please be on your way. Be sure to apply the medicine to the child faithfully, and her rash will heal."

Mr. Harrison looked as though everything was now called into question and that he wasn't prepared to accept any advice whatsoever. He grasped the bottle of gentian violet and gazed from Addison to Esther and back again.

"If you say so. Then we'll be going."

"Of course, we won't keep you any longer."

The family left, and Addison and Esther stood on either side of the treatment table staring at each other. Addison was dismayed that Esther was looking at him reproachfully.

"You could've been a little more helpful," she said, appearing aggrieved.

"I did the best I could. You could see he wasn't amenable to the vaccine idea."

"He is no doubt outside telling everyone waiting that the doctors in the City and County Hospital are trying to infect their patients with smallpox!"

"I doubt that, and I don't see what else we could have done. We can't force people with a government order."

"Well, then we need to do that."

"My dear Doctor Strauss," Addison said, but she interrupted him.

"Don't 'my dear' me, Doctor. Don't try to placate me. We better move on to the next patient."

Addison closed his mouth and left the room. Outside, he ordered the nurse to ensure all patients who had concluded their treatments be told to leave immediately to make room for others. He hoped he could prevent a general spread of panic and they could perhaps inoculate a few members of the population without causing widespread hysteria. He was disappointed on Esther's behalf, frustrated for both of them, and, most of all, deeply chagrined that he hadn't been able to help her achieve what she wanted.

At the end of the afternoon, after the last patient had left and Esther and Addison concluded their notations and gave all the records to the nurse for filing, they returned to Esther's office. They'd persuaded about half the patients to accept vaccines. It was sometimes a frustrating thing, Addison reflected, to be an infectious-diseases doctor.

Esther sat rather heavily behind her desk and swiveled her chair, staring at the floor.

Addison perched on the straight-back chair facing her. He was unsure what to say that would comfort her without seeming either overly familiar or condescending. "Well, Doctor. We've made some progress. I hope you can embrace the idea of the glass as half full rather than half empty."

She looked up and at him, her eyes boring into his. "It's not good enough. You know as well as I, San Francisco is a seaport.

Disease comes in with the tide and we've few weapons to fight it with. Vaccinations are crucial. I saw what happened in New York, and I saw the success we had."

"Doctor, I agree with you wholeheartedly. But, as you know, it's complicated."

"When we enlisted the help of the mayor and the city council, we were able to make public our efforts and our needs."

"There's the rub, though. Without the government, our hands are tied. It's not the same in San Francisco as it is in New York." Addison thought of the plague cases and Dr. Kinyoun's dilemma. Esther might not be able to mount an effective campaign for smallpox vaccine, but she would welcome involvement in the fight against another disease. "We're not facing down a smallpox epidemic at the moment, but we could well be on the verge of a bubonic plague outbreak."

She stared at him, clearly not comprehending.

"Yes. I haven't spoken of it because I don't want speculation and too much publicity." He described the fate of Beth's patient from the Presidio and Kinyoun's frustration with the city officials. He was gratified to see her mood lift as she eagerly asked him questions. He promised to keep her informed, and she said she would watch for any other potential plague cases.

"I'd welcome it, as well, if you'd offer your perspective to Nurse Hammond. She's currently preparing to take the entrance exams for the University of California Medical Department next year. I'm sure your advice and experience would help her immensely."

Esther tilted her head and regarded him with some interest, appearing as though she'd suddenly just understood something about him. In some way, it seemed his request changed her opinion of him.

"Well," she said. "So that's what you wanted all along. You have a protégé and think she might learn from me."

Addison couldn't tell if she was teasing. Her tone was playful. She'd transformed from the downcast woman of a few moments before to a joyful one at the prospect of both the plague and another aspiring woman doctor. He wasn't inclined to try to analyze the change too closely. He was just pleased her mood had improved.

"I'm certain she could. Allow me to arrange a meeting."

"I look forward to it," Esther said, and they beamed at each other.

❖

Kerry waited until well after the dinner service was over and the kitchen was winding down for the night before pulling Davey aside. She'd heard the Palace was going to be the site of another famous and elaborate banquet. Something about the Mexican ambassador visiting San Francisco in a month and the California governor hosting a gala dinner there. She wanted to play a part, a significant one if she could.

She was always on the lookout to catch Chef Henri's eye. The competition among the cooks was intense because that's how he liked to run the restaurant. She was the only woman and Chef tolerated her and depended upon her in many ways, but she wanted more. Davey was sympathetic but could do only so much. Chef had effectively enslaved him and held the ever-imminent supposed failure of the kitchen at some crucial moment over his head. Davey had to marshal the troops for Chef and would only be blamed for failure and never rewarded for success. It was Chef's way. He was a temperamental and mercurial Frenchman. She had to be better than all the cooks, or otherwise Chef would give her the boot without a second thought.

"Davey, if we're going to cook a banquet, I want to prepare an entrée. Tell me when Chef creates the menu. I'll think of something. Is he going to have a contest?" Chef often would have the cooks compete to make dishes and would choose the winners to cook for the special banquets. It was considered a great honor. Quite often she managed to be among those who received Chef's blessing, and she was determined to continue.

"I don't know how he'll be organizing this one. He didn't mention a contest. Your guess is as good as mine. If he does, I'll make sure you're one of those chosen." At least Davey had the power to name exactly who'd compete. If some cook was a little lazy or mistake prone, Davey would be justified in denying that cook a chance to perform. After that, it was Chef's decision.

The next day, Davey called his crew together before lunch, saying that Chef intended to make an announcement. They formed a big circle around the kitchen, and into the center strode Chef Henri with Fermel, his nephew and new game chef, at his side.

As Chef looked around at the assembled cooks, Kerry silently prayed he would tell them they could cook for the big banquet if they could produce an extraordinary offering of French cuisine in the Palace style.

"Once again," he said, "it is our great honor and privilege to produce a magnificent dinner for a notable guest. Senor Alvarez, Mexican ambassador, is a guest of the hotel, and Governor Graham wishes to honor him next Friday. It will be a dinner for one hundred and fifty. Monsieur Fermel will choose the theme, devise the menu, and select the cooks who will prepare dishes for the banquet. In him, I have the utmost confidence."

The year before, for the dinner for President McKinley, Chef had said exactly the same thing of Jim, the hated sous chef. Kerry and Davey had fixed that. But they didn't dare attempt something of that nature this time. She was sure Monsieur Fermel wouldn't choose her even though she was one of the best, and Chef had told her so in private. He'd never said anything to anyone else.

"Thank you, Chef. I've observed the work of all cooks of the Palace for the past two weeks and have made my decision." Monsieur Fermel named Davey and five others, but not Kerry. She stood, itching to say something but knowing that was impossible. She clenched and unclenched her fists. Her only chance was to speak to Chef.

After the end of dinner service that evening, Kerry searched for Chef Henri and found him in his office off the lobby. Monsieur Fermel was with him. After she asked to speak to Chef and he agreed, Monsieur Fermel glared at her and rose to leave.

Kerry gathered her courage when they were alone. Chef seemed nervous, drumming his pencil on the desk, and wouldn't meet her eye.

"Chef. I want to cook for the Mexican ambassador. I would like—" Here she took a very deep breath, knowing what she was asking, "—you to ask M. Fermel to take me on. It is only fair. I've been here longer than either Shannon or Telford." She named two cooks.

"It is done, Miss Kerr-ie. I have allowed M. Fermel full control. He is of the opinion that women cannot perform in restaurant cuisine."

"But you know that isn't true." Kerry was chagrined to be reduced to pleading.

"For you I've made the exception. Though I am of the same opinion, I will not attempt to change Chef Fermel's mind. You would be best served by not making the, how you say, the scene about it. Like a woman."

Kerry couldn't believe it. She'd never, in six years, behaved as a woman in the way Chef meant. She was tough, she was reliable, and she never complained. She was furious but could only fume silently, unable to change his mind.

She said no more but stood up and left without another word and got outside before she started to weep. It was good that no one was around to see how frustrated and disappointed she was. She'd likely never rise any higher than grill cook. As good as she was, she was a woman and hence would never be good enough. She wiped away her tears and decided she owed nothing more to Chef.

She couldn't and wouldn't give her notice. She had Beth to think of and medical school. They had to save their money. The savings account in the Bank of California that her father had begun so many years before contained several hundred dollars, but they'd need much more if they were to pay for Beth's medical-school tuition and survive without Beth's pay *and* buy a house. Kerry would probably be unable to find any other work that paid as well as the Palace and so had to stay there.

She put on her coat and walked up Market Street in the dark to the cable-car stop. Beth would be waiting at home, and the thought comforted her. Then she recalled that Beth would have left for the hospital to work the night shift an hour before.

Kerry turned up her collar and hunched against the wind that blew down the street from the ocean, made harsher by its passage between the buildings of the financial district. She was bitter and discouraged about her employment at the Palace, but so be it. She had to think of Beth and their future together. The gripman clanged the cable car bell and engaged the clamp on the underground chain that pulled the car up the California Street hill. Even late at night, the car was crowded, so Kerry sat outside, trying to ignore the chill. After the heat of the restaurant kitchen, it was refreshing in a way, but tonight she was colder than usual.

At home, she took off her clothes and finally, exhausted, slid into the empty, cold bed. It was a long time before she slept.

Chapter Seven

Kerry awoke abruptly as Beth got into bed and barely opened her eyes. It was probably seven thirty or so. It was difficult to tell from the tiny slit of gray, fog-suffused light under the shade. To be able to sleep during the day, Beth kept the shade down as tight as possible.

Beth moved closer to her, seeking warmth no doubt, but her movements were small and quiet so she wouldn't awaken Kerry. She settled on her back. Kerry looked at her from under her eyelids. She was staring at the ceiling. She blinked once, then again. Then her eyes stayed closed, though she wasn't asleep. When Beth was asleep, her breathing grew deep and even, and her face relaxed. Kerry touched her shoulder and she turned over.

"Oh, love, go back to sleep. I didn't mean to wake you."

"I was awake. Don't worry. Are you well?" Kerry worried she didn't sleep enough when she was on night turn.

"Oh. I suppose. I'm fine. What about you?"

"Missing you very much. It seems we see less of each other than ever."

"I know. It's a heartache."

"Beth? Are you very tired?" Kerry touched her shoulder, and the warmth from Beth's solid arm flowed from her body through her nightgown into Kerry's palm, up her arm, and coursed along her nerve endings, igniting desire.

"No more so than usual."

"Oh? Well. Then. Perhaps?" Kerry unbuttoned Beth's nightdress and lifted the opening. Even in the dimness, she could see the outline of Beth's breast. She took a deep breath because that sight had such an effect on her. She imagined taking the hard pink nipple in her mouth and fingering the soft velvety flesh around it.

She lifted the button placket higher and giggled slightly. Beth exhaled. "You…"

Kerry could tell she wasn't irritated but was almost certainly feeling the same in her body as Kerry: the need for touch, for warmth and wetness and smooth skin. Kerry reached under the covers and pushed Beth's nightgown up. She was naked underneath. Kerry wore only a light singlet herself. They wouldn't have far to go to get as close as they could be. Kerry smoothed her hand along the inside of Beth's thigh. Beth murmured and moved her leg restlessly, the muscle tensing. Kerry smiled to herself. She rolled on top of Beth and kissed her. Neither of them had cleaned their teeth in a while, but it was no matter. Kerry pressed their mouths together, and as she probed with her tongue, Beth gasped and opened her mouth fully. It was the prelude to the opening of her body Kerry knew so well and craved so desperately, though she willed herself to go slowly. Beth had gently reproved her before for being too fast. They pressed their bodies together.

Kerry whispered in her ear, "Shall we go on?"

Beth whispered back, her voice charged with need, "Yes. Please."

Kerry was determined to have nothing between them so she sat up, pulled Beth upright, and yanked her nightgown up and over her head. Beth did the same with Kerry's singlet, and they fell together with twin sighs.

Kerry kissed her neck and shoulders and breasts, taking first one then the other into her mouth as Beth whimpered. She snaked her hand down Beth's torso and stomach until it came to rest between her legs. Beth opened her legs, and Kerry plunged her fingers inside her. She was slippery and soft, and each movement she made, every sound she made echoed in Kerry's own body. Beth's head whipped from side to side, and her heavy hair brushed Kerry's face and neck. Kerry smoothed it down so she could immerse herself in its scent as she made love to Beth.

When they'd first become lovers, Beth hadn't exactly been shy, but she'd been tentative and unsure of being touched. Because of her abuse at the hands of the family pastor, she'd had no pleasant associations with her body being stroked. Kerry was patient, tender, and considerate, and in a short time, Beth had relaxed and come to fully enjoy Kerry's caresses.

Kerry found it a wonder and was more than grateful; she was awed and humbled. She was sure those feelings would never leave her. Every time she made love to Beth, she prayed her touch would erase the terrible damage just a little more. The look in Beth's eyes when she would finally open them and gaze back at Kerry with such adoration always made Kerry gasp.

As she quieted this morning, Kerry held her silently. Beth's hand moved weakly to her her breast, but Kerry gently put it aside. "No, love. Later. Sleep now. You must rest."

Beth yawned and snuggled closer, drowsy and satisfied. "What of you?" She was so close to sleep her voice was nearly inaudible.

"Never mind." Kerry hugged her close and held her until she was fully asleep. She herself dozed off but awoke in plenty of time to go to work.

❖

At Beth's meeting with Addison the following week, he told her, "I've a new medical colleague I'd like you to meet. She's quite astute and well trained as a physician. I believe you'd derive some benefit from your acquaintance with her. She can, I would say, offer you concrete advice on the path upon which you're about to embark, having traveled that same path herself."

"She…?" Beth was taken by surprise and somewhat mystified.

"Yes. Dr. Esther Strauss, from Bellevue Hospital in New York City, is currently house staff at the City and County Hospital. She is, as are we, keenly interested in the study of infectious disease."

"Why yes, certainly. Of course." Beth had heard Addison refer to women doctors with whom he'd shared medical studies at the University of California, but she'd never expected to meet one in the flesh. The prospect fascinated her.

"Very good. Now as to a meeting, I thought supper at my home would be the easiest. Even if you're off to work at the Presidio, you'll have time. We'll take you after we've all enjoyed a leisurely meal and conversation."

We? Something about the way Addison used the word intrigued Beth. He never spoke of women since Laura had left. What was he thinking?

"Will Kerry be able to join us?" he asked.

"I'll inquire. Perhaps you could set a date for a few weeks hence so she'll be better able to manage taking leave of her usual dinner shift."

"Certainly. I quite understand. Shall we say two weeks from tomorrow?"

Beth woke Kerry up when she returned home the next morning. "Kerry, dearest, sorry to wake you but we must talk. And now is the only time."

Kerry rolled onto her back and put an arm over her face to block out the light, then removed it and moaned. She looked more tired than usual, and her eyes had dark smudges under them. She opened them with some difficulty.

"Yes, love. What is it?"

"Addison has invited us to supper in two weeks. Would you please, please say you'll come with me?"

Kerry turned on her side, propped her head up on her hand with her elbow crooked, and stared back at Beth. "This is important to you?"

"It is, so very much. Not only do I want you to try to reconcile with Addison, but he's introducing me to a woman who doctors with him at City Hospital. He thinks it'll be good for me to make her acquaintance."

"Oh." She closed her mouth, and the silence was so long Beth was afraid she might refuse again.

"I suppose I'll have to say yes then."

Beth stared at her for a moment, then squealed with delight and hugged her. Kerry nuzzled her neck. Though her voice was muffled, Beth could readily understand her as she said, "Anything for you, love. Anything."

❖

Mrs. Evans, Addison's housekeeper, had evidently been instructed to make the meal memorable, and Kerry, though slightly critical, was still impressed. She was proficient at French cooking, but she still admired and liked to eat basic good western American cuisine. Mrs. Evans had roasted a rabbit and trimmed it with turnips and carrots, and they'd finished with a cherry pie.

Throughout dinner, Kerry had been quiet, content to let the conversation flow amongst the medical people. When she watched Addison, her psyche was at war with itself. In the Barbary Coast, not much was of value to anyone save money, but loyalty was still important. In spite of his many kindnesses, Addison had been disloyal to her in bowing to Laura's wishes. He was her guardian, her foster father, and she owed him a huge debt of gratitude. She was still sore, however, that he'd let his hateful wife dictate to him.

Beth had pleaded with her over and over to forgive him and leave it in the past, but she couldn't. He seemed, though, to not have any ill will toward her. He greeted them warmly at the door and made introductions to his new friend. Was she being unreasonable? He was, after all, tutoring Beth so she could pass the entrance exams and begin her medical studies. He'd brought them over to have supper. Though she was of two minds she decided it wasn't necessary to do anything at the moment except be pleasant.

Beth was obviously much taken with Dr. Strauss, and Kerry regarded her with some interest as well because she was unfamiliar with this type of woman. She recalled what it had been like the first time she'd gone to find Addison at his hospital and had encountered a nurse. She'd never met any women who weren't either prostitutes or barmaids or some combination. The only "respectable" woman she'd ever met was Addison's wife Laura, who was, happily, no longer in the house. Beth said she'd returned to her parents in Kansas, thank goodness.

Beth eagerly questioned Dr. Strauss about her medical studies. Addison sat at the head of the table in his accustomed chair, but he wasn't saying very much. He simply smiled in a benevolent fashion and let the two women converse. Kerry saw, however, with some amusement, that he looked quite warmly at Dr. Strauss.

"You were at the Sorbonne for a year then, Doctor?" Beth asked.

"Please do call me Esther." The woman's dark eyes sparkled when she smiled. She wasn't beautiful, Kerry thought, but something in her lively dark eyes and forthright manner of speaking was deeply attractive.

"I was privileged to study with Doctor Hellman, the foremost anatomist in Europe. He takes on only three students a year, and two of them are always French." She laughed. "You may think the French doctors wouldn't take kindly to a member of the fairer sex in their midst, but oddly, because I was an American medical student, I believe they didn't equate me with the stylish and servile females of their race. To them, I was another species altogether." She took a bite of roast and chewed it thoughtfully, then glanced at Addison with the same warmth in her gaze as Addison.

"Shall we leave these two to chat, Kerry, and repair to the parlor?" Addison asked, startling her.

'Yeh-yes. I guess." Kerry was surprised, but his suggestion was logical. Beth would have to go to work in a while, and she needed to make the most of her time with Dr. Strauss. It was a bit dismaying to Kerry, though, that she and Addison would have to be alone together. She truly didn't know what to say to him and preferred to not have to try to think of something. The stress of being in his home again was enough

When they sat down in the front parlor, Kerry remembered for some reason the first time she'd done so, many years before. She was nervous then and she was nervous again, though she didn't need to be uneasy.

"So, my dear Kerry. How is your employment progressing?"

"Well enough, I suppose."

"You are still employed at the Palace, I understand. Do you like it?"

"Yes. I am. Yes, I do." Kerry wished Addison would begin one of his avuncular monologues and relieve her of the burden of trying to converse. He was, however, staring at her without a word, evidently waiting for her to expand on her statement.

"I'm well established as a cook, and I'm able to work many hours because the sous chef likes me. This may change though. The chef de cuisine has brought in someone new, and we aren't yet certain how this will affect the rest of us."

"I recall all your tales of the kitchen when you were residing here, and I'm certain not much has changed." Addison fell silent and folded his hands over his waistcoat, so she told him about M. Fermel. She found, to her great surprise, that she wanted to talk about it. She'd purposely kept quiet around Beth, not wishing to disturb her study. But Addison was a kind and attentive listener and had always had time for her. As she talked, her anger at him dissipated and she relaxed.

❖

"I was a student at the Women's Medical College of Pennsylvania. The founders of that institution were frustrated that other schools of medicine refused to admit women so they founded one especially for us," Esther told Beth.

"My goodness, classes entirely made of women. It seems too fantastic to contemplate."

"It was a gift, Beth, but there's still the cold reality of the world outside the cloisters of a women's college. We have to get along in a world still directed by and structured for men. I assume you know that well since you've worked as a nurse.'

"Yes. That's true. But strangely, the one person whom I thought would welcome my ambitions the most turned out to be the one who seems to understand them the least. My friend and superior at the hospital, another nurse, doesn't approve of my becoming a physician."

Esther smiled ruefully and shook her head. She seemed to be thinking of something but only said, "Sometimes our sisters aren't our allies, though we expect them to be. Nonetheless, you'll prevail, I'm certain, especially with Dr. Grant to mentor you. How long have you known him?"

"Around three years. He taught us bacteriology and infectious disease in nurse's training. Then he recommended I serve as a contract nurse for the army during the Philippines war. We worked together on a hospital ship there."

"I see. So then you know him fairly well?"

The question startled Beth, who sensed something more than casual interest behind it.

"I believe I do, yes. He's the kindest, most generous of men. He's quite respectful of women, the most respectful doctor I've ever worked with, as well as the most intelligent."

"Stellar recommendations. I believe you'd always tell the truth."

"I certainly hope so, Doctor."

"Is Add-Doctor Grant married?"

Esther's neutral tone was deceptive for the question was provocative. Could she be interested in Addison as more than a fellow doctor with whom to cooperate in medical problems? She had to answer truthfully. "Yes, he is."

"But that drab woman in the kitchen. Surely she's not his wife?"

"Oh, no. That's Mrs. Evans, the housekeeper. His wife, Laura, is in Kansas city visiting her parents presently." Beth thought she should say no more than that.

Esther gazed off into the distance with a sad air. "Ah. Well. I see. So tell me, Beth. What drives you to become a doctor?"

"Oh, that's easy. Disease. It's Addison's example and what we've encountered here in San Francisco. It's the study of infection, of microorganisms that fascinates me."

"I understand. That interests me as well, but not as an academic exercise. To me, the eradication of disease is the only way we'll be able to lift people out of poverty. Public health is the key. At Bellevue, we had several programs going on that I'd like to replicate here."

Beth listened avidly as Esther described her experience treating the poor of New York City.

Kerry had mostly exhausted her repertoire of restaurant stories and had fallen silent again. Addison was watching her and she wondered what he was thinking.

"You know, I was terribly disappointed that I had to evict you and Beth. I don't blame you for being angry. I had made a promise to your father, but I broke it to placate my wife."

"I understand. Beth told me I shouldn't blame you, but I was angry anyway." Saying it aloud made it seem trivial and petty.

"And are you still angry with me, Kerry?" The way he asked the question showed he really wanted an honest answer. "You've avoided any contact with me these last months. I thought I knew the reason."

"I'm ashamed for the way I behaved. I just thought I'd be at least as important to you as Laura. You'd always led me to believe that was so."

"I've always considered you like a daughter. Laura, well..." He paused. "I thought I needed to let her have her way. She always made out I was a beast for bringing you into our house. I wanted her to be happy. It seems, though, that nothing would make her happy, and her cruel spying on you and then going to Beth's parents shocked me." He looked at Kerry, his face drawn.

"She'll never come back. I don't want her to. But she'll also never grant me a divorce, so I'm still chained to her one way or another. I don't have any recourse. I can't fall in love with another woman, find happiness, remarry. She won't permit it. That's her ultimate revenge. She's won in the end." Addison spoke matter-of-factly, but Kerry could see his anguish.

"That's not fair!" she burst out, angry anew at the woman who'd made her adolescent years miserable and caused Addison to betray her.

"Indeed, it isn't, but that is how it remains. Come. Let's see if Beth and Esther are deep in medical talk. We have to think of taking a ride over to the Presidio to deliver Beth for her work shift."

With that, they rejoined the two women in the dining room. When Esther and Addison deposited Kerry back on Divisadero Street and bade her good night, she thought deeply as she prepared for bed. Esther was a lively, intelligent, strong-willed woman, not headstrong and devious like Laura. She would be an ideal mate for Addison.

She would have to talk to Beth about it and see what she thought. She was glad she'd agreed to attend the dinner. The conversation with Addison had lifted a burden from her heart she hadn't known she carried.

Chapter Eight

The year passed quickly. Between their work and Beth's studies, they scarcely had time to breathe. It was July, and in one more month, Beth would sit for her entrance examinations and they would see soon enough if their sacrifice had been for nothing or would pay off. Kerry was of two minds, and she didn't want to share either of her conflicting feelings with Beth. Either would be a heartache to her, and Kerry would rather die than cause her any pain.

If Beth failed to gain a spot in the university medical department, it would devastate her, but it would solve the problem of how they would pay for it. Beth and Kerry had sat together with a pencil and paper and the university's register and calculated the cost of Beth's education. The price had staggered Kerry, but she hid her chagrin.

"You must concentrate only your studies, Bethy. You'll need every ounce of your strength and time and fortitude."

"But how will we pay our expenses?"

"I've got that figured, love. I have my savings, and I'll just work more hours at the restaurant. They have to let me do that."

"But our house? You want that so much. How will we—?"

"Just you let me worry about that. You mustn't bother with anything else right now but your preparations for the examinations. They're just a few weeks away."

Beth kissed her then and said, "You're the most wonderful, most faithful, most loving person. I love you so much." She kissed her again, and Kerry accepted the kisses happily, but she didn't deserve them. She secretly hoped Beth wouldn't pass the tests. Then they could stay as they were and Beth could work, and in a few more years, they'd buy a house. She was ashamed of these thoughts. They were unworthy but they were true. If what Beth wanted came to pass, it would gladden her, but it would be very difficult.

A few months earlier Kerry had done all the figuring with Teddy, and the numbers didn't add up. They couldn't have both Beth's schooling and a house. They couldn't even have one or the other if Beth's salary wasn't part of the scheme. When they finished and Teddy and Kerry were looking at one another bleakly, Kerry said, "Remember what I asked you last year?"

"Yeah, I remember."

"Well. It's still true. I have to get more money somehow."

"But you could iffin you was amenable to have some girls workin' for—"

"Shut up. I told you no to that. What about something with gambling? You boys always have some kind of bet going."

"That's just small time and ain't no sure thing. I just don't know, Kerry. It's a puzzle."

"Who's still around from the old days? Someone who could put us onto something on the BC." Teddy frowned at her.

"You ain't thinking of crimping, are you?" Teddy meant kidnapping sailors, an operation Kerry had learned with her father, Lucky Jack.

"Nah. I ain't crazy. What else is there?"

"I heard someone bought the Grey Dog. Someone respectable."

Teddy's father had run a warehouse on the wharf before drink had killed him. Teddy hadn't mourned very much. Old man Black had beat him every day of his life until he got away at fifteen to be a bellhop at the Palace. They both came from the Barbary Coast, but Kerry sometimes thought she'd gotten a much better deal even though her dad had been murdered. She'd gone to live with Addison, gotten an education and a real job, and met Beth. That surely amounted to a whole lot of good. Teddy was still kind of a no-account and was only going to be a bellboy his whole life. She berated herself for thinking mean thoughts about her old friend.

"How's he respectable if he runs a saloon full of whores?"

"He don't have the girls do that no more. They just serve drinks."

"Well, how's he going to help me?' Kerry was being ornery because of her anxiety and taking her fear out on Teddy. It wasn't fair to him but she couldn't help it.

"You're asking me and I'm tryin' to think of stuff. Leo's still there. You could ask him."

"Yeah, yeah. Fine. I suppose. Just tell me if you think of something. If Beth gets her wish, I'm going to have to get me some more money, and a steady stream of it."

Kerry left Teddy to go back to work before she was missed. The past year had seen the gradual ascendance of Monsieur Fermel to sort of co-sous chef with Davey. Chef Henri never said anything one way or another, but that was how it was, and Kerry had to struggle to get enough work. If she slipped up at all, Fermel would get rid of her and that would be that. No medical school, no house near the bay, and she and Beth would likely be on the street, begging for bread. Kerry shivered at that thought. It wasn't going to happen, if she had anything to say about it and if she were to use her head. What she needed was a little luck.

❖

Beth stared at the equations on the page. The numbers and letters were meaningless. Just the day before, she and Addison had sat together in his dining room as he patiently took her through solving a quadratic equation. They'd saved mathematics for their last subject because Beth had wanted that particular discipline's details fresh in her mind. She'd mastered everything else to Addison and Esther's satisfaction. Esther had taken up a part of her tutelage, much to her enjoyment.

Esther turned out to be in her early thirties and from a Jewish family in Manhattan. Beth had encountered Jews a few times, but they'd seemed like anyone else. Esther was different, though it was hard for Beth to say why. Her manner of speaking, for one. It had taken Beth a while to get used to it. Esther had told her a little about her background.

"My father, like many devout Jews, has a great respect for learning and books. Having no sons, he decided to educate me. In our tradition, there is no greater honor for a child than to be a doctor. The only greater profession is rabbi. But that's out of the question." She laughed heartily.

"So I decided to be a doctor. My father's *shul* were bewildered and my mother objected, but my papa could be very stubborn."

Esther told her more about New York City, Philadelphia, and the hospitals where she'd studied in London and Paris. Beth's imagination was fired, and she wondered if she'd ever be able to see those places. She'd only been abroad once, only to Manila where there was a war. She'd thought she was very worldly until she met Esther, and then she knew how provincial she actually was. She was enchanted with Esther because she was so different, and she realized that Addison was equally enchanted. Esther talked about him sometimes, but it was hard to discern her feelings. When they were all three together, they concentrated on Beth's tutoring. Between the two of them, Beth thought fondly, they'd managed to beat a great deal of learning into her.

But would it be enough to make up for her lack of education? It was obvious why Mission High School wasn't accredited by the University of California. Their curriculum had a long way to go to meet the standards of the exacting state university system. She would only see if her tutoring worked after she took the exams in two weeks. Between now and then, she had to master these wretched equations.

She had no idea what good they would do for a doctor. Addison could only say that some mathematical disciplines were considered good for the brain. Doctors had to do arithmetic just like nurses, and Beth was reasonably adept at that. She held her head in her hands and struggled to focus. This entire process was somewhat like a Christmas goose being fattened for the slaughter. Well. Soon it would be done.

❖

Addison hung up the hospital central phone and rubbed his chin thoughtfully. The telephone call had come from Dr. Kinyoun. He had asked if Addison would care to be part of a team to visit Chinatown as part of an inspection team to look into some other possible plague cases. He would go, and he decided to ask both Esther and Beth as well. Beth would benefit from the real-life experience, and Esther would be gratified.

He looked for reasons to spend time with Esther apart from their daily work at the City and County Hospital. He was overjoyed when she'd agreed to help him tutor Beth, and the three of them spent many hours together. She always came to consult him on any difficult case she had, and he did the same. The other doctors smirked and commented, but Addison was unfazed. She was an excellent doctor, but she was a remarkable woman in other ways. Just a few months after their acquaintance, he'd told her the story of how he'd come to be Kerry's guardian and Beth's mentor.

They had been sitting in the doctor's lounge having a coffee break, although Esther preferred tea, and happened to be alone. When Addison told his tale, Esther listened closely, and when he met her eyes, they were uncommonly focused. He couldn't tell if it was his story or him, but her intense attention unsettled him a little.

"So, when I was teaching the nurses, Miss Hammond became a favorite of mine, and we subsequently shared overseas duty. She came to live with us for a time, and she and, er, Kerry formed a strong bond that endures to this day." He didn't want to say anymore because he was protective of them. He wasn't sure what Esther would make of it if he hinted at the true nature of their relationship.

"They're lesbians then?" She asked without emotion.

"I'm sure I don't know what you mean." He'd never heard the word but had an inkling of what it might connote.

"Oh, Addison. Don't be silly. That young Kerry, I knew it the moment I met her at your home. It's not that uncommon. I wondered about Beth. She speaks freely of Kerry but not of anything intimate. It's caused me to speculate about their bond, as you call it. She may not be aware of it."

"I'm not familiar with the word, but if I take your meaning to be women who prefer other women, then yes, but I want to maintain discretion. I…" He was uncomfortable discussing this subject with Esther.

"It's not a bad word, Doctor. It's taken from the Greek island of Lesbos, birthplace of Sappho."

Addison wasn't fond of poetry but didn't want tell Esther. So he nodded in what he hoped was a sage and worldly fashion.

Esther continued. "They call the men homosexuals. Some people use the word 'invert,' especially to describe the person who takes on the characteristics of the other gender. I'd suspect Kerry is an example. Yet they find that normal-appearing and acting people also harbor desires for their own sex. So I don't understand it completely. The new discipline of psychiatry is replete with descriptions of human behavior, some of it contradictory." Esther laughed. Then she fixed her eyes on Addison and became serious again.

"I was familiar with a number of such people in New York City. With San Francisco's reputation for harboring all sorts of people and behavior, I can't believe the phenomenon is unknown here."

"Er. Beth is quite aware of their bond, as you call it. They confided in me." Addison felt defensive on the part of himself and his city. "To be sure, the phenomenon, as you call it, isn't unknown in the city, as it wasn't unknown in my birthplace, Boston. It's just not spoken of. I'd never heard the words you refer to."

"Ah. Well. They're new terms, I suppose, for something that's no doubt as old as human history. The Europeans are well ahead of us in most matters. Anyhow, I have no particular objection to such folks, if that's what concerns you. I'm a follower of the anarchist philosophy, and they hold that the matters of the human heart are best left to the direction of the owners of those hearts and not to any law of society."

"Oh, certainly." Addison agreed, though he didn't know exactly what she meant and didn't want to seem more ignorant than he was sure she considered him already. Esther always either impressed or annoyed him, and both reactions made him berate himself. He'd finally admitted in his mind that he was attracted to her, but he forced his behavior around her into a tightly wound, though not formal, neutrality. To apprise her of his feelings and risk rejection was one thing. For them to become intimate and then for him to be unable to offer her a future seemed infinitely more painful. He decided he must be professional and that was all. To be otherwise would be unfair. He could sometimes see a glimmer of something more personal in her eye contact, but he never encouraged it.

"I'm glad you don't take the priggish moralistic tack that so many men seem prone to. That's admirable."

The compliment took him off guard but pleased him. She didn't think he was a simpleton for not knowing what "lesbian" meant.

"Thank you. I must admit, I'd like to hear more about these so-called anarchists of yours. We're not very political around here. The politics of San Francisco revolve around making money and not much else."

She laughed. "Well, that's true everywhere. Oh dear, it's grown late. It's time I got back to the ward."

They'd returned to work, but Addison was more intrigued than ever.

He thought of that conversation and the many others that had previously occurred. He was unused to considering intellectual attraction as a means of relating to a woman. He'd truly had been naive to marry Laura. He should have had a lot more experience with women so he'd have spotted her faults before her looks had captivated him. He was now stuck in a marriage that existed on paper only but that he couldn't extricate himself from in order to pursue another woman.

It was astonishing how powerful a connection could be that was not based on looks. Their professional and intellectual relationship, though similar to friendships he enjoyed with other men, was its own form of intimacy. However, rather than giving him the ability to distance himself from her, it made it more difficult to deny his feelings.

❖

The night before she was to take the Medical Department's entrance examinations, Beth couldn't sleep. She was still lying awake when Kerry slipped into bed. "Hello, love," she said, softly.

"Oh goodness! You're awake. You startled me," Kerry said, then looked at her closely.

"Are you nervous, sweetheart?"

"Yes." Having to say that word aloud made the simple truth of it more real.

Kerry gathered her up in her arms and stroked her hair. "Shhh. All's well. You'll do fine."

"I don't know which worries me more, succeeding and gaining admittance or failing and just going back to carrying on as we are."

"You're not going to fail."

Beth wished she could be so clear in her certainty. Kerry was always the more definite of the two of them. She'd determined they belonged together and took steps to ensure that happened. She'd found their room to rent. She was the one who seemed surest that Beth would become a doctor. She never wavered. Compared to Kerry, Beth felt weak and unsure, although she was anything but. Kerry's arms around her and her soft reassuring voice helped. Beth relaxed and finally slept.

❖

Beth numbly accepted her exam booklets, found a seat, and pulled out her four sharpened pencils. She listened to the proctor's directions, then bowed her head and said a short prayer. She opened the first book and read the questions, took up her pencil, and began to write. She would have to wait for two weeks to learn whether she'd scored high enough to be admitted to the Medical Department.

Addison had invited them over to supper that night. It was just he and the housekeeper. He took pains to keep the conversation on subjects other than the examinations. Beth was tired but relieved. It was good just holding Kerry's hand under the table. She was unsure what had transpired between Kerry and Addison, but they seemed to be getting along very well. She was grateful for that. It had been distressing when Kerry wouldn't see or speak to Addison. She'd have to ask her what happened.

Addison beamed at Kerry and Beth from his chair at the head of the table. "This is a pleasure, isn't it? Just like the old days." Beth decided not to mention that it was better than the "old days" with Laura glowering at Kerry from her side of the dinner table and ignoring Beth.

Addison handed the food that Mrs. Evans brought out around to each of them. To Beth he seemed in an especially good mood. She was drained after her long day and wanted to go home and sleep, for she'd be up again at dawn and back to the Presidio General Hospital to face Marjorie's displeasure. Marjorie had only reluctantly permitted her a day and a night off. It wasn't as though she didn't have a substitute. Sometimes being needed so much wasn't all that gratifying. Beth had to pull her attention back to the present and try to attend to what Addison was saying.

"I heard from Dr. Kinyoun again, and he's been asked to take a group of physicians into Chinatown to check for plague victims. I'm expecting it'll be quite a difficult undertaking. The Celestials are notoriously closemouthed. They hate white intrusion into their neighborhood. I imagine they can't be happy to be accused of harboring the plague. The police will accompany us."

Kerry spoke up suddenly. "People are cruel to them 'cause they're different. I liked to visit there when I was a kid. They never paid me any mind."

"Ah, Kerry, that's the truth. If you leave people alone, they're not inclined to make a fuss. This time we can't though. Kinyoun doesn't want to risk the plague getting out of Chinatown and into the rest of San Francisco. Beth, are you game for another adventure?"

Beth was surprised. She wanted to go, but she was feeling bad about leaving Marjorie in the lurch. Of course, if she was admitted to the Medical Department, she'd truly be gone, and she feared that would spell the end of their friendship.

"I do, but I don't know if I can," she said.

"Nurse Reynolds?" Addison raised an eyebrow.

"Yes."

"Beth, my dear, let me talk with her. It's well for her to depend on you, for you're quite reliable. However, you're about to embark on a new chapter in your life, and Marjorie must learn to cope without you."

Beth glanced at Kerry, who was looking at her with an unreadable expression.

"All right. I'd very much like to go if you can convince Marjorie."

"Leave it to me. Dr. Kinyoun has permitted me to bring Dr. Strauss along. She's always telling me that patients are sometimes easier when their doctor is female. I'd like to put that to the test with reluctant Chinese. It would prove interesting." He grinned.

Later that night when they were in bed, Kerry said, "It's not what I thought you'd be doing as a doctor. I only thought of you in a hospital with white people."

"Kerry, dearest, what are you worried about?'

"You getting sick or hurt...I don't know."

"*You* went to Chinatown yourself, when you were a kid. Why is this different?"

Kerry turned over restlessly and put her arm over her face. "I want to protect you."

Beth embraced her. "You're the best and bravest and most loving person, but you can't always protect me. I want to do this kind of work, and I'll need to go to unsavory places. I find it most amusing that you'd worry like this when you grew up on the Barbary Coast. I assure you, I'll be perfectly fine with Addison, Esther, and Dr. Kinyoun, and the police will be there, for goodness sake."

Kerry fell silent, having no answer for Beth. She couldn't quite articulate her feelings. Not only was she nervous and anxious about Beth becoming a doctor. But now it seemed she'd have to worry about where Beth might have to go as one. It made no sense in the end. Beth was always around sick people, but she never got sick. This worry of hers was only a symptom, Kerry supposed, of her general dread of not being able to make sure nothing stood in Beth's way. Again she silently berated herself for entertaining thoughts that it would be better if Beth couldn't realize her dream. That wasn't how she wanted to feel, and she told herself to just wait and see.

Chapter Nine

On the day of inspection, Esther, Beth, and Addison traveled to the San Francisco Health Department offices downtown near city hall. It was a large group, composed of twenty-five volunteer physicians and several burly and grim-faced policemen. As they listened to Dr. Kinyoun describe their task, Esther whispered to Beth and Addison. "If they're taking police with them they must expect trouble. But this isn't a particularly suitable way to conduct public-health operations."

"We've chosen to take our surveys in the evenings in hopes of finding the residents at home. Please make sure to emphasize that we do not wish to jail or deport anyone. We want to treat the unfortunate victims of the plague. We are lucky to have in our company several volunteer translators who will assist us in our endeavors. It's of utmost importance we gain the confidence of the citizens. Their civic leaders have asked for cooperation. We will disperse in our teams and meet back here at the health department at ten p.m."

Dr. Kinyoun gave out assignments for different areas of Chinatown, using a large map with lines drawn on it. Addison, Esther, and Beth would be part of a team of six doctors and medical students, along with three police officers. Their destination was the area bounded by Dupont, Stockton, Sacramento, and Jackson Streets. Dr. Kinyoun had pointed out a tiny alley, Waverly Place, where he said they should pay particular attention because of cases previously reported.

It was still sunny in the late afternoon, but the western wind was kicking up. Beth settled into a wagon with the rest of their party. One of the policemen drove, and two of them sat in the back with the other medical people.

They were quiet at first, but then Esther spoke to the policeman sitting across from her.

"Have you done this before, Officer, and if so what was the outcome?"

The police officer, a large, middle-aged man with the red-veined nosed of a drinker, sniffed and seemed to consider spitting but thought better of it. "Them Chinks got no truck with the likes of us. White devils, they call us. They think we want to poison 'em or throw 'em in jail."

"Why do they think that?" Beth watched Esther's face and saw, from her peripheral vision, that Addison was watching the exchange closely as well.

"They're dirty as well as ignorant. We was down there last month trying to disinfect the neighborhood and they nearly rioted."

Esther spoke. "Officer, er, Maloney, is it? Your attitude might contribute to their lack of trust. We are, after all, going into their homes. A little respect and restraint might be in order. Did this disinfection help?"

"Naw, just made 'em madder. The stink of sulfur, I reckon. And look, here we are going back, so no, it didn't help."

"I heard from Kinyoun they'd had a few more suspicious cases, but the people were denying up and down they had the plague," Addison stated. "He said the governor of California had his own doctors in to say it wasn't the plague. People won't trust us if we can't agree. The state's doctors claimed that bacillus couldn't cause the disease."

Esther's eyebrows went up and she pursed her lips. "What sort of untenable situation have you gotten us into, Addison?" Her eyes flashed.

"Truly, Doctor. I don't know, but we've had a few cases of the plague and surely there's more. If we are to stem the tide, we must identify them. Kinyoun thinks it can't be allowed to get out of Chinatown."

Before Esther could say anything, a young man who'd introduced himself as a medical student from San Francisco Homeopathic

Medical College spoke up. "I, for one, am not taking any chances with this contagion. I don't care about the rest of you, but I hear the filth of this place'll kill you. I'm prepared." He pulled a small cloth bag from his coat and anchored it around his neck. The smell of camphor drifted into Beth's nose.

"Do you believe that'll help protect you from the plague?" she asked, incredulous that a medical man would have such medieval superstitions.

He looked abashed but said no more. The cart clattered down Market Street, then turned north on Kearney Street. The fine masonry buildings of the financial district began to lessen in number as ramshackle wooden and brick structures jammed close together on the narrow streets replaced them. Beth looked at the cages of live chickens and other animals piled on the sidewalks.

The streets were crowded with Chinese people, dressed in quilted jackets, both men and women. The men wore their hair in long queues trailing down their backs. Coolies hauled unbelievably large burdens on their backs. The lampposts were covered with flyers in Chinese characters. To Beth, they'd left San Francisco altogether and been somehow magically transported to an Oriental city.

Their cart pulled up at the entrance to Waverly Place, where they alighted to split up into groups, each with a policeman and a translator. Esther took Beth's arm and pulled her close to speak into her ear. "This is going to be rough, I can tell. I don't know what this policeman is going to do, but if I can keep him out of the way and speak to the translator, we may have a chance. Addison!" she called. He walked to them. "If Officer Maloney starts bullying people, I want you to stop him. I don't believe he'll listen to me, but he may listen to you. But I want to do the talking to the residents through the translator. Beth will help me. They'll respond to us women better than either you or that blustering policeman."

"Esther, I want to believe you're correct, but we've got police escorts so we aren't harmed—"

"You're being naive, Addison. The police don't care what happens to us. They want to intimidate these poor people. I went through a similar exercise with Polish and Russian immigrants in the Lower East Side tenements in New York City. These people can't speak English, they're suspicious of us anyhow, and if the police get involved they'll clam up. We'll not get anywhere unless the Chinese can be made to trust us somehow."

"I think you're the one who's naive, Esther, but shall we proceed? We've come here for a purpose." He consulted the list of addresses they'd received. "The first one is right here."

Beth listened to their conversation, fascinated but apprehensive. She was excited to have been asked along on such a delicate but vital task, and she could see the sparks fly back and forth between Esther and Addison. She almost giggled but managed to keep a straight face. There *was* something between them, but they were keeping it under wraps. They walked into the dank, fetid alley, and Officer Maloney pounded on the first door and shouted, "Health department. Open up!" The translator glanced nervously back at them and then shouted himself, only in Chinese.

The door opened a crack, and before the translator could say a word, Officer Maloney threw his weight against the door and pushed in. The four of them followed.

In the dim light, Beth saw an older woman cowering in a corner, a younger woman embracing her and obviously trying to protect her. A man stood in the middle of the tiny room, clearly ready to defend his family. There was but a single light in the room, which was perhaps ten by fifteen feet. Cots lined one wall, and a tiny stove belched black smoke. Beth could scarcely imagine how they could live in such cramped conditions. And, in spite of her scientific knowledge of bacteriology, she sensed her own tendency to attribute disease to the unsanitary conditions of the Chinese home.

Addison put himself in front of the policeman and stuck his chest out just a little. He was nearly as tall but not as bulky as the policeman. "Officer Maloney, could you wait outside, please? If we require help, we'll summon you. These folk will not harm us."

"Doc, I—" He seemed ready to assert his authority but looked at Addison and then nodded and left the hovel.

"Mister Chow?" Esther addressed the translator politely and in a pleasant tone. "Please introduce us to this family, make our apologies for the abrupt entry into their home, and tell them the purpose of our visit."

Beth followed the twin gazes of Addison and Esther, who were looking closely at the old woman in the arms of the younger one. She could see why. The old woman looked ill, very ill, as a matter of fact. She was sagging, barely able to stand. Her eyes were glassy and feverish, her hair lank and disordered.

Mister Chow bowed and spoke rapidly in Chinese to the man. The man drew back, appearing angry.

"I told him you are doctors and have come to see if anyone is sick. That you don't wish anyone any harm. He says the only people who live here are himself, his wife, and her mother."

"Ask him if any the family has been ill.?" Esther said. Her voice was even, but Beth could hear the tension underneath.

After more tense, rapid-fire Chinese sentences between Mr. Chow and the man, Mr. Chow said, "He says no one's sick."

"Tell him that his mother-in-law is clearly ill, and we want to examine her," Esther said.

The translator looked uncertain, but he went ahead. The man was obviously becoming quite agitated. "He says she's not sick. There is no need."

Addison said, "Esther, we need to get Maloney in here to add some force to our request. It's clear that woman is sick, and we have to determine if it is the plague."

"If we bring in the policeman, we won't get any cooperation, Addison. Let me try again."

Esther smiled at the Chinese man, then pointed at herself and at the two women. "Ask him if he would allow his family to speak to me."

The translator obliged, and the Chinese paterfamilias seemed to soften a little. He turned and spoke to Esther. "He says all right but no men!"

"Very well. May I have this young woman help me?" She indicated Beth.

The Chinese man nodded. Esther made her expression encouraging, clearly hoping he would respond. He didn't. Beth kept her gaze toward the floor.

"Mr. Chow, you and Addison please go stand by the door and turn your backs."

"What!" Addison was clearly astounded.

"Do what I ask, please." Esther turned to the Chinese man and put her hands together and bowed slightly, as she'd seen the translator do. Beth did the same. The man stepped aside.

Esther motioned to Beth, and they stood in front of the two women. Esther brought out her stethoscope. The women cowered.

"Mr. Chow, please explain that we won't hurt them. I want to take Mama's temperature and listen to her heart." Esther whispered to Beth, "While I'm doing that, you stand right next to me and palpate her neck. We won't be able to get her to disrobe, so I'm hoping we can tell something from the inguinal lymph nodes."

Beth tried to breathe to calm herself and stayed alongside Esther, who was smiling and bowing as she drew out her thermometer and, by pantomime, got the old woman to open her mouth and accept it.

Beth placed her hands on either side of the woman's neck and pressed gently under her chin. She palpated the swellings. Looking closely, she could see the beginning of discoloration. The old woman very likely had the plague, but they needed a sample of saliva. How were they going to do that? They really needed the translator. Esther paused, looking nonplussed. She mimed opening her mouth and pointed at the old woman to ask her to do the same. She complied, but when Beth tried to insert a swab, she screamed and started to cower against her daughter.

Addison stood at the door, facing away. "Is all well?" he asked, sounding impatient.

Before Esther could answer, the door flew open, nearly hitting both Addison and Mr. Chow. Officer Maloney pushed between them, his nightstick out and exceedingly agitated.

The two women drew away, babbling in Chinese.

"What's going on?" Maloney shouted.

"Officer!" Esther spoke sharply. "You're not needed. Please leave!"

"I heard yelling. I want to know what the trouble is."

The Chinese man suddenly leaped forward and threw himself at Maloney. Maloney was much larger than he and had no trouble fending him off and hit him with his nightstick. The two women screamed again. Mr. Chow was shouting frantically in Chinese. Addison grabbed Esther and Beth by their arms and pulled them away.

Officer Maloney sat on the Chinese man. He looked triumphant, as though that was what he'd wanted to do all along. "He's under control now. You can do what you need. You need me to turn him over?"

Beth saw Esther was nearly apoplectic with rage. "He's not the problem. You've certainly ruined any chance we have of cooperation, you imbecile. Would you let him up, please, and go back outside and wait for us. I'm begging you."

"No, miss. I was told not to let you alone. I tried it your way. But I've got my orders. I'm not leaving."

He folded his arms. Esther snorted and turned away. Addison started to say something but stopped. Beth saw that he was willing to let Esther make the decision on how to proceed.

Esther finally told the poor translator they wanted to take a saliva sample. He translated, but the man shook his head so adamantly that they all knew it was hopeless. She tried asking if the mother could come with them, but they didn't need the translator to understand that the response to that request was "no." With the glowering presence of Officer Maloney, they couldn't accomplish anything further.

Addison wrote in his notebook that the plague was suspected at that address, and they went on. For several hours, they knocked on doors, and their reception veered from utter confusion to outright hostility. They finally stopped because it was close to ten o'clock and they were due to return to the Department of Public Health. The meeting with Dr. Kinyoun went on until almost midnight and included many complaints about the clumsy behavior of the police and the refusal of the Chinese residents to act in their own self-interest.

Addison was dejected. "Observations were one thing, but samples were crucial for us to definitively diagnose the plague. We haven't been able to obtain any samples or convince any possible plague victims to go to the hospital."

"We obviously don't know what we're doing and we deserve failure," Esther said. "We ought to go back without any policeman, just with a translator."

"I don't believe that would be a very good idea, Esther. Perhaps we need to convince the police to take a different approach,"

"Oh, Addison, that won't be possible. I thought the city of New York was bad in the treatment of its poorest citizens, but San Francisco's worse. The language barrier monstrously complicates this. At least my poor Polish patients knew some English, but we're confronting a tremendous cultural and language divide."

"It's worse than that, Esther, because the leaders of Chinatown won't cooperate and encourage their citizens to do the same."

Beth was distressed by what she'd seen and by her two mentors' discussion. She was disappointed at how badly they'd failed in their mission and how impossible it seemed to make any sort of headway in trying to stem the spread of the plague among the Chinese. If this was how the practice of public health would proceed, she wasn't sure she truly wanted to pursue it. Being in the hospital and treating patients who were at least nominally cooperative seemed more rewarding.

Chapter Ten

K erry was wakeful and unsettled after she returned home from work. She was worried because Beth hadn't returned. She needn't be concerned because Beth was with Addison and Esther and was safe, but she worried anyway. She thrashed about, tangling her limbs in the sheets. The bed linen carried Beth's scent, and concentrating on that finally calmed her and she dozed until the sound of the front door closing woke her up. She debated feigning sleep but decided that was silly because Beth would probably want to talk anyway.

Beth brought a wave of cold night air as she dropped on the bed in her clothes to embrace Kerry. "Oh, Kerry. I'm glad to be home. It was terrible." She described the night's adventures, but she wasn't excited or happy. She was perturbed.

"We could do nothing really. The people didn't trust us. No one can be taken care of if he doesn't trust his doctors. They don't speak English, but it was worse than that."

"Shhh, love. It's not your fault." Kerry stroked her hair.

"Oh. But if I'm to be this kind of doctor, I've got to be better. I need to be like Esther. She's wonderful—so smart and so sensitive. I believe she and Addison have something between them."

"Truly?"

"Yes, but also they're at odds, and I think Addison won't court her because he's still married to Laura."

"Do you think that's it?"

"I'm not sure. I know she cares for him because she came right out and asked me if he was married. I don't know what they'll do. Well, I must go to sleep."

She got up and put her nightgown on as Kerry watched in the dim light of their one lamp, loving her and still worried.

Beth's last sleepy words were, "I'll hear soon from the university, by next week, I hope. But it's back to the Presidio General Hospital at the crack of dawn."

And Kerry wondered again in her heart how she'd feel when the time came and they found out Beth would go to school to be a doctor. She'd never given much thought before to the difference in their education. Beth certainly never mentioned that Kerry had only learned to read a few years before they met. If Beth became a doctor, would the gap in their educations affect them? Another concern to add to the ones she already had.

She held Beth as she fell asleep and worried that she not only wouldn't be able to support them, but that Beth was on a path that would take her far away and leave Kerry behind.

❖

Addison was sitting in his office, writing notes on his patients, when Esther appeared at his door and sat down without ceremony. He looked up, his pen poised, and she stared at him in what he interpreted as an unfriendly fashion.

"Dr. Strauss? May I help you?"

"You are an obtuse man," she said, abruptly.

He was astounded and a little hurt. "What would cause you to characterize me as such?"

"In spite of my best and most persistent efforts, you've failed to notice me."

"Oh? It's nearly impossible to not take note of you, Doctor."

"Esther. It's Esther when it's just us."

The phrase "just us" saddened him. There was no "just us," not in the sense he'd like, and there never would be.

"All right, then. Esther. Please explain further."

"Why have you never, not even once, invited me to a social occasion? You've been talking with me and have summoned me numerous times to join you and Beth so we can study with her and impart our wisdom. We've attempted the plague investigation in Chinatown."

"And did any of that displease you? If so, I would've thought you would decline. You're not one to do anything you don't wish to do."

"It didn't displease me in the least. I've enjoyed it, but I'd rather we had some time when Miss Hammond wasn't present."

"I see. Well. I'd imagine her presence lends a certain propriety to any interaction we have outside of the hospital and you would welcome that." He hated how cool he sounded, but it was necessary. The sidelong glances and soft confidential tones she adopted when speaking to him were the symptoms of what he feared. Esther was developing certain expectations, and he must disabuse her of them as soon as possible without alienating her.

"Well? Maybe I would like to see you without Beth's presence." Esther raised her eyebrows, challenging him. Addison paused, not knowing what exactly he could say that wouldn't be offensive.

"Well, what do you have to say?"

She was verging on being demanding, and that helped him. "Nothing. I have nothing to say because it's not appropriate, what you're suggesting."

"Not appropriate?" She was clearly offended.

"I'm sure you understand."

"I'm sure I do. Very well. You're a prig as well as obtuse. Consider the subject closed." She arose and strode out, slamming the door.

The sharp sound made him jump. He sat, wondering why he felt so bereft and if his response was really the correct one.

❖

It was a slim envelope bearing the seal of the University of California in blue. Beth's hands shook as she stared at it. She'd walked into the house and found it in the mail piled under the mail slot by the front door. She listened and couldn't hear any sound, meaning Mrs.

Thompson wasn't home. She was relieved. She also was happy Kerry wasn't here either. She was alone with her fate. She hung up her coat on the peg and walked, envelope in hand, to the parlor and sat down. She smoothed her hand over her name on the front, the handwriting legible and elegant.

The letter was wonderful looking, but what was the news inside? Was she to be matriculating along with the rest of the class of 1905, or was she to continue as before as a faithful but underappreciated nurse for the Sixth Army at the Presidio General Hospital? She put the envelope on the sofa and went to the kitchen drawer for a knife to open it. She didn't want to make a mess of it by tearing it open with her finger.

After she returned to the parlor, she sat down on the divan, knife in hand, and looked at the envelope again. She hesitated, then shook her head, inserted the knife, and tore a slit on the top of the envelope. It was time to know. She took out the letter and unfolded it.

Dear Miss Hammond,

With great pleasure, the Regents of the University of California invite you to become a member of the incoming class of 1905 of the Medical Department of the University to pursue the degree of Doctor of Medicine. Your examination results qualify you for a place in our program. Kindly inform the Office of the Registrar of your intention to matriculate so that your place is preserved. They...

It seemed unreal. Beth read it again and decided it *was* real. She'd done it. She was to attend medical school, to study to be a doctor, to *become* a doctor. She was breathing hard from the shock. She looked around wildly but she was alone. She wanted to tell someone, but she couldn't. Mrs. Thompson didn't have a telephone so she couldn't phone the City and County Hospital to tell Addison or Esther. She couldn't telephone the Palace Hotel restaurant. She had to content herself with imagining how she would share her news and how those closest to her would react. She suddenly thought of her mother and father. Should she tell them? They hadn't spoken in almost two years. They hadn't approved of her becoming a nurse so they'd scarcely be happy she was going to be a doctor. She decided not to tell them.

❖

They had a dinner party because it because seemed the right thing to do. Kerry put on her social persona and smiled until she thought her face would crack from the strain. Across the table from her, Beth was radiant. She hadn't looked like that since the first night they'd spent together in love. Kerry wanted to be ecstatic for her but was relatively silent as Beth conversed animatedly with Esther and Addison.

Kerry watched the interaction between Addison and Esther. Beth's opinion of their feelings for each other fought for her attention alongside happiness at Beth's joy and her dread about their future. Beth would need to concentrate on her studies, that was what they said, and she, Kerry, was steadfast in her promise that she would take care of things, take care of Beth, no matter what.

She'd come home to find Beth wide-awake and sitting in bed with a letter in her hand and an expression that telegraphed immediately what had happened. They'd talked, and Kerry had made the proper expression of congratulations, but she wasn't being completely honest about her fear. But she refused to let her uncertainties perturb Beth, who would have enough to handle as she pursued medical studies.

"Are you really, truly sure, Kerry, dearest?" Beth had said. "I'm not compelled to attend. I've only been given the opportunity."

"Of course you'll go! This is your dream and you must pursue it to its end."

And so Kerry had said nothing and they made love and Beth fell asleep in bliss. Kerry held her close and swore Beth would have what she wanted, nothing less, and she'd do whatever it took to ensure that.

Now they sat with the remains of their supper, and everyone was having another glass of wine, and Beth was flushed. She kept looking at Kerry with her eyes sparkling from joy as well as intoxication.

Addison said, "You'll want to try to get Dr. Montgomery as your advisor. He's the most respected faculty member and is also a bacteriologist. You'll want to specialize early—"

Esther interrupted him. "Oh, Addison, leave the girl be. There's enough time for all that later. Let's enjoy the moment."

Addison seemed, to Kerry's great surprise, to almost pout at Esther's mild reproof. But then he rolled his eyes and grinned at her.

"Yes, by all means, Esther. We must leave Beth to make those decisions. But classes start in three weeks. She'll have much to do to prepare and become organized. Beth, one thing, have you given notice yet?"

Beth was uncharacteristically hesitant, and Kerry wondered what she was thinking

"I will next week. I want to stay as long as possible."

"You'll need to get over to Parnassus and enroll. You have books to buy and laboratory supplies and what all."

"Yes. But I do want to give Marjorie time to get used to my leaving."

"Yes, certainly. I just want to ensure you're fully ready to take up your studies."

"I promise you I'll be ready."

In the pause that followed, Kerry saw the look Esther gave Addison, and it somewhat resembled the way Sally used to look at the customers in the Grey Dog whom she hoped to seduce. Beth was right about them.

Kerry would have rather speculated about Addison and Esther than think about the future. Four years of medical school, followed by a year of internship, meant Beth wouldn't be earning any money for a long time.

"Well," Beth looked around the table, "I want to thank each of you from the bottom of my heart for everything you've done to help me. You have my everlasting gratitude." She became a little teary.

"I'm truly blessed by your friendship." She raised her glass in a toast. Kerry looked over her glass at Beth and made sure her face was arranged in an expression of joy. Despite her misgivings, she didn't want Beth to ever be troubled by her doubts but to always feel her love.

❖

Beth knocked lightly on the door of Marjorie's office, and Marjorie called, "Come!"

She pushed the door open slowly. Marjorie raised her head and their gazes met. Beth couldn't read her expression. Two weeks previously, when she delivered the news to Marjorie and gave her a letter of resignation, Marjorie had said little aside from issuing a list of items she wanted attended to prior to her departure. It was now time to say good-bye.

"I've made extensive notes on all my current patients. Here." She handed Marjorie a number of sheets of paper. "I've talked at length with Nurse Simmons."

"I'm grateful. Your keys?" She held out her hand.

Beth detached the ring from her belt and put it into Marjorie's hand. Her arms hung at her sides. She didn't want to simply leave, but she wasn't sure what to say.

Marjorie took the keys without a word and dropped them into a drawer and shut it. She folded her hands atop her desk and looked at Beth quizzically. "Anything else, Nurse?"

"No, I believe that's all." She was hurt that Marjorie was being so cold. It didn't seem right after their long and close association.

"Thank you for everything. I'll always remember you with great affection and respect. I would want to continue our friendship, but I understand if that's not possible."

After a long pause Marjorie said, "Although I don't agree with your choice, I have to accept it. I'll miss you very much."

"I'll miss you as well. If you're amenable, can we meet again sometime?"

"We'll see. I must return to this task." Marjorie gestured at some papers on the desk.

"I understand. Take care of yourself. My best to Florence. Good-bye."

There would be no hug or even a handshake, Beth saw. After a moment, she turned and walked out the door, shutting it gently behind her.

❖

Kerry sat on the divan with Beth as they looked through the university's register and catalogue, and she watched Beth's face as she turned the pages. She glowed with excitement and read out loud the parts she liked and every so often told Kerry to help her remember something. She thumbed to the part that detailed the fees that would be due and showed Kerry. The yearly fee was one hundred fifty dollars, plus another forty-five for laboratory equipment and books.

Kerry swallowed at the sum but smiled. "Of course, love. Just tell me when and to whom I must send the fee. At least we don't have to pay for your board." Just saying that made Kerry feel better, if only a little.

"Oh, I agree. I can continue to live at home and take the streetcar to Parnassus. I'm lucky we don't live that far away. Neither of us would want me to have to find a room up there. Kerry, dearest..."

"Yes?"

"Truly, I want you to be honest. Are you sure we can afford this?" Beth looked her, her expression concerned, and Kerry gulped. She'd never lied to Beth before and she hated to start, but there was no other way. If Beth knew the truth, she'd insist they must save for the house. If she didn't go to medical school, it would break her heart. Kerry was determined they would have both. She would find a way, she had to, for Beth's sake, for both of them.

"We can. I can bring home some food from the Palace sometime. I'll talk to Mrs. Thompson about cutting our rent in exchange for me helping her with something. I have the savings."

"I'm perturbed you won't tell me how much you've saved, but I understand that for us, even still some things are private. I trust you."

Beth grinned at her and Kerry grinned back, concealing her true feelings. Between the school fees and living expenses, the savings would go down quickly. They'd managed to save some during the last year, but not enough. Kerry listened to Beth run on about her plans for school, but her mind was working at a furious pace. She had to find another source of income, and quickly too.

Chapter Eleven

Kerry contemplated her *mis en place*. She was in a very bad mood because she'd told M. Fermel the week before that she'd be pleased to work more hours, but he'd ignored her. She heard from Davey that they were short staffed most days at dinner, so she couldn't understand why her services weren't welcome. Davey was none too happy as well since M. Fermel had gradually but definitely undermined his former power as sous chef, and Chef seemed to be oblivious.

"Why not go to Chef ourselves and talk to him?" Kerry asked. But Davey sighed and spat on the kitchen floor. Kerry had never seen him do such a thing.

"That'll do no good. Chef will just lose his temper and order us back to work. He's got no time for us. He's away even more than usual, and he lets that bastard Frog run wild."

"I guess it'd be no good to ask *him*?" Kerry knew the answer before Davey could open his mouth."

"He hates you even worse than Jim did. I think Chef told him he had to keep you around though. Otherwise, you'd be gone."

"Well, then, I suppose I'm on my own as usual." Kerry swallowed her anger and put on a brave face for Davey.

Later, she went to find Teddy Black at the bellboys' office and dragged him out for a smoke. "You got to help me, Ted. Don't you know someone who needs help with something and who's willing to pay?"

"I told you all's I know! Why don't you ask Leo? He might know about something."

"And I told you I don't never want to go back there!"

"Yeah, but how in the hell you going to find the work you want 'less you do, Kerry? You told me you don't want nothing to do with no women, and that's all's I can tell you."

Kerry wanted to grab his neck and shake him until his teeth rattled like she did when they were little and he made her mad, but she couldn't do that. Kerry went back to the kitchen, still frustrated. She didn't have a choice: she'd have to make her way back to the Barbary Coast and talk to Leo. She'd have to go before noon, but Leo might be there early since he wasn't a drinker but an insomniac.

She didn't tell Beth where she was going because she saw no need to worry her. Beth knew all about her past and certainly didn't hold it against her, but she would be concerned that Kerry was going to pay a visit to the place where she grew up since Kerry had such mixed feelings about it.

They'd made one nostalgic visit together to see the Cobweb Palace and Beth had understood more clearly about her childhood, but as Kerry rode the cable car downtown to the Ferry Building she remembered what Beth had said while they were looking at the pictures of women. She'd said Kerry had to be good because she could never love someone who wasn't.

Beth had left home early in the morning to go to the university to register for her classes and otherwise get organized to start the following week. She'd talked to Esther, and one of the things Esther had suggested was to pay a call on her professors and tell them she'd be attending school and that she would appreciate respect but didn't expect any special treatment because of her sex. Kerry was glad for the time to slip away downtown without having to tell Beth why she was leaving so early or to have to lie about going to the restaurant. It was better that way.

Other than the prospect of difficult and time-consuming study, which she actually looked forward to, Beth regularly talked about her concern with the reception she'd get from her fellow students and her professors. If Kerry hadn't been consumed with worry about money, she would have shared Beth's concern. Beth could handle anything, though, and she'd find a way to cope with whatever was presented her. Kerry was grateful she was so caught up in her school plans that she didn't see how quiet Kerry had become.

Kerry made her way the few blocks from the Ferry Building to Jackson Street. The streets and the buildings caused a flood of memories. Her old life had come to seem so far away and disconnected from her present life with Beth, she'd mostly forgotten about it. But here, all at once, the reality came rushing back and she recalled how on New Year's Day she'd stood with Beth looking out over the Golden Gate and sworn she'd never go back to the old life. She'd never take up crimping again, but she was about to reenter the criminal economy of the Barbary Coast. This was different, though, because it was for a vitally important reason. She had to ensure hers and Beth's future.

The Grey Dog Saloon, the place where she'd been born and spent her life up to the age of fifteen, was before her. All around were the familiar sights and sounds of the Barbary Coast. It was too early for the real revelry, but saloons were still open at dawn. Kerry heard the sound of raucous piano music and muffled shouts and curses. The seagulls swooped and shrieked. Behind her was the San Francisco Bay. The Grey Dog had changed. It had a new coat of paint and a new door. The new owner must be seeking to refurbish it a bit.

She walked into the dark interior of the barroom. Well. The inside hadn't changed. As her eyes adjusted to the dimness, she saw Leo behind the bar. He was tall and thin, with a hooked nose and sharp expression that hid the kindness and loyalty he rarely showed anyone. He'd been the one to tell her that her father, Lucky Jack, had been murdered, and they went to the morgue to identify him together. If she asked him, he'd help her, even though they hadn't seen each other for more than a year and a half. That didn't matter.

"Hey, Leo," she said. His back was to her and he stood up, and before he turned around, he said, "Kerry?"

"It is. In the flesh."

"I'll be damned, girl. What the hell are you doing down here? I thought after last year you was gone forever." He didn't move out from behind the bar to embrace her, but that didn't surprise her. She was just happy no one else was around, especially Sally. Their last parting hadn't been friendly because Kerry had left her side to follow Beth.

"I didn't expect to ever come back, but here I am."

"Should I get Sally up? She might have gotten over being mad at—"

"No. Don't. I didn't come to see her."

The emotional storms, romances, and feuds of the pretty waiter girls were familiar to Leo, who just nodded. "Oh. Well. Then what brings you back to these parts?" Leo looked suspicious, and she supposed he had a right to. If she was him, she'd be wondering just what was up.

"I'm hoping you could maybe help me get in on some scheme. Not crimping though," she added, hastily.

Leo rubbed his unshaven chin and lowered his brows. "Hmph. You ain't got no gambling talent. You willing to kill for hire?"

"I'd rather not, if possible." Kerry hadn't even entertained the thought of murder. She was hoping for something less bloody.

"Eh. Too bad, cause there's money in that." He laughed. "I can't think of anything else, but I'll ask around. There's always somebody got something going. Come back here in a few days. I'll see what I can scare up. You sure you don't want to see Sally?"

"Nah. Give her my best but I got to scoot. Thanks, Leo. Be seeing you soon."

"Don't thank me yet, kid. I don't know what I'm going to find, and you may not like it."

Kerry went back uptown to the Palace Hotel. While she might not like getting involved with crime back in the Barbary Coast, she didn't really have a choice.

❖

Beth clutched her list in her hand and stared at the directory on the first floor of the Medical Department building. She'd carefully timed the trip from home to the university campus. Barring any mishap, she'd be able to travel from home to school in twenty minutes. She had gotten off the streetcar and stared at the Affiliated College buildings. The Medical Department was on the far left after the Dentistry and Pharmacy buildings. It was actually the last structure on the street. It was a testament to the power of the University of California that here beyond the residential area, they'd extended a streetcar line to serve the campus.

As the university register had promised, it was an attractive location. A partially wooded hill rose behind the buildings, which seemed nestled beside its protective bulk. Beth had read that Mr. Sutro had donated the land to the University of California. The wind in her face wasn't unpleasant. At the top of the hill on Parnassus Avenue she could see clear to the ocean, and across Parnassus, to her right, stretched Golden Gate Park and a view similar to the one near their home on Divisadero Street. The sun was out and it was an altogether pleasant experience. She would enjoy coming here every day.

She went inside the Medical Department and consulted the directory, then gathered her courage and, picking one of the names from the building directory, Dr. Montgomery, Professor of Microbiology, she sought his office.

He answered her knock with a shouted, "Enter!"

She found a bewhiskered middle-aged man behind the desk who stared at her questioningly but not unkindly. "Yes, miss. May I help you? Are you lost?"

"No sir, I'm not lost. I came to introduce myself to you. I'll be in your class next week."

"You don't say! Well. That's a treat. What's your name, miss?"

"Elizabeth Hammond." She decided formality was called for.

He scanned a sheet of paper. "Ah, here it is. E. Hammond. I would have interpreted it as Edward." He raised an eyebrow.

"Yes, sir. If it's not too forward of me, I wanted to meet you and say that I hope you wouldn't think I would require any special courtesy or treatment from you due to my sex. I want to be just another student and pursue my studies without fanfare."

"Hmm. I see. Brave of you to seek me out to make this announcement. I've had young women in my classes before. It has gone well and it has gone poorly. I hope you'll be up to this. I may say, in my opinion medicine isn't a suitable calling for a woman. It's not that I doubt your intelligence or that I don't believe you'd be good with patients, especially women patients, but the study of anatomy, in particular, can cause much embarrassment to all at certain times."

"Dr. Montgomery. I have worked as a nurse for several years. The human body interests me. It doesn't disgust me. I assure—"

"Wasn't you I was thinking of, young lady, but the men students. There'll be fellows as unused to seeing a woman next to them at the dissecting table as they would to find a Chinaman or a Negro amongst their number."

Beth's mind touched briefly on their recent foray in Chinatown, but she said only, "I anticipate that, but I assure you I can conduct myself with the utmost professionalism. I only wish for others to do the same."

She held her head up and looked Dr. Montgomery straight in the eye. He didn't recoil, but he tilted his head and peered at her through his spectacles as though he was settling something in his mind.

"I see then. Very well. I look forward to our course of instruction together. Now, if you would be so kind, I have things to do." He gestured toward the door; she was dismissed.

"Of course, sir. Thank you for your time." She shook hands with him and went on to the other professors.

The ones she found in were cordial but noncommittal, though she encountered no hostility. Esther had related a story to her of a special lecture course she'd attended. Esther's alma mater was, of course, specifically designed for teaching medicine to women, and its classes, while taught mostly by male doctors, consisted entirely of female students. She went on to further study and enrolled in a course at Columbia's medical school she'd chosen because of the reputation of its instructor as an outstanding anatomist and lecturer.

She'd said she was wholly unprepared that when the other medical students discovered a female in their midst, they began to hoot and holler for her to leave. The famed anatomist seemed at a loss and didn't reprimand them. She'd stayed but was subjected to all sorts of taunting and bad treatment. She didn't allow that to deter her, she'd told Beth, but it was quite unpleasant and the most difficult episode of her career. It was prudent for Beth to warn her professors ahead of time because they were the only ones who could effectively squelch that kind of behavior. Beth fervently hoped she wouldn't have to confront that situation, but she wanted to be prepared.

She wandered through the medical school, taking note of the location of various laboratories and classrooms and something called a "student room." No one was about since it was summer, and she was just as happy to conduct her tour in peace. She imagined herself at various tasks in the laboratories and sharing a cup of coffee and medical discussion with her fellow students in the student room. On the first floor were storage areas where students could stow books and overcoats and other personal items.

She walked back out to the street and looked again out across the Bay, shivering with anticipation and mental excitement. She'd be back at this very place the following week to begin her great adventure.

Addison's life felt a bit empty after Beth was accepted and enrolled in the Medical Department. He'd always looked forward to his meetings with her and their studies. He also missed the times he'd spent with Esther. He still saw her every day, and they generally took time at least once a week to have luncheon or coffee together to discuss their current cases. It was, he saw, not the same as the times when they were away from the hospital and engaged in preparing Beth for her examinations. He simply missed her more than he thought he would, and he saw no real way to manufacture any more reasons for them to spend time together.

She sought him out frequently to discuss patient issues and seemed truly happy when he took the initiative to talk to her. He still feared she harbored feelings toward him that he couldn't reciprocate. Or rather he *did* reciprocate them, but he was unable to act upon them. He was enthralled by her mind certainly, by her acuity and organization and energy. She'd, finally, launched a weekend clinic, whose attendance was increasing every week, and some of the patients were persuaded to vaccinate their children against smallpox and a few other maladies.

Esther's powers of persuasion were remarkable. She enlisted a couple of the nurses to help with mother-and-infant instruction. That these individuals, who worked themselves to exhaustion during their regular workweeks, could be induced to devote a little of their free time to Esther's clinic was astounding.

She was one of a kind, for sure, but Addison endeavored to keep his distance without being rude or unfriendly. However, he loved being around her. She didn't flirt, and she didn't primp or preen or try to elicit compliments and attention from him, as Laura had. She had a perfectly professional demeanor except...He could see her looking at him some times in a manner that warmed and alarmed him in equal measure. They'd be together examining a patient and it would be like conferring with any other doctor, except, somehow, her hand would brush his. Or she'd turn her head with its dark curly hair toward him, and her black eyes would be on him. She could be asking something mundane, such as, "Doctor. I feel this person shows signs of neuralgia. Do you concur?" However, her face and her expression would be saying something else altogether.

He couldn't, for propriety's sake, say anything to her. For him to imply that her feelings toward him were other than professionally friendly would be presumptuous and ungentlemanly. But he wanted to see her outside of the hospital, and he no longer had the excuse of helping Beth to offer. That saddened him. He wanted to let it go, but he was continually casting about for something, anything that could substitute. He wanted to manufacture some reason for them to spend time together, but he couldn't think of anything that wouldn't seem as though he wanted to court her, which was what he really wanted but couldn't. It was a conundrum that appeared to have no solution.

Soon after, they were in the cafeteria and having lunch together, and after thorough discussion of the current cases, they both fell silent. Addison stared at his empty coffee cup. He said, "May I get you something? I'm off for another cup of coffee."

Esther appeared distracted, quite unusual for her. She looked at him as if she'd been summoned back from a daydream. "Eh?"

"I beg your pardon. I wondered if I could fetch you anything more to eat or drink?"

She raised her eyebrows slightly. "No. Thank you."

When he returned to the table, she still seemed lost in thought. "How do you suppose Beth is faring at school?" she asked, as though she'd been thinking of the question for a while.

"It's been a few weeks, and I've not had word from her. Not that I expected any communication. She'll be quite taken up with her preparations. I recall my first few weeks at school, and it was a whirlwind."

"Oh, indeed. But in another week or so, she may be more settled. We could meet at my house. What do you say to a supper? I'm not much of a cook, but we could bring in some food. I know of a place that serves a decent roast of beef with cabbage. We should invite your young Kerry as well, if she's able to come." And she smiled so brilliantly at Addison, he caught his breath.

She'd been thinking of a way to see him, and it was Beth once again who provided a convenient reason. Take away Beth as a reason, and it was almost as though she was eager to see him socially just because she wanted to. The thought terrified him but he found himself agreeing in spite of that.

"Why yes, that would be splendid, I agree. I'll write her and Kerry. Shall we say two weeks from Wednesday? Perhaps Kerry would be better able to acquire that evening off with sufficient time."

"Yes, certainly." Esther beamed at him. "That would suit me perfectly. Shall we get back to the ward?"

"At your pleasure, madam," he said with mock formality, and pulled her chair out for her.

Chapter Twelve

Who's this fellow?" Kerry had asked Leo when he handed her the name and address.

"It's Irish Mike McGee. He owns the Emporium on Pacific. He's in the saloon business same as me."

Kerry was suspicious. "So what good does that do me?"

"Irish Mike, can I say, has a way of getting his booze that don't have the government involved. He turns a pretty penny in that saloon of his. I told him I got a lively, smart lad to work for him. I told him you was a cook and he seemed real interested in that."

"You told him I was a boy?" Kerry was taken aback because she'd gotten out of the habit of passing. The kitchen help and everyone else at the Palace knew the truth. Maybe strangers on the street didn't see that she was a girl, but that didn't matter. This could be something else altogether.

"What? Do you think if you was a girl, Irish Mike would want you in on his business? You're dreamin'. Come on, you can do it. You been doing it your whole life. I'm not saying you got to court him or nothing."

"Is he a testy type? Like to lose his temper?"

"Don't know him well, but I never heard nothing about that. Around here the men that are dangerous get the reputation. Irish Mike ain't a choirboy, but I never heard he was a murderer or nothing. Just go talk to him. He's expecting you. Get on with yourself."

So here she was in front of the Emporium. She crumpled the paper and scrunched her cap down low over her face and pulled her coat tight. It was August and chilly, so that made it not seem odd that she'd be wearing a coat.

Kerry looked at the slip of paper in her hand. It bore an address, one she was vaguely familiar with. It was yet another Barbary Coast saloon, but located a few blocks away from the Grey Dog on Pacific Avenue, in the heart of the district. The noise and activity level were even worse than on Jackson Street

Leo, true to his word, had found someone for her to talk to. He'd been on the BC his whole life and knew everyone and everything. If someone was up to something, Leo knew about it. He kept himself out of trouble, but in the Barbary Coast, survival by any means was a way of life. And any means often included illegal and unsavory methods. Money could be made provided you were willing to do what it took. Kerry had made her choice and drawn the lines she had to. No murder, no more crimping, and no women. All else would be open for consideration.

She shook herself and went inside the saloon, which was twice as big as the Grey Dog and much noisier. It was only ten in the morning but the place was full of drinkers. She strode up the bar and slapped a hand on top and, deepening her voice, called, "Whiskey!" The barkeep came over and eyed her for a moment.

"You Kerry O'Shea?" He poured her a shot.

"Yep." She growled. "Is Mike around?"

"Uh-huh. He's 'spectin' you. I'll tell him."

She tossed the whiskey down, and it was the harshest stuff she'd ever tasted. It hit her stomach like a lead weight, then shot straight to her head with a punch. She didn't recall ever tasting whiskey quite like that. She was glad she'd eaten breakfast. Drinking this on an empty stomach could be fatal.

"Hello, boy." Hearing a deep booming voice, she looked up, and behind the bar stood an enormous Irishman in a white shirt, cravat, and braces. He wasn't tall but his girth was truly impressive.

"Hello, Mr. McGee. I'm Kerry O'Shea."

"I know your name, boy. Got it from Leo. He told me your dad was Lucky Jack O'Shea. I never made the pleasure of his acquaintance, but I can surely be of service to the son of someone from the old sod. The Irish have to stick together." He laughed heartily at his own words, then slapped her on the back so hard, she nearly fell over.

"Come with me, boy. We'll talk in private. Call me Mike."

They went into a cramped office off to the side of the bar, and Irish Mike motioned her to take a seat. "Old Leo tells me you cook at the Palace. Swanky place."

"I guess so. Kitchens, though, they ain't swanky no matter what kind of restaurant they be in." Kerry kept her voice mumbly so it wouldn't sound too girlish. Lucky she already had a sort of deep voice.

"That's a fact. But here's the deal. I make my own whiskey. I don't like having to give the county any of my profit, and I got to do that iffin I buy from a wholesaler. I got me a couple a stills south of Market, hidden away nice and safe like. But manufacturing whiskey's an exacting process or you come out with pure slop. I like to serve a decent product. That takes time and it takes manpower. Them stills got to be served just about twenty-four hours a day. I need me another boy for the work. You get a three-percent cut of the sales. You might get more if you could help me out a bit with material?"

"How's that?" How much would three percent of Irish Mike's whiskey sales amount to?

"Corn is cheap, for sure, but it takes a lot of it to make mash. If you work in a kitchen, you get access to corn, am I right?"

"Yeah. I suppose." Kerry's mind was working furiously. "How much corn we talkin' about?"

"Two bushels a week."

"I have to see, but sure, I could help you out."

"You got some smarts, Leo told me. I expect my boys to be able to fix the works and keep it going. I don't make whiskey, nobody makes money. You got that?"

Kerry sensed the menace behind Irish Mike's genial manner. What was she getting herself into? "I have to hear what my take's going to be if I have to babysit a still. That's a lot of time."

"Oh, you work it out with the other boys. I don't expect no twenty-four hours a day." He waved his hand as though it wasn't a difficult subject.

"Look, Mike. I got a job already. I want some extra money and I'm willing to work, but I have to know what it's worth for me." She stared at him. All her old Barbary Coast attitude came back to her.

Never show fear, never be afraid to demand what you wanted. Be smart and be quick and cautious and you got respect. There'd only been one man who ever got the better of her: Big Moe, her dad's murderer.

"Hmph. You think you're a tough guy, I bet." He was testing her.

"Not so tough but not stupid." She answered back lively but still respectful.

"Good boy." He slapped her back again. "You reliable, you keep up, I can guarantee you ten dollars a week."

Ten dollars a week was enormous. Kerry was staggered. That would pay for Beth's school and then some.

"How much do I get if can get my hands on two bushels of corn a week for you?"

Irish Mike laughed and said, "Boy, you're a caution. You tell me what you can do, and I'll tell you what I can give you. Now off with you. Come back next Friday."

They shook hands.

On her way to the Palace, Kerry wracked her brain on how to explain what looked to be long absences to Beth. It could be working all night to help prepare special banquets for the Palace, or she was making more money by cleaning the kitchen at night. That sounded better. There would only be so many special banquets. The lies were really piling up, and the need to lie to Beth made Kerry feel sick to her stomach and down at heart. She shook the feeling off, grimly. It was necessary; it was vital to earn the money to make all their dreams come true.

Now the next problem was how to convince Davey she could be in charge of produce ordering. How difficult could that be? Cooks were inherently lazy and always looking for shortcuts. Fermel had foisted the food-supply ordering on Davey while he reserved for himself what he liked to do, such as choosing who got to cook what. Davey would be glad of help but might be suspicious of Kerry's offer. She didn't see any good way around that unless she brought him in on the scheme, and that was a problem. Davey was too upright and honest, unlike her. She shook her head. She'd think of something.

❖

"Is this seat taken?" The voice in Beth's ear was mellifluous, with a slight drawl. She turned to meet the glance of a young dark-haired man who looked at her with a polite but hesitant expression.

They were in the anatomy laboratory and about to embark on their first day of class. Beth wrinkled her nose at the stench of formaldehyde. As a nurse, she'd encountered innumerable unpleasant smells, but nothing quite prepared her for the pungent, slightly sweet odor of anatomic specimens. They were arrayed in jars everywhere in the lab. Some were easily identifiable body parts and some weren't. She supposed in due time she'd be obliged to learn the identity of all. Rough wooden benches with tops were finished in some mysterious material. Beth had unrolled a cloth that contained scalpels and forceps, wooden sticks, pins, and other implements she'd been told to buy that she surmised would be used for dissection. She had been engaged in arranging her tools and papers and books in a pleasing fashion when her concentration was broken.

"Not at all. Please feel free to take this spot."

"With pleasure, miss. May I present myself? Charles Scott Wilton of Charleston, South Carolina." If he'd been wearing a hat, he would have no doubt swept it off and bowed. Beth had encountered a few Southern boys in the army hospitals, but they were of the lower-class variety. This fellow was obviously a different sort.

He settled himself in the backless bench next to her and proceeded to do exactly as she had and arrange his workspace. She didn't want to presume further conversation.

That didn't matter, because within a moment he was addressing her again. "And with whom do I have the honor of sharing this table? I didn't expect to encounter such an attractive young lady within such a setting."

"I'm Beth Hammond. It's a pleasure to meet you, Mr. Wilton."

"The pleasure is entirely mine, Miss Hammond. Shall we follow the relaxed custom of this fair city and address one another by our Christian names?"

"I don't see why not. Please call me Beth."

"And you may call me Scott." They shook hands.

"You're far from home, Scott."

"That I am. I wanted to come out West because it seemed a perfect place to make a new start. I was tired of the stultifying atmosphere of the South Carolina low country. Both its society and its weather are enervating. What of you, Miss Beth?"

"It's just Beth, and I'm a San Francisco native. I grew up in the Mission District just a few miles away from here."

"Beg your pardon, miss. It's not customary for a gentleman to omit a lady's title." She looked at him a moment and concluded it was useless to argue.

"I see. So you were saying…?"

Scott smoothed his mustache and grinned. "San Francisco's a right fair city, from what I've seen of it. It's not as rough as I would have thought, but it is not, shall I say, as prim and proper as Charleston."

"It's quite sophisticated. Have you heard of the Palace Hotel?"

"I believe so."

"It's the most luxurious hotel west of the Mississippi and it has a French restaurant. My, er, friend works there." Beth was embarrassed about stumbling over who Kerry was but had been at a loss as to what to call her.

Scott raised his eyebrow and asked, "Oh? And where would this famous hotel be located?"

Before Beth could answer, the instructor swept into the room and dropped a pile of books and papers on the front desk. "Your attention, please, gentlemen and—" he looked right at Beth, causing all in the room to follow his eye-line and look at her as well, "lady. I'm Mr. Hardesty and this is anatomy." She blushed under the scrutiny.

"Please open your notebooks and your textbook to page sixty-five. We will begin with the lowly pig. It is a creature, however, whose anatomy presents some interesting similarities to that of man." He waited while the class prepared themselves.

Two hours later, Beth and her new companion, now laboratory partners by order of the instructor, bent their heads over the tray containing the disemboweled carcass of a baby pig. The class had sniggered when Mr. Hardesty had made the assignments, but Scott took it in stride.

The formaldehyde made her eyes water, but Beth concentrated on trying to make a fair sketch of the guts of the pig, which bore little resemblance to the illustration in the textbook. She glanced over at Scott's work. "Your drawing is much better than mine."

"Perhaps." Scott looked at the pig and added a tube to show its intestine. "But I'm flummoxed by the task of memorizing Latin names. I was never any good at that language. I received a gentleman's C grade for the course, and that was a generous estimation of my abilities." Beth absorbed this news silently, but it eased her fear of being intellectually inferior to her college-educated classmates.

"I've got an idea," Beth said. "Since Mr. Hardesty has assigned us as partners, let's make use of it. We'll use your drawings, and I'll help you memorize the names of body parts."

"Done!" Scott said, and they shook hands again.

His grin was genial, and to her surprise and relief, she could detect no hint of flirtation. His elaborate courtesy seemed to just be part of his personality and not an effort to impress her. She recalled Esther telling her it was likely her male classmates would have one of two reactions: either they would be hostile or they would be overly polite. Beware, Esther said, of both types because even good manners could mask deep hostility. Scott, so far, seemed to fit into neither category. As they gathered their belongings to prepare for their next class, Beth saw the other young men looking at the two of them with curiosity.

❖

Beth struggled to stay awake until Kerry came home at midnight, but she succumbed finally and dozed until Kerry got in bed. Beth reached over to touch her shoulder and Kerry rolled over to face her.

"You're still awake, love?"

"I was trying to stay awake until you came home. I must talk to you, and I didn't want to try to wake you before I leave for Parnassus tomorrow at seven." Kerry took Beth in her arms and they kissed sleepily. Beth caught the smoky scent from Kerry's hair mixed with a slight smell of sweat. She always associated those two smells with love and comfort, the love she had for Kerry and the comfort of her physical being.

She said, "I wanted to tell you about my first day of class, but I also want to ask you something."

Kerry's arms tightened around her and she snuggled in close, their bodies' combined warmth filling the space under their quilt. Kerry kissed the top of her head, and Beth outlined her experience briefly.

"I like Scott very much. I like my classes, but I'll have to work hard. There's so much to learn."

"You'll be fine, I expect, Bethy. No one's smarter than you."

"Oh, love, I not only have to keep up, but Esther said I have to be better than the men because that's the only way they'll respect me."

"Well, she knows best, I'm sure, but I said, you'll be fine. What did you want to ask me?" Kerry yawned, and Beth was sorry she was keeping them awake after a long day.

"Esther has invited us over to her home for an order-in supper in two weeks. Addison will come as well. I'm *sure* she's interested in him." Beth giggled. There was a long silence, though, and Kerry was uncharacteristically silent.

"What do you think?" Another pause

"I can't go. Sorry, my love."

"But why not? Surely with two weeks' time, you can arrange for—"

Kerry cut her off almost rudely. "There's no one who will take my place. I must be there, and I've agreed to stay after and clean the kitchen."

Beth leaned back to scrutinize Kerry, who remained impassive under her gaze. "Is it Addison? Are there still ill feelings?"

"No. All's well between us, as I told you."

"How will you get any rest if you are to cook and then clean the kitchen?" Beth was genuinely alarmed.

"I'll ask Teddy to get me into an empty room, and I'll sleep for a few hours."

This was one of those rare times when Kerry's tone indicated there would be no more discussion. It had happened before, and Beth ultimately had agreed but not happily. She hated to have disharmony between them, and she hated the idea of them sleeping apart.

Kerry hugged her tight and whispered, "Try not to worry. All will be well. Let's go to sleep, love."

Beth had always believed Kerry. She never had a reason not to. She was dubious but finally settled her mind on the fact that Kerry had reassured her.

❖

Addison drove Beth home after their supper at Esther's home. He let his horses meander back to his house as he thought about the evening. They had had a lively discussion, and he and Esther had a friendly rivalry over giving the best advice to Beth as she pursued her medical studies. Beth reported success in the short time she'd been in school and had seemed excited and absorbed by the challenge.

But during times she wasn't directly answering a question or telling some story, she had looked distracted and a little sad. Did Kerry's absence have anything to do with Beth's manner? However, he hadn't wanted to ask, aside from a perfunctory question on her current state, which Beth had just as briefly answered before changing the subject.

His other and more troublesome train of thought concerned Esther. If it were proper, she would be asking him to accompany her on some sort of social outing. She did nothing of the sort, but he was deeply aware of her looking at him as she talked with Beth, and she went out of her way to touch his arm or brush his hand. He was flattered and warmed and attracted, but he was sorrowful. To pursue this would be madness, and he couldn't tell her without seeming either presumptuous or silly. She must think him a dolt, but he couldn't explain. More to the point, he didn't want to explain. He didn't want to have to tell her about Laura and watch her face fall and her turn away from him in embarrassment.

He straightened up in the carriage seat, snapped the reins to rouse the horses, and headed home, gloomy and discouraged.

Chapter Thirteen

The next day, when he asked Esther to meet him at eleven in the hospital cafeteria, her cold demeanor wounded him.

"I've no time today. Dr. Grant. I have seven new patients, all in dire straits."

"Later on in the afternoon perhaps, after you've gotten them settled and their treatments begun? Nurse Shaw will be on the ward and she'll surely have matters well in hand."

They were standing in the hallway outside the infectious ward and Addison, though this hadn't bothered him before, was terribly aware of their lack of privacy.

"Dr. Grant. Nurse Shaw is certainly competent, but the diagnosis and treatment plans must be in place. That's my responsibility."

"Of course. I only meant to say that perhaps by then you would be ready to take a slight break."

She seemed about to say something and then changed her mind. "I don't have the time today, Addison. Try to understand."

He was devastated by her cool manner and couldn't control his own emotions. "What's the matter, Esther? Is something wrong?"

"No. Nothing's amiss. I'm just busy."

"Let me assist you then, I've—" He started to touch her arm, but she glared at him, shook off his hand, and said, "I said, I've no time for nonsense today."

She walked off down the hall as he stared at her back. He wanted to run after her, but that wouldn't do. He stood helpless and unsure as she disappeared around the corner in a flurry of skirts. One nurse, coming from the other direction, looked at her curiously, then at

Addison, who raised his eyebrows in an expression of mild confusion. He went to attend to his own patients.

Several hours later he heard a knock on the door of his office, and when he responded, he was astounded to see Esther walk in, seat herself abruptly in front of his desk, cross her arms, and fix him with an expression of what looked like complete exasperation.

He was writing, and he put his pen down and folded his hands over the top of the paper and waited.

"You're an annoying man!"

His mouth dropped open, and then he closed it and swallowed. "What," he asked with as much patience as he could summon, "could you mean by that?" He thought he understood, however, and was slightly ashamed that he was more than willing to place her in an uncomfortable position so he wouldn't have to be in the same discomfort. It was unmanly and he wasn't proud of it, but there it was.

"How can you be so stupid?"

"According to you I'm stupid, and annoying. Very well. Please enlighten me as to the reasons for your low opinion of me, and I shall try to improve." He couldn't help the edge to his words and saw they angered her even more.

"How can you not know? How can you not perceive what I want you to do? In the year and a half we've worked side-by-side, I've given you as many indications of what I wish as I possibly can without literally throwing myself at you. I think you're interested in me as well, yet you appear to lack the words to express it."

"Esther, I'm afraid you'll have to excuse me. I don't wish to hurt your feelings."

"You *are* hurting them!" She was nearly shouting. "I feel so foolish forcing your hand. What could be holding you back from expressing the interest in me I think you have? Is it because you want to keep our relationship professional? You don't think I'm attractive?"

"No. Stop right there. You're deeply attractive, and you're intelligent, compelling. You're an amazing woman."

"Then, why?"

"My dear Esther. I can't see you socially because I'm a married man." It was horrible having to say it out loud, to acknowledge the reality that, even in her absence, Laura controlled his fate.

"I'm aware that you're married. However, I've seen no evidence of a wife. I'm not sure I believe you."

"My wife, Laura, lives in Kansas City. We're separated. But if you're aware that I'm married, then I'm not clear—"

"She's left you? You're pining for her?" Esther's tone indicated that she knew *that* wasn't true.

"No. Not at all. It's a long story, and an ugly one. I don't wish to go into it."

"I see. So since you're married, you need to keep your distance."

"I cannot, with honor, do anything else."

"Honor." She sighed and slumped in the chair.

"You must understand why, Esther. I can't get a divorce, and even if I could, no respectable woman could receive attentions from me."

"Respectable." She raised her chin to look at the ceiling as though some sort of wisdom would be written there. "But you didn't want to tell me because it would be painful to you?"

"I thought it might be painful for both of us. I'm aware of the feelings between you and me. I'm not nearly as obtuse as you think, but we have no future. I didn't want to encourage any anticipation of one."

"Do you love your wife?"

He leaned back and met her gaze, "No. I no longer love my wife."

"You don't love your wife. Then you could, in theory, give your love to someone else?"

"I'm not able to offer the future of marriage so I consider whatever professions of love I might make to be empty promises, devoid of substance."

"You're equating love with marriage then?" Her black eyes glittered and she spoke through her teeth.

"What other state could a woman accept?" Her statement truly confused him.

"You're a man of honor, Dr. Grant. That's certainly unfortunate. Ah, well. Then I'm sorry for embarrassing you and taking your time."

She got up from her chair and left his office, and he sat motionless behind his desk, sadder than ever.

❖

It took Kerry nearly forty-five minutes to find the still. The black, moonless night wasn't helpful. The location she had been given was buried in the ramshackle warehouses and unidentified buildings in the area south of Market Street and west of Rincon Hill. There were no street numbers or even any landmarks. Kerry reckoned Irish Mike thought this was the best place to hide something illegal that would produce noise and smell but not draw attention.

She lit a match to look at the scrap of paper Irish Mike had given her with the directions to his still. Shaking her head, she pinched the match out and then, in complete darkness, listened. She could hear faint noises that might have been conversation, and she followed that sound. She could hear and smell a wood fire and knew she was getting close. She decided to risk lighting a lamp, held it up, and looked at the doors of the wooden sheds that lined the unpaved dirt street. There it was: a small X on the doorframe. She knocked three times, then paused and knocked three more. She heard men's voices, and then from the behind the door she heard the words she expected. "Who goes there?"

"Emporium. Mike McGee."

The door opened and a short, unkempt man with a scraggly beard appeared. "Hey. You here for the night watch?"

Kerry stuck her hands in her pockets and growled. "Yup."

"Come on in."

She followed the man through the shack to a small backyard. There sat a second man on a crate, smoking and staring at a complex metal contraption that steamed and hissed. The fire burned brightly under a huge closed kettle. Metal tubing snaked and coiled around in a complex shape. Small glass jars full of clear liquid were ranged about on the ground.

"Make yourself to home, such as it is," the first man told her. Home was apparently a wooden crate to sit on and little else.

"There ain't much to do, the second man said, "'cept making sure this fire never goes out. You can drink a little bit, like testing, you know, but not much. Old Man McGee'll know if them bottles is short, and he'll beat on you."

Kerry had no intention of consuming any of the vile product. She didn't really want to talk much either, because it strained her voice. She wanted to spend her time, do the necessary work, and then get over to the Palace to grab a few hours of sleep. She pulled up the collar of her coat and settled down.

"Hey, boy, don't get comfortable. You need to go fetch some more wood."

"Where?" she asked, her voice raspy.

"Over yonder." The second man vaguely pointed, and then the two men laughed.

Without a word she got up and went out the back gate. It couldn't be that far away. They'd be too lazy to walk any distance just to get wood. She lit the lamp and scouted the alleyway.

Suddenly a gate to her left opened and a big dog barreled through, barking loudly. It leaped on her and knocked her over, and she instinctively put up her arm to protect her throat and ward off the animal. It seemed forever, but finally, the dog went away. Kerry propped herself up on her elbows. The scraggly bearded man was laughing hysterically, and the second, bigger man was holding the writhing dog.

"Hahaha, you got the spit scared out of you by old Muggs. He don't like strangers none. Hahahah." So this was their little joke.

Kerry was shaking from fear and anger, but she took several deep breaths and hauled herself up off the ground. She mastered her emotions and brushed dirt off her coat. All she said was, "One of you jokers want to show me where the wood's kept and introduce me to the stupid dog so's he don't try to tear me up every time I set foot out here? Name's Kerry, by the way. You got names or should I just say, "Hey, you!" and leave you to figure out which 'you' I'm talking about?"

Her harsh words worked. They stopped laughing, and the bigger man said, "Name's Jake. This here's Sam. Sorry 'bout the dog. Here, Muggs, here, boy. He patted the dog, who'd calmed and started to wag his tail. Kerry approached and offered her hand. Muggs sniffed then licked. She patted him.

Back at the still, Sam and Jake were genial enough, and the three of them divided up their times to watch and settled in for the long night.

❖

In the days after the confrontation in his office, Addison avoided talking to Esther, and she didn't speak to him. They didn't seem to have anything more to say. It saddened him deeply that he should be deprived of any possibility of love. It hadn't mattered before Esther because no woman had captured his attention as she did. He missed her; he missed talking to her, missed seeing her. He had nothing to look forward to, nothing to be thankful for, and wondered what she was thinking.

At last, he decided this situation was untenable. They had to learn to get along as colleagues. They had no reason not to, even if they would never have the possibility of more. He found her on the ward and, after waiting patiently for her to finish with her patient, he was disappointed she didn't turn her bright, black-eyed gaze on him and ask, "Dr. Grant, what do you think?" Instead, she just looked at him, her eyes dull and sad. "Yes?"

He was deprived of speech, overwhelmed at the change that had come over her. "I, uh, er. I wondered if you would join me for a coffee at four?" That had been their usual time.

She stared at him and said, finally," Do you have a case you wish to discuss?"

He divined what the right answer should be and said, "Eh. Yes, if that wouldn't be too much trouble."

"No. None at all. I'll see you then." She turned back to her patient.

He was slightly encouraged.

In the cafeteria, he fidgeted as he sat waiting. In truth, he didn't know what to say but concluded that the only thing to say was what was in his heart. The truth.

She flew in the door and he watched as she acquired a cup of coffee, her movements quick and decisive, like her mind. She sat down across from him, and he was silent as she added milk and sugar and stirred briskly. She took a sip and at last looked him in the eye over her coffee cup.

"So. Doctor. What can I do for you?"

He cleared his throat. "I'm dismayed at the change in our relationship. It troubles me, and I wonder if there is any way to repair it."

"I don't know what you're talking about."

It seemed obvious to him. "We're coworkers, but we don't seem to be working together as well as we did and as well as we could."

"I'm sure I don't understand."

Now who was being obtuse? He grew frustrated and angry. "You're no longer friendly with me. You judged my character and found it wanting. I want to know if you can put aside your judgments and we may once again be as we were."

"My dear Addison, it's not that your character is wanting. It's the opposite. Your character is entirely too pristine."

Again, he was dumbfounded and confused.

"You've told me you can't have social interactions with me because you aren't in the position to either court me or offer marriage. Did it ever occur to you that I don't require either?"

"Eh, no, it hasn't. I've wondered why you aren't married but concluded that the demands of our profession don't leave room in your life for it. I only didn't wish you to get the wrong idea of me that I would, at last, perhaps be a potential candidate. I didn't want to mislead you."

"First, it's somewhat true that marriage to a woman doctor isn't an attractive proposition for many men. Most men wish the care and attention of a wife focused on themselves and their children. I, obviously, am not in a position to offer that. Secondly, I am not philosophically oriented to marriage. So that is not my objective in pursuing a more personal relationship with you."

"Ah." That was all Addison could think of to say.

"So," Esther continued, "if you could come down from your high-minded mountain of propriety, perhaps we could find some common ground. I hope I don't need to be more explicit than that."

"Eh." He wasn't sure he understood what she was saying, still but he had an inkling.

She waited, looking at him closely.

"I see. Well, Er. Very well. I would appreciate your company at dinner next Wednesday."

"Perhaps. Are you inviting the Misses Hammond and O'Shea?"

"No. I'm not planning on it, but I—"

"Please, Doctor, I'm not suggesting you do so. I was just inquiring."

"Eh. No, then. Say seven p.m.?"

"That would be quite acceptable." She arose from her chair, smiling at him brilliantly, said good-bye, and was gone.

He sat for a long time and his thoughts raced ahead. He no longer knew what to expect either from Esther or, for that matter, from himself.

❖

Beth lay awake looking at Kerry, who was soundly asleep. She hadn't been home for three days, and Beth had become seriously worried. Beth had been awake when she dropped into bed but hadn't said anything as Kerry immediately had fallen into what looked like a deep, exhausted sleep. To Beth this situation was worse than when she'd worked the night shift at Presidio General Hospital. On a few occasions, their paths would cross long enough for some conversation and, if both weren't too tired, some love. Otherwise, they were separated by absence or by sleep.

Neither conversation nor love had been possible between them for many weeks. Beth was caught up in her classes and her studying, but not so much so that she didn't long for Kerry's company. More than that, she was worried. Something was wrong but she couldn't quite identify what. She had, at last, asked Scott to make her excuses to Mr. Hardesty for missing his eight a.m. anatomy lecture and to take copious notes for her. She was determined she would be at home when Kerry awoke and that they were going to talk.

She brought a steaming cup of coffee to Kerry to awaken her. That method never failed to make her sweetheart happy. She waved it under Kerry's nose, which wrinkled in an adorable way. Kerry didn't awaken, however; she simply groaned and turned over. Beth was dismayed because Kerry would need to leave soon for the restaurant. She shook her gently. Kerry moaned again and opened her eyes, then struggled to focus and rubbed her face and sighed.

"Beth" was all she said.

"Good morning, love, I've got your coffee right here." She handed her the cup.

Kerry pulled herself semi-upright and took a big gulp. "Ah. Good."

Beth scrutinized her. She looked thin and weary, as though she hadn't had a good night's sleep in weeks. Perhaps she had, but Beth wouldn't have any way of knowing, which further reminded her of their separation. "I'm glad you're home this morning. I've been missing you very much, and I'm worried you aren't getting enough rest."

Kerry stared at her knees and sipped her coffee. "I'm fine. I'm getting enough."

"Kerry, dearest, look at me." Kerry slowly raised her head. Beth tried to discern what she was thinking but she couldn't. This was new because Kerry always had every emotion she experienced written on her face and charging her voice. Now, nothing. It was terrifying and inexplicable.

Beth put a hand on her cheek. "You'd tell me, wouldn't you, if something was wrong?"

Kerry nodded slowly. "I would. And I miss you, too. But this won't last for long."

Beth persisted. "When will we be…together?"

"Soon, Bethy, soon. I promise." Kerry leaned over and kissed her.

Beth wanted to be reassured and she was. Somewhat.

Kerry smiled wanly and said no more.

Chapter Fourteen

In the month and a half since Beth began her medical training, her anxiety about not being good enough ebbed, and she regained some of her old poise and confidence. She made no friends except for Scott, to whom she'd become close. Mr. Hardesty gave the class the choice of switching partners, but Beth had no qualms about staying with Scott. He was quite unlike the other young men, who either ignored her or treated her with a sort of faintly uncomfortable jocularity. Esther's predictions had come true:

They won't know how to behave with a woman in their midst. So be compassionate. If you can avoid outright hostility, that is the best outcome.

Scott was different. He continued to treat her with elaborate courtesy, but other than that, his attitude was perfectly friendly, untinged by contempt or veiled attraction. She was in no mood to attempt to figure out why this was so; she was just grateful. The other students sometimes would glance at her, then whisper or giggle, behaving exactly like the young nurses back during her nurse's training when they were embarrassed. When she pointed this out to Scott, he guffawed, causing her to laugh almost uncontrollably as well. For the most part, she only cared for the good opinions of her professors, which she seemed to have.

They were about to embark on their most ambitious and complex dissection: the cadaver. Beth and Scott discussed this prospect and formed their plans.

Scott said, "We must make this a logical process from start to finish. There will be a great deal to memorize. We must ensure all the drawings and all the notes are organized so we can review them properly."

"I agree. We can make a code for all the drawings and have all the notes coded as well."

Scott drummed his pencil on the bench. "I'm nervous. I don't want to faint or anything of that nature."

"Oh, I'm sure you'll be fine." Beth was surprised at such an admission from him. She'd heard the other students joking and boasting about their eagerness to begin cadaver work. It was likely to cover up their unease.

The big day finally arrived, and as they filed into the anatomy lab, they found a room full of tables holding draped forms replacing their low benches and chairs. They would be standing for this part of the instruction. The sweet, pungent odor of formaldehyde filled the room. Each table had a tray underneath to catch drips and pails to hold various body parts.

"Gentlemen, today begins two months of cadaver dissection and study. I trust you've chosen your study partners well, for they will be your key to success. Put on your aprons and gloves and pull the covers back and roll them at your cadaver's feet. We'll begin with an overview."

Scott glanced at Beth and then grasped the cover near the cadaver's head and rolled it toward the feet. With the cover removed, the odor of preservative became almost unbearable, and it made Beth gag. Scott paled but grinned confidently at Beth. The male corpse was somewhat unreal looking with its soggy gray-green skin and stiff limbs

Mr. Hardesty said, "Note the gender and age of your cadaver. Age is given on the tag. Now, beginning with its head, make note of any significant features or aspects."

Hearing a scuffle and a thud behind them, Beth and Scott twisted around and saw that one of the men had fainted. The others gathered around him.

Mr. Hardesty said, with no sympathy whatever, "Ah, our first casualty. Throw some water in his face so that we may proceed."

The fainter stood up and shook himself and straightened his clothes, looking much abashed.

"Mr. Summers, you would do well to inure yourself to the sight of death. Even our representative of the fairer sex, Miss Hammond, seems steady on her feet."

Amid scattered laughter, all the students turned to Beth again. Several members of the class elbowed Summers, who scowled.

Mr. Hardesty, a follower of the Socratic method, often directed questions to those he knew least capable of correct answers. He also would call on Beth who, to her great pride, always had the right answer. She surmised this incident would only add to the resentment of those who had been shown up by her before. But she had no time to worry about the other students' feelings. She and Scott were determined to perform this dissection as perfectly as they could.

The next morning, when they uncovered their cadaver, he sported a white shirtfront and formal tie and white gloves. A small hand-lettered sign covering his privates read:

Miss Hammond, would you please marry me? Although I cannot speak, I feel we've come to know each other intimately. I hope you'll look with favor upon my suit, even if I must pursue it in writing rather than verbally.
Yours truly,
Hartley A. Wake

Scott and Beth looked at each other, then at the corpse bridegroom and then back to one another, and they began to laugh. The other students, who had all been unusually quiet earlier that day, were watching and listening closely. What had they expected she would do? Scream? Cry? Have a temper tantrum? The folly of young men perplexed her.

"Hmm," Scott said. "As a husband, he wouldn't be much of a conversationalist, but he would certainly be less trouble than most husbands."

"I should say so. Perhaps I should give this proposal serious thought." Beth grinned at Scott, and they prepared to go forward with the first dissection.

The very next day, after yet another lonely night without Kerry, Beth was distracted when she arrived at the Medical Department and went to prepare for her day. The separation from Kerry was painful, but she would steel herself to concentrate on her studies and tell herself that it wasn't forever. But she longed for her lover and missed their intimacy.

She unlocked her locker and yanked the door open, and a cadaver wrapped in white bandages tilted out and fell into her arms. She started violently, took a step back, and nearly fell. She could hear laughter and saw the other students peering around a corner, where they'd obviously hidden to watch. She shoved the corpse off herself and onto the floor, then turned and confronted the group of students.

"Would one of you be so kind as to assist me in getting this body back to the lab?" she said through her clenched teeth. She hoped the formaldehyde hadn't ruined her clothes.

With effort, they stopped laughing, and one stepped forward and said, "Yes. Certainly. Let me fetch a cart." While two of the students removed the corpse, Beth went to the ladies' room to clean up. Hours in the anatomy lab had so accustomed her to the formaldehyde smell, she barely noticed it anymore. Even though it had been present in her locker, she hadn't been able to smell it. She was shaken, though, as she scrubbed her dress with a wet towel but finally gave up. The stain would require much more work, but at least it gave her time to compose herself before going to the laboratory.

When she arrived, Scott was standing like a sentry by their cadaver. "Are you all right?" he asked, his concern evident.

She glanced at the two members of the class she suspected of engineering the cadaver prank, and they looked away. They were the two least likely to provide correct answers to Mr. Hardesty's questions. "I'm fine though *I* now smell like a cadaver, I'm sure." She pitched her voice loudly enough for those nearby to hear. Scott grinned and then said in a low voice, "I heard them talking, and I think, like the trick with the note yesterday, they were disappointed they couldn't cause you sufficient distress."

"Well, that's a relief. I hope they've exhausted their pique at my presence."

"I heard one say, 'She may go to Hardesty.'"

"I've no plans to do any such thing. Good grief, what do they think I am?" She allowed herself to express her frustration to Scott.

"It has less to do with you personally than with their generalized resentment and jealousy of you. I'm positive. I'm sorry I was late today."

"Today of all days." But she grinned to show it wasn't he who'd upset her. Far from it. "Why, Mr. Wilton, are you so different from the rest?"

"Ah. As I've told you, I was raised to treat women with respect." He spoke matter-of-factly, but something about his voice told Beth she wasn't hearing the whole truth.

"Well. That may be, but I suspect that other members of the Southern male species would apply that respect only to the women who remained in the proper womanly sphere. The ones that know their places, not upstarts like me."

She focused on him in a slightly challenging manner, but before he could answer, Mr. Hardesty appeared and class commenced.

Kerry dragged herself downstairs to the basement kitchen at the Palace. She'd been asleep for perhaps four hours. This was the fourth day in a row of watching the still, and it was wearing on her. She drank multiple coffees and splashed cold water on her face. This still-tending was difficult enough, but the deceit she had to practice with Beth was far more devastating. She was actually happy to not be at home to see Beth's wounded and doleful expressions. She should be far more available to hear Beth talk about her studies and the challenges she had to face.

That had always been the way for them: to listen, to reassure and comfort. That made all the trials they faced separately and together more bearable, and now they were deprived of that. Kerry planned to tell Jake and Sam that she wouldn't be showing up the following night. They could make of that what they would. She would talk to Irish Mike about it as well. She needed more sleep, and she needed Beth as much as Beth needed her.

Things in the kitchen were miserable because M. Fermel was merciless. But he was an excellent chef and Chef Henri doted on him. The tension between Davey and Fermel kept them all on edge. Davey, who was usually so amiable, was testy and depressed almost all the time.

Kerry poured out her troubles to Teddy. "You just give me the word and I'll beat his frog ass." He meant Fermel, but, like everyone at the Palace, he was afraid of Chef.

Kerry didn't pay any attention to his bravado though.

He asked her, "But how you gonna keep up with that whiskey-making? You got to sleep sometimes."

"I don't know, Ted. It's a puzzler. I got to talk to Irish Mike."

She dreaded that because she hadn't been able to figure out a way to swipe enough corn from the kitchen to make it worthwhile for Irish Mike to give her a bigger cut of the profits. At some point, she'd have to go back to her savings to withdraw more money for medical school, and she'd already had to tap it for their rent. She couldn't discuss any of these problems with Beth, and the burden of carrying them along with the deceit was becoming unbearable. But she was determined to take care of them while Beth pursued her dream. She'd made a promise and she intended to keep it, no matter what the cost.

The next day, she obtained an audience with Irish Mike. As they faced one another, he smoked a huge cigar and blew great puffs of smoke in her face, just to see what she would do.

She cleared her throat. "I can't figure how to get enough corn to help you out. The chef who orders the food would know if I swiped any. We only get a certain number of bushels every week."

Irish Mike frowned and chewed his cigar, squinting through the smoke. "I thought you was a smart lad."

"I thought I could do it, but I can't. If you have any other ideas, I'd welcome them."

"Hmph." He tapped his cigar on the spittoon, then spit as well. Kerry was disgusted but didn't blink. She had on a newsboy's cap, scrunched low over her face, and a heavy coat she kept buttoned up. She'd even taken some soot to her face so it would look like a beard shadow. She prayed Mike wouldn't be suspicious.

"That swanky hotel youse work at? They got a bar?"

"Yep. They do."

"Iffin someone wants to drink in their room, do they bring it in or do they buy from the bar?"

"Don't know."

"Find out," Mike said.

When she told Teddy about Irish Mike's question, he rolled his eyes. "Rodney's got that all sewed up."

"What do you mean? I thought he had the girls?"

"Yeah. He's the one who gets the hotel guests whatever's not on the menu."

Teddy meant that if someone wanted a whore, Rodney was the one to take care of it.

"But he sells whiskey, too?"

"Some, but he has to buy it and sell it expensive to make any money."

"Can you find out how much he has to mark it up?"

"Yeah, but Kerry, you ain't thinking about trying to compete with Rodney, are you? Remember what happened with Big Moe?"

"Oh, bother, Teddy. That was years ago and this ain't the Barbary Coast." Kerry was really angry he'd brought up Lucky Jack's death. He hadn't spoken of it in years and neither had she.

"Sorry, Kerry, didn't mean to rile you."

"Never mind. Just find out how much Rodney charges."

"Right."

❖

On the evening of his meeting with Esther, Addison wanted to ask Mrs. Evans to prepare supper and then leave, because he wanted to have complete privacy with Esther. He refused to allow the full implication of that enter his mind, but he wanted, above all, that he and Esther be able speak freely, and the presence of Mrs. Evans wouldn't permit that.

He approached Mrs. Evans with some reluctance but steeled himself for her inevitable questions about his break of routine and, surely in her mind, with propriety.

"Mrs. Evans?"

She looked up from stirring a pot of onion soup. "Yes, Doctor?"

"Please complete dinner preparations, and then you may leave."

"What about the full cleanup sir?"

"I will put away the food and stack the dishes."

"I see. Any special time you want me back tomorrow?"

"No. The usual time is acceptable."

"Very well." She went back to stirring her soup.

That done, the next issue would be to get Mrs. Evans out of the house before Esther arrived and the food became cold.

"Oh, Mrs. Evans?"

This time she scowled at the interruption. Of what exactly he didn't know, but she valued routine and liked to be left alone in the kitchen.

"You may leave as soon as the meal is cooked."

"You don't want me to serve, Doctor?" Her tone was incredulous.

"There is no need, Mrs. Evans. I shall handle that myself as well." He tried a smile but got no response.

"How much longer until you'll be finished with cooking?" he asked an hour or so later. He wanted to fetch Esther and bring her back and be sure Mrs. Evans would be gone. All this subterfuge was wearing on him and making him feel guilty.

"In fifteen minutes or so, I expect."

"Ah, excellent. I'll be going out and shall return presently, but please feel free to depart as soon as you are able."

As he drove the carriage over to Esther's home, he was nervous, but the nervousness was of a pleasant, excited variety. He scarcely knew what to expect, but the uncertainty fueled his anticipation. He realized that he hadn't looked forward to something so much in many years.

Typically, Esther didn't wait for him to help her into the carriage but swiftly and deftly seated herself next to him and gave him a radiant smile. Addison noted that her dress was of a warm burgundy color, with some lace around the neck and wrists. It was far different from the drab, serviceable dresses she wore to the hospital. *She has made herself attractive for me.* That was hugely gratifying, but again, his innate conservatism surged and he dismissed it.

His wandering thoughts had caused him to miss something she said.

"…and what do you suppose has been her reception?"

"Eh, pardon. I wasn't listening."

"You've just arrived to take me to your home and you were woolgathering?" she asked, but with a hint of humor.

"Not precisely, but please start your question over." And he grinned in what he hoped was an apologetic and friendly fashion.

"I was wondering how Beth was faring at school. I remember my first few months, and they were difficult."

"Oh, most certainly. I recall the same."

"A young woman has an extra amount of anxiety."

Esther spoke earnestly, and Addison could detect behind her declaration a history. He berated himself for his insensitivity. "Yes, I can see that. But, Miss Hammond, as you know, possesses a strong and confident character."

"Oh, I agree, but I'm still concerned for her." They spoke of trivial matters as they made their way to Addison's home.

When they arrived, Addison asked Esther, "Would you like to come with me as I stable the horses or remain here?" She looked at him closely, and in that pause, he saw, in her expression, a fire he hadn't noticed before. He swallowed as he waited for her response.

"Ah, I'd rather go inside and freshen up a bit." Their trip through the city had lasted only twenty minutes, and the dust hadn't been bad.

"I believe the door's open. Please feel free to make yourself comfortable." He raised his hat and clicked the horses into motion, anxious to get them settled and to return home. To Esther.

When he walked into the front hall, he saw Esther sitting in the front parlor, her hands primly folded. It was such an unusual occasion to see her at rest and she looked so pretty, he stopped in the process of taking off his hat and coat and simply stared. They were several feet apart, but that distance only enhanced the strength of their connection. It was as though she was his wife and he her husband, happy to return home to her after a long day of work. But Mrs. Evans appearing in the hall, in her coat and tying a bonnet around her dull gray hair, interrupted this brief and astonishing fantasy.

"I asked Miss Strauss did she want some refreshment, and she said, no, she'd wait for you. Supper's cooked and I'm leaving like you asked." Mrs. Evans's expression indicated that she'd developed complex and prurient fantasies about would take place after she left. This was exactly what Addison had been trying to avoid.

"Thank you, Mrs. Evans. That will be all. I will see you tomorrow evening."

"Very well, Doctor. Miss Strauss." She gave Esther a curt nod and left, closing the door with what Addison considered unnecessary force.

"I don't think Mrs. Evans approves of my being here without say, Beth, to chaperone." Esther appeared to be greatly amused, which both annoyed and charmed Addison.

"Mrs. Evans's opinions don't concern me," he said, stiffly.

"Nor do they concern me. Come, forget that sour-faced old biddy. We're having a supper party. Let's enjoy it." Her enthusiasm was infectious, and Addison forgot his dismay at Mrs. Evans and let himself be drawn in by Esther's enthusiasm. At her suggestion, they went to the kitchen and prepared their plates together, set the table, and fetched glasses of wine.

Finally, seated at the dining-room table and eating soup and roast beef that Mrs. Evans had cooked, they began to talk.

"Tell me about your experience in medical school. Tell me all about your training."

Esther obliged, and he watched her eyes sparkle and flash either from happiness or anger if she was describing some doltish treatment by a male doctor. Both emotions enlivened her. Her East Coast accent became more pronounced as she drank more wine. Addison remembered he'd been a bit put off by that at first, and now he thought it delightful. *She* was delightful, lively, articulate, passionate, challenging. Again, seated at his dining room, just the two of them, he thought of what it would be like to be a married couple. His thoughts progressed to how it would feel to go upstairs with her and prepare for bed. He shivered. This was madness. It was impossible, and he had to take hold of his emotions. Again, he'd missed something she said.

"Addison? Where have you gone?"

"Oh, sorry. What did you say?" Her eyes flashed at him, making him nervous.

"I was asking you to tell me about yourself as a boy in, where did you say, Boston?"

"Ah, yes. I came out to San Francisco to attend the University of California."

"Why would you do that when there are fine schools in Boston?"

"I just wanted a change of scenery. There's an air of possibility in San Francisco, a sense of excitement. The opportunities abound. You yourself have indicated the same thing."

"Yes. I was hoping that the West would be more welcoming to a woman doctor."

"And have you found that to be true?"

"Yes and no. But, tell me. You're married but you rarely mention your wife."

Addison grew uncomfortable and was unreasonably irritated that Esther had brought up Laura. She sat quietly, obviously waiting for him to say something.

"She returned to her parents in Kansas City. We weren't getting along, and she hoped a separation would help."

Esther scrutinized him and took a large sip of wine. "And did it?"

"I can't speak for her, but for me, nothing has changed."

"Addison, you said before that you don't love your wife anymore."

Her directness startled him again and he struggled to meet her gaze. "No, I don't love my wife."

"And yet you remain married." She spoke softly, but her tone had a distinct edge.

"Laura would never agree to divorce. Besides, she has to have a reason. I've given her none, and she has left me."

"That seems like abandonment to me."

"Perhaps, but I instigated it."

"You're on the horns of a dilemma, aren't you?"

"What do you mean?" Addison had an idea what she meant, but he wanted to hear what she would say.

"You're married to a woman you don't love, and you believe you can't obtain a divorce. So you're too honorable to pay attention to another woman because that would violate your marriage vows. Where precisely does that leave you?"

Her accurate and succinct description of his situation amazed Addison. "It leaves me with no route of escape."

"What if a woman you met has no expectation of, indeed, no desire for marriage? What would you think then?"

She was talking about herself and she was issuing a challenge to him. "I'm not sure."

Esther persisted. "Would you think she was below your standards, unworthy of you?"

Addison was silent. Was that how he would think? He'd never considered the idea of relations outside marriage. He'd never used prostitutes because the idea was distasteful to him, and he had no experience with women other than Laura.

"I wouldn't want to think that way, but others might."

He thought of Mrs. Evans and then wondered why he cared for the opinion of a housekeeper. He *was* a weak man

"Addison, you invited me to supper at your home. You made sure we'd be alone together. I've let you know as subtly as I can about myself and my feelings. Yet still you seem to hesitate. You're a man with normal needs and—"

"Stop. Please let us not discuss my needs. Even with you that's too much."

"Well, then what of my needs?" She looked at him.

"I don't believe that is quite the same for a woman."

"Oh. Now we're getting somewhere. What makes you think that, pray?"

Addison was becoming quite uncomfortable with the direction the conversation was taking. He cursed his decision to go through with this social event. "It is, I believe, the consensus."

"Consensus among men. I don't believe anyone has bothered to ask women what they think." That last sentence was etched in acid.

"Well, Esther. I won't presume to think I could tell what's in your mind or your heart. You would certainly think me wrong whatever I might say. Wrong for even attempting to discern your thoughts as well as wrong about you." He was feeling attacked and was sorry for his sour tone, but he couldn't help it.

She tilted her head and looked at him for a long time. "Addison you're not all that stupid, and I'm sorry for implying that you are. I'm just frustrated. If you weren't who you are, then I wouldn't feel as I do. You're an attractive man, a deeply attractive man. I'm certain you don't mean to shame me. You're not a cad, and you'd never take advantage of a situation. For that I am grateful. But still, you leave me in my own dilemma."

"I respect you very much, and you're beautiful and intelligent. I can't offer you anything, however. How could I?"

"You could offer me a great deal, but you're too custom-bound to see that."

"Whatever do you mean?"

"Oh, never mind. Thank you for supper. Tell Mrs. Evans I enjoyed it. Would you take me home, please?"

It wasn't very late, but Addison urged the horses to gallop. He was at sea and disappointed. He'd let Esther down. What was really his original intention in asking her to supper? Did she think he meant to seduce her? It seems she had, and when he didn't, she was angry.

Women wanted marriage, and in spite of all his fantasies, there would be no marriage for him ever. Not with anyone except Laura, which was no marriage at all. He was going to be alone for the rest of his life.

Chapter Fifteen

Teddy and Kerry sat outside in the alleyway behind the kitchen entrance. It was an unsavory place, strewn with garbage, and rats skittered in and out of the piles of refuse. The rank unpleasantness ensured few people came there and helped make it a safe place to talk.

"What news?" Kerry asked. She was dead tired and seemed to have caught a cold somewhere. She had to struggle not to sneeze on the food she was cooking, and she'd only seen Beth twice in two weeks. Both times she was asleep and Kerry wouldn't awaken her. The money she was getting from Irish Mike was good, but she thought she might die of exhaustion before Beth graduated from school more than three years in the future.

Teddy drew hard on his cigarette and blew out a cloud of smoke. "I asked some of the other boys, casual like, about Rodney's ways. They said he did more business with the girls than anything else. He could get a bottle if someone asked for it, but he didn't advertise that the way he instructed the other bellboys to talk up the whores, in a discreet way, of course."

"Then I ain't steppin' on his toes if I can offer the guests some liquor they can get cheap."

"Guess not, but cripes, Kerry. You know how them boys yak. He still might get hot under the collar if he finds out, and then well. Nothing good can come of it. Rodney can be a mean bastard."

"That's where you come in. You tell a couple of them, the ones that can keep their mouths shut, that I'll cut them a deal to get me business and not rat me out to Rodney."

"Well. Yeah. I suppose." He was still reluctant.

"You get something too, Teddy. I won't forget you."

"I don't want nothing to do with it. I'm going to get a promotion soon. I need to keep my nose clean. I don't even want to hear about this, Kerry. You shouldn't take these risks. You told me you was done with all this. What does Beth—"

"Shut up and don't mention Beth to me! I've got my reasons. I said I'd leave you outta it. You told me what I need to know, anyhow."

Kerry boldly proposed to Irish Mike that she could turn over twenty bottles a week of his moonshine.

He chomped on his cigar and smirked at her. "Right. Show me and we'll talk numbers."

"Fine. I'm off the still watch except for one night a week."

Kerry collared the two other bellboys, and they promised to get buyers when she told them the difference in price between the bottles of moonshine and the whiskey that Rodney sold under the table. And when she told them what they could expect for themselves for each bottle sold, they were enthusiastic. It turned out Rodney bullied them into helping him and seldom if ever did they see a dime. So they were eager to help and would be energetic salesmen.

Two weeks later, Kerry and her two confederates had managed to turn over fifty bottles, most to repeat customers. Kerry noted with grim satisfaction that the swells who frequented the Palace were thirsty men and the plentiful cheap moonshine suited them.

Kerry started getting more sleep and was in a better mood. Beth was still much involved with her schoolwork though. She spent dawn to dusk at school up on the Parnassus Hill and no longer had time for anything but school. Mrs. Thompson's piano sat silent. Kerry seldom saw her. That was hard but probably just as well. She still fretted about the underhanded way she had to go about making money, but she rationalized it as what she had to do to make ends meet, and it would only trouble Beth if she knew about it. It was a heavy load to carry by herself though. Teddy's question made her feel worse because it reminded her of the subterfuge she was using. She shook her head and dismissed it from her mind.

❖

"I believe we need to find some extra time and a more congenial location to study," Beth said to Scott on the day they received the news that their midterm anatomy-lab practical was the following week. They stood together over their thoroughly dismantled cadaver and looked at one another.

"We must know the names of the parts as they appear on the body," Scott said.

"Your drawings are so good, and I tend to become nauseated from the preservative when we stay here too long. It's unpleasant."

"Where do you live?" he asked.

"Oh, er. Divisadero near California. You?" Beth was hoping he wouldn't suggest going to her home. She didn't want to try to explain her domestic arrangements, and she didn't think she could lie about Kerry.

"I've got a room here. I can't, obviously, have a young lady in."

Beth thought deeply. "I believe we can use my friend Addison's house on Fillmore Street. He's at the hospital all the time, so he wouldn't mind."

"You have a doctor friend?" Scott was obviously interested and impressed.

"Yes. I can tell you more about him later. It's getting late. Let's finish the digestive tract. How about tomorrow evening after dinner?"

"That would be most agreeable."

Addison was amenable and even offered Mrs. Evans's services to cook dinner for Beth. She started demur but then agreed. It was better than staying home with Mrs. Thompson and missing Kerry, who would be at work.

Scott appeared at the appointed time, and they spent two hours with his drawings, their anatomy texts, and notes. They fired questions at one another until they were satisfied they knew the Latin perfectly. Beth said, "Now that's done, can I offer you a glass of something? Addison said we could have whatever we wanted."

Scott raised his eyebrows. "I'll leave that to your discretion, but you promised to tell me more about this benefactor of yours." Beth glared at him but she was playful. He was too charming to be angry at. She fetched them a couple glasses of red wine.

They each took their first sips in silence. Scott leaned back in his chair. They were at the dining-room table with their study materials spread out. Beth was more comfortable here than in the anatomy lab with its chilliness and the ever-present stench of formaldehyde, the cadavers, and the other students. She enjoyed the warmth conferred by the wine, combined with relief at their task being done or, more accurately, well begun, since they had many hours of study to go.

Scott twirled his glass and stared at it a moment before setting it on the table, folding his hands, and fixing her with stern gaze. "Now, you promised to enlighten me concerning this doctor." His green eyes twinkled, and his cheeks lifted his neatly trimmed mustache.

Beth wasn't averse to being forthcoming about Addison. It wasn't something she needed to hide, but simply venturing into personal territory disquieted her.

"Oh, he was my favorite instructor during nurse's training. He told me I should be a doctor and helped me prepare for the exam. I lived here for a time when we both worked for the army at the Presidio. We went abroad to the Philippines war together."

"I see. He sounds like quite a fine friend and mentor."

"He is. Very much so. I owe him a great deal."

Scott was quiet for a moment, then, grinning broadly, he asked, "Is marriage in your future?"

Beth was shocked and quite irritated. "Of course not. He's already married! We're not involved in that manner. I can't think why you would ask such a question."

The chill in her voice must have been evident because he was instantly chastened. "I beg your pardon. I was just curious. I do apologize. I didn't mean to be offensive."

"All right. I didn't mean to be so touchy. I want you and I to be friends."

"I feel as though we are already," Scott said with great enthusiasm. "I'm far more fond of the company of women than I am of men's society, and I was overjoyed when we met on our first day. I couldn't believe my luck that we were assigned as laboratory mates."

"I'm happy as well that you're my partner. I don't think the other boys, and I do think of them as boys, would be too happy to be in your position."

"It's to their loss and to my gain, Miss Beth. Again, I apologize for my impertinent question. That's my fault. I love to delve into people's lives too much. My sisters would beg me to tell them all about everyone and pretend to be shocked, but they loved to hear much as I loved to tell."

"Then tell me about your sisters."

They talked about Scott's family for a time, and then Beth yawned.

"Please let me see you home," Scott said

"Oh no, I cannot…"

"But you must indulge my Southern manners, Miss Beth. A gentleman never lets a lady wander the streets unescorted."

"We aren't in the South, Mr. Scott. We're in the far West, but I will allow you since I'm very tired."

"Excellent. I'll get my little cart."

After Beth told Scott good night and when she was settled in her empty bed and trying to relax into sleep, she wondered if Scott had asked the question because he intended to court her. She hoped that wasn't the case. He didn't seem to be at all interested in her in that fashion. She couldn't quite say why she knew that, but he behaved as a brother and as a friend, almost as though she were another young man.

It was comforting, and she didn't need to worry they would drift into romantic territory. She'd handled such situations before and would again, if necessary. As she drifted off to sleep, she vaguely wondered when she would see Kerry again.

❖

Kerry appeared finally several days later, dead asleep as usual when Beth arose to prepare to go school. She thought again of awakening her to talk but refrained. Her anxiety about the upcoming practical, however, had her on edge, and if Kerry had been available to talk to, they might have ended up arguing. It was better to wait until after the exam. In the silent room, Beth moved as quietly as possible, struggling to quell her resentment. She wanted to talk to Kerry and to get her reassuring hugs. She looked at her sleeping lover, caught between tenderness and annoyance. It was time to catch the cable car, and when she returned, Kerry would be long gone.

She should be thinking about her studies, but it was useless. Her mind had disengaged from anatomy and latched onto her absent love and speculation as to when they'd be able to have any interaction. She thought rapidly. This morning she had anatomy laboratory as usual, then a physiology lecture. If she could make it home before noon, she could catch Kerry before she left again for the Palace Hotel.

❖

Kerry forced herself awake. After a dinner shift at the restaurant, followed by picking up bottles and delivering them to her two bellhop confederates, she hadn't arrived home until three in the morning. She'd had to stick around to make sure to collect the money. It wasn't that she didn't trust the two bellhops, but it was necessary to keep a sharp eye on things.

Teddy told her Rodney had started asking questions and the two boys had kept their mouths shut, but he warned that Rodney wouldn't rest. Kerry wanted to make sure nothing happened to disrupt her operations and the flow of money from the illicit booze. But it was nearly as tiring as minding the still all night. She still was getting barely any sleep, and she worried that Beth was wondering about her.

She rolled out of bed and groaned. She could smell herself. She hadn't bathed in weeks because she hadn't had time. Should she ask Chef for a night off? No, she couldn't leave John and Bob to their own devices, so she'd have to return to the Palace Hotel. It wouldn't do any good unless she took the entire night off, and she couldn't do that. Every nickel counted, and she refused to let any opportunity to make money slip by. She pulled her clothes on and splashed water on her face. While she was staring at her weary self in the glass, she heard the front door close downstairs and Beth calling her name. Her stomach turned over. She was stuck between desperately missing Beth and dreading having to look her in the eye and talk to her with all that she was keeping secret.

She went to the top of the stairwell and called, "Hello, love. What are you doing home at this hour?"

She hoped nothing was amiss because Beth was predictable; if she was to be at work, she was at work, and she was always at the university every day, all day.

Beth raced up the stairs two at a time and threw her arms around Kerry, who had to fight the inclination to stiffen and draw away. Beth must have sensed something because she leaned back and tilted her head.

"What's the matter, are you ill?"

Kerry put Beth's arms back to her sides and said, "No, but I haven't bathed in quite a while. I don't want to embrace you, because..." She dared to meet Beth's stare. She was concerned and looked hurt.

"Oh, Kerry, dearest, that doesn't concern me. I'm so happy to see you. Awake. It's a miracle. Come downstairs. Let's make some coffee and talk."

Before Kerry could stop herself she said, "I can't. I'm sorry. I'm late."

"How in the world can you be late? You've got hours before you have to be there. I've come home expressly to see you and talk to you. I'm missing my afternoon lecture. Scott will give me notes later."

"You ought to go to school, Bethy."

"But—"

She looked stricken, and Kerry felt worse than ever. Kerry found her cap and sat to tie her boots. She wouldn't meet Beth's eyes, but she could feel the anger coming in waves from her usually loving Beth.

"I don't understand. Just spend a little bit of time with me. I've rearranged my day to be home. We must talk."

Kerry stood up, buttoned her shirt, and looked at herself in the glass. "Is there something we need to talk about?" She went downstairs to the kitchen and Beth followed her. She looked in the icebox and then at Beth. "I may be able to bring home a couple of legs of lamb tonight if some are left over from dinner."

"Kerry O'Shea. I'm not here to discuss legs of lamb with you. Will you please sit at this table and have a proper conversation with me!"

Kerry couldn't resist Beth's formidable tone of command. She let Beth make coffee for them, and as she did so, Beth rattled off random facts and questions that Kerry could only meet with silence or monosyllables. Beth finally sat down and, with a cup of coffee in her hands, beamed at Kerry.

"It's so good to see you. Dear me. You still look tired. Aren't you sleeping? Are you cleaning the kitchen after supper?"

"Yes. Whenever the night crew is shorthanded, I step in." Kerry could scarcely get the lie out because it was so painful to see Beth just blink and shake her head, then touch her cheek.

"You're a hard worker, but this can't go on, my love. You have to sleep. And I miss you with me in bed. I miss you so very much. We're like strangers."

"Bethy, it's just for now."

"That's what you told me three weeks ago."

"I—" Kerry was at a loss for words. "I know, but it will end soon."

Beth looked skeptical, her eyes narrowed.

"You and I have to take at least an afternoon together. This is most difficult for me. I know I'm always at Parnassus and you're always at the Palace, but I must see and talk to you for more than a moment. More, if possible." Her hazel eyes flashed.

Kerry smiled in spite of her anguish. Beth was extraordinarily desirable when she wasn't even trying. A hint of this kind from her was unusual and made her even more irresistible. Kerry thought fast. She could take one night off. She would make up something to tell Chef. Her helpers could take care of themselves for a night.

"How about next Sunday?"

"I have an enormously important examination on Tuesday. I'll be studying for it." Beth hesitated, then said, "All right. Next Sunday."

Kerry took a breath. "Then it's a date?"

"Yes! Yes! I love you."

Beth had leaped up to embrace her again and they kissed. For just a moment, Kerry stopped thinking about moonshine and lies and making money and just kissed her lover.

❖

The woman had come in to the hospital complaining of a high fever and body aches, and Addison was summoned to examine her. She was quite pale but flushed and clearly feverish. The admitting nurse had recorded her temperature as one hundred and four degrees. He listened to her heart and lungs, and her lungs sounded congested. He frowned. It could be so many different things.

"Madam, eh…" Addison looked at the chart, "Mrs. Graham. Is anyone in your household ill?"

"Nah. It's just me and the mister. He don't never get sick."

"What is his profession?"

"Garbage man."

"Do you work outside the home?"

"Yeah. But must you pester me with these questions?" She was peevish, as anyone this sick would be.

But he needed her to give him information. He scrutinized his patient carefully. She was middle-aged and rugged. Not fat but solid, substantial, with arms corded with muscle. "What's the nature of your work?"

"Washerwoman. Empire Hotel."

"What part of the city does your husband ply his trade in?"

"Chinatown."

Addison looked up from the chart he was writing on, suddenly more alert. "He's not ill, you say?"

"No, he ain't. Look, can you give me some medicine to make this go away?"

"I shall. Once I've determined what 'it' is." She sighed and hmphed, flopping back on the cot and causing it to shake.

"Where is the Empire Hotel located?"

"Stockton and Grant."

"Near Chinatown?"

"One block away. How come you asking me all these crazy questions?" she asked again, her face scrunched with suspicion.

"It may have something to do with your illness."

"Ain't no Chinks ever stay at the hotel. The manager won't have none of their filthy kind."

"They're not filthy, Mrs Graham. Just different."

"Huh." She didn't believe him. She was typical of the crowds of ignorant working people who populated the city.

"I am going to lower your blanket, raise your dress, and examine your abdomen. Is that acceptable?"

"No, it ain't. You a pervert or what?"

Addison sighed. "I'm a doctor, madam, but very well. I will fetch another doctor, a woman."

She eyed him suspiciously. "A woman doctor, you say?"

"Yes." He was happy in a way since he and Esther had barely exchanged ten words in the last three weeks. He had an excuse to call her in to consult.

He sent the nurse to find her and, as he waited, continued to question the woman. "When did you begin to feel ill?"

"Day afore yesterday."

"Have you been bitten by any fleas that you know of?"

"I always get bitten by fleas. My mister brings 'em home. We keep a dog too."

Addison grew excited. Near Chinatown, fleas. Yes, it could be the plague. He had to have Esther examine her more thoroughly.

Esther appeared, looking put out, so Addison tried a supplicating smile. "Doctor, I need your expertise."

She didn't change expression so he outlined what he knew. As he spoke, her face became intent, her eyes wide and focused. When he finished, he saw her turn her "patient smile" on the sick washerwoman.

"Mrs. Graham, it's unfortunate you had to come to the hospital. You must indeed be feeling poorly. Tell me about it."

The patient launched into a litany of woe. Addison stood well back, but he could tell that as she spoke, Esther was rapidly and discreetly examining the woman's body from top to bottom. When the woman finally fell silent, Esther pulled her dress down and the bed cover up.

"Well, my dear lady, you are very ill. It's well you came to us. I must confer with Dr. Grant for a bit. Nurse Shaw will make you comfortable." She turned and spoke to the nurse standing by. "Clear fluids, please take a urine sample, and check her temperature every two hours."

Esther took Addison's arm and led him out of the ward.

"Well?" he asked.

"You may need to report. She has spots on her torso but no buboes appearing yet. The location of her hotel and her husband's garbage route and—"

"It must be the plague. She isn't achy, as happens with the influenza, but she said she was nauseated and had vomited several times."

"Oh it's likely. I'll give Shaw orders to move her to isolation. Shall we come back tomorrow and examine her together?"

"Of course. Say ten a.m.?"

Esther nodded and turned away. He watched her walk down the corridor and was overcome again by regret. Before their last conversation, she'd at least been pleasant, but now she'd become withdrawn. That was to be expected, he assumed, but still it was painful. He shook himself and went on to see the other patients.

Chapter Sixteen

On their Sunday off, Beth woke up without the benefit of the alarm, ecstatic that at last she and Kerry could spend some time together. In spite of her absorption in her studies, she longed for Kerry.

She planned to spend an hour or so with her anatomical terms and Scott's drawings before she awakened Kerry. The human-cadaver laboratory practical examination was coming on Tuesday, and she had only two more days to prepare. But it was essential that she and Kerry have most of the day. She crept downstairs to the kitchen table.

It was late October and the light was dim, so she lit a kerosene lamp and spread her papers out. Scott's exquisitely detailed drawings would win the day for them. He'd generously allowed her to take them home with the promise they would meet early Monday. She tried to concentrate, but it was difficult. Images of herself and Kerry on the train to Sutro Baths, strolling the shops, and then later in bed kept intruding. She persevered as long as she was able. Then she just gave up and went back upstairs to the bedroom.

She shook Kerry's shoulder gently. "My love, time to wake." No response. She shook more firmly, and Kerry turned over and opened her eyes. She didn't smile as she usually did when she first saw Beth, her eyes hooded with sleep.

"What time is it?" she whispered, her voice hoarse.

"It's eight in the morning. I thought we could get an early start." Beth spoke apologetically.

"Hmm. Could I sleep for another hour?"

Beth was surprised and irritated. "Can you sleep later? Kerry, dearest, I'll have to study for my exam when we get home from the park."

Kerry groaned and hauled herself up and put her feet on the floor. She hunched over, her head hanging down. Beth wanted to touch her but instead said, "I'll go get some water for you to wash." Kerry nodded.

Beth went outside to pump some water, wondering how to help Kerry get in a better mood. She must be tired, poor dear. Beth wondered why. Kerry had said she'd no longer be staying late to clean the kitchen.

When she came back in the bedroom, Kerry was staring at herself in the glass with a dull expression. Beth poured the water into the basin, and Kerry splashed her face and hair. Beth handed her a towel and watched as she dried her face and combed her hair.

"I thought we could have a picnic and stop for tea at the tea garden."

Kerry turned to look at her and only said, "We can't afford it."

Her harsh tone shocked Beth. "But it's just a cup of tea."

Kerry was pulling on her pants and shirt and she looked away, seemingly lost in thought.

"Still. We must be careful."

"I know, love, but just the once?" Beth struggled to keep her voice light and even. In truth, she was upset. Kerry seemed far away and unhappy. Beth couldn't understand why, on their holiday, she wouldn't be her cheerful and enthusiastic self. It was an unpleasant mystery, but Beth didn't want to start an argument by trying to solve it.

In the kitchen, they prepared a basket of fruit, bread, and cheese and a couple slices of pie that Mrs. Thompson, not Kerry, had made. Kerry hadn't done any cooking at home for quite some time. Beth thought it was because she was too busy, but she wondered why she didn't have time now. Again, this wasn't the time to ask. Perhaps when they were in the park and Kerry had been outside for a bit, she'd cheer up.

It was midmorning when they arrived at Golden Gate Park, which was crowded with Sunday holidaymakers. As was common in autumn, the sun was shining and the temperature mild, which brought out the crowds, eager to enjoy their park before the winter rains started.

Kerry had said little during the train ride, though she smiled when they arrived. Settled on a blanket on the grass in front of the conservatory, she chewed on a piece of grass, and Beth admired her profile with its sharp nose and cheekbones and her dark eyes. Beth loved the way she looked. She was neither boy nor girl, masculine nor feminine, but some mysterious creature in between—handsome and beautiful at the same time.

They nibbled on their picnic lunch and watched the parade of carriages and bicycles on the promenade just below them. Kerry seemed to be in a better mood. She reached over and brushed a lock of Beth's hair back from her face and touched her cheek at the same time. That simple gesture of affection made Beth's heart melt. All would be well.

"Is the restaurant busy?" Beth asked as she took a bite of bread.

"No more or less than usual."

"And are you being given some new things to cook?"

Kerry scowled. "I have my grill station. Fermel doesn't like me, and he never wants me to do anything else."

Beth was angry on her behalf. "How can Chef let him do that?"

"You know Chef. He's happy to let someone else run the kitchen so he can plan parties and oversee all the special requests. If some nabob asks for candied pheasant or some such nonsense, Chef must see to it."

"What about Davey?" Beth was fond of Davey because Kerry liked him and they got on well.

"What can he say? Chef is chef."

"Poor Davey. He must be angry."

"He tries to pretend all's well, but yes, he's very sore."

"What if you and Davey would look for another restaurant?"

"There's no future in that." Kerry savagely tore off a chunk of bread and gnawed it

"But—"

"I have to stay at the Palace! I wouldn't fit in anywhere else."

Kerry was obviously upset. "I'm sorry, love. I didn't mean to anger you. I just wondered."

"But it would be hard for me to find a position. I only got this one by accident. Chef just keeps me because I'm reliable."

"You're so good at cooking. He ought to be more grateful."

"Well, he's not, and that's that. Say, did you think to bring any beer?"

"We didn't have any."

"I'll go over to the vendor and get some." Kerry leaped up from the blanket and strode off, leaving Beth to wonder why it was permissible to buy beer but not a cup of tea. Kerry returned with two bottles and handed one to her. Beth sipped it slowly. She didn't care for the taste but it was there. Kerry downed her bottle in a moment.

"Goodness, but you're thirsty today," Beth said. "Here, take mine." Kerry accepted it with a muttered thank you and then fell silent. Beth decided a change of subject was required.

"I've been so lucky to have Scott as my laboratory and study partner. He's such a pleasant and friendly man. After hearing Esther's stories, I didn't know what to expect of my classmates. Some of the others were standoffish at first but have come around a bit. A few just will not even acknowledge I exist. Scott's much different."

Kerry was still drinking the rest of Beth's beer, and she drained it. "Are you certain he's not after something?"

"Oh, no. Not in the least." Beth was taken aback. "He only wants me to help him memorize anatomy terms."

"If he ever makes the least wrong move, tell me. I'll put the fear of God in him."

"Kerry. Whatever has gotten into you? Scott is a perfect gentleman."

"So he seems, but you've only known him a short time."

"I should say not. He and I share all our lectures, and we spend hours together in the anatomy lab, and we're studying for this exam. Tomorrow, I'll be with him in the laboratory nearly all day long."

"I hope you'll be careful and not lead him on. You know how the men get."

"Kerry, you mustn't equate Scott with those naive, uneducated soldier boys." Beth had often been the object of adoration of some lonely army man who she'd been nursing.

"Men are men, no matter where they come from, and you are too attractive a woman. Not that that would matter to most of them."

"Kerry, dearest. Please." Beth wasn't happy with this line of conversation, and she was cursing herself and wondering how in the world they'd reached this impasse.

"I'm just saying that you can't be too careful, Bethy."

"I can't be too suspicious either, or else I'll never get through my course of study, let alone through life. I can't afford to be on guard all the time. You ought to understand that."

Kerry lay back on the blanket and put an arm over her eyes. "I want to protect you."

"When I need protecting, I'll be sure to inform you." Beth was unhappy with her tone but helpless to moderate it. This day had all gone very wrong and she didn't want to blame Kerry, but she was sure she wasn't the one who'd started out in a bad mood.

They were quiet for a while, and their silence, so often peaceful and tender, was instead tense and strained. Beth longed to have things put right.

"Kerry, my love, let's not quarrel today. I so want us to be happy. I wish for *you* to be happy, and you don't seem to be. Whatever is the trouble?"

"It's nothing. I'm sorry for being unpleasant and quarrelsome. I'm not sleeping well." Kerry's apology was sincere, but she spoke in a dull tone. She was still troubled in some way.

"What is the matter, love? You can surely tell me."

"It's nothing. Believe me, Beth. All's well. I swear."

Beth didn't believe her but questioned her no more.

On their way home, Kerry stared out the window of the train at the passing houses and streets. She was conscious of Beth close to her and sad at how they hadn't enjoyed their outing as they usually did. It was her fault. She couldn't look at Beth or speak to her without thinking of the secrets she hid. It was almost impossible to bear. They'd be at home soon, and Beth had whispered that she'd spend just a little more time with her anatomy study before they could retire.

Hearing the tenderness in her voice, Kerry understood Beth wanted them to make love, but she wouldn't come right out and say so. How would she manage that intimacy without breaking down completely? If talking was hard, if just looking at Beth and knowing she wasn't being truthful was even more difficult, then how in the world was she going to able to touch her? She had no idea.

She sat at the kitchen table and tried to read a book as Beth studied but couldn't concentrate. It was a Charles Dickens novel and she generally loved his stories, but she was in a quandary. Beth kept looking up at her and smiling and then glancing back at her drawings and notes, still smiling.

Kerry willed her mind to be quiet but it wasn't cooperating. She could only think of her worry about money and her deceit. It hadn't been nearly this hard to keep secrets when she was a youngster on the Barbary Coast. She hadn't had a person whose feelings needed protection. That was the problem. She recalled New Year's Day of 1900, when they were just starting out. She'd sworn to herself she would never go back to the Barbary Coast, but here she was all the same. She was the person she thought she'd left behind. She was living that life she'd thought never to be part of again. And worst of all, she couldn't allow the woman she loved to hear of any of it.

Beth gathered her papers, stretched her arms, and yawned, then turned her hazel eyes on Kerry. They were bright and alert. Kerry smiled back. It was hard not to respond to Beth. They said good night to Mrs. Thompson and boldly went upstairs together to their room.

Beth closed the door and immediately fell into Kerry's arms, kissing her feverishly. Kerry kissed her back, unable to resist. It had been so long since they'd been together in love that lust took over and Kerry's mind went blessedly blank. She immersed herself in the feel of Beth's body, the sound of her urgent murmurs, and the smell of her hair and her skin. It was this finally that made her forget her anxiety and her guilt. Their love would save her.

Beth pulled her hand between her thighs, demanding release, and Kerry obliged her. It was as if she were granted a reprieve and that somehow her touch could make Beth forgive her for what she had no knowledge of but for which Kerry needed forgiveness. She could attain grace by giving her lover the ultimate pleasure.

When Beth had rested a few moments, her hands and lips desperately sought Kerry's. Kerry wanted her just as much, and she succumbed happily to Beth's touch. Her respite from reality was secure for the moment, and she gave herself over to Beth as completely as she usually did. At the moment of her release, however, her mind tumbled back, unbidden, to reality, and with physical ecstasy came mental anguish.

She burst into tears, causing Beth to embrace her fearfully and ask, "My love, what can be the matter? Did I hurt you?"

She sobbed, not speaking, afraid to say a thing lest she confess the truth. Beth held her tightly, the tension in her arms saying more than she could say in words how worried and confused she was. Kerry finally got her tears under control and patted Beth's cheek.

"Oh no, love. I'm just so overcome with loving you. The feelings are just too much sometimes. It's nothing to worry you. I'm fine, truly." She could see, in the dark, Beth peering at her, eyes bright with concern. But in the end, Beth only nodded and they hugged close and stayed that way as Beth fell asleep. Kerry lay awake. She'd just told another lie. There seemed to be no way to stop the lies from piling up. They would bury her eventually.

❖

"Her condition is deteriorating, Doctor, and I'm afraid she's not going to make it. However, I haven't seen the characteristic buboes yet. As you noted, her torso is covered with spots. Her fever is in its fourth day. She coughs weakly and her sputum's bloody." Addison described Mrs. Graham's condition to Esther in grim tones.

She listened without comment, then asked, "Would you like me to examine her?"

"I would be most grateful if you could and share your opinion with me."

After questioning the nurse on the patient's urine and fecal output, temperature, and the like, Esther withdrew her stethoscope from her pocket. Each of her dresses had a pocket sewn into it for that purpose. Her no-nonsense practicality still charmed him. She approached their patient quietly and shook her, but the woman appeared to be unconscious. Esther gripped her shoulder, turned her over, and as she did so, the patient coughed, violently spewing bloody mucous onto Esther's dress before she could step back. To his horror, Addison saw flecks of the material on Esther's face.

"Esther, are you—?"

"Stay back!" she said. She motioned to the nurse, who passed her a towel with which she wiped herself off.

"Are you quite all right?"

"I am. I don't believe I've got any in my mouth, though I may have breathed in, and if this is pneumonic plague, I could be infected." She spoke dispassionately but the words chilled Addison. If this was true, then the patient was almost certainly terminal. Pneumonic plague was far worse than bubonic plague.

"I'll attempt to culture the sputum so we can verify if it is the plague. I believe it is, but only a positive identification of the bacilli will be definitive."

"If I develop the plague, that will be definitive as well."

And at this, Addison heard the slightest quaver in her voice. So she was capable of fear.

"I only know of one person in the city who may have Yersin serum," he said. "If you were to succumb, perhaps—" Addison referred to the only known antidote to the plague, a serum developed by the original discoverer of the cause of the plague, a French doctor named Yersin.

"Let's not get ahead of ourselves. Take this to the laboratory, and in three days we'll see the results of the microbiological culture and the state of my health." Addison wrapped up the bloody towel and, unable to think of anything further to say, left Esther alone.

Sure enough, three days later, the bacteriologist showed Addison the *Yersinia pestis* bacilli under the microscope. He went in search of Esther to give her the news but was informed she hadn't come to the hospital that morning. She wasn't feeling well, the desk nurse said. A spike of fear jolted Addison. It was certain she'd contracted the plague from their patient.

He found another staff member to see to his patients and, urging his horses up to full speed, raced across the city to Esther's home. When he knocked on the door, calling out her name, he heard a faint answer from within, but no one came to the door. It was locked so he threw himself against it until it gave. He was frantic with worry, and when he reached her bedside, she turned over, showing him a face filled with such misery, he nearly started to weep.

"Esther, we must take you to City hospital. Now, my dear."

"Don't touch me, Addison." She could just manage to speak.

"Don't be ridiculous. It's not that infectious unless you cough on me and I breathe it. Here, put this on your face. I'll be well. I'm taking you to the hospital myself."

"If you say—" She passed out.

He tied his handkerchief around her head and over her mouth, then carried her downstairs and drove the horses as fast as they would gallop, with one arm wrapped around her to keep her from sliding off the carriage seat. She moaned, her head dropping to her chest. In his terror and haste, Addison whipped his horses as he'd never done in his life.

❖

"I'm telling you, we must at least try!" Addison pleaded with Dr. Kinyoun to give him some Yersin serum.

"It's only experimental, Grant. I haven't managed to save more than one monkey. I have no idea if it's good after a week in cold storage. You'd be taking a monstrous risk with Dr. Strauss's life."

"But this is pneumonic plague, Kinyoun, and hardly anyone recovers from it!"

"Of course, man, but you'd be better off letting Dr. Strauss's own body fight it off than giving her this antiserum. The French have only just developed it in the past few years. It's far from perfect and, by even their boastful reports, kills more animals and humans than it cures."

"I don't care. We have to try it."

"As you wish. She's young and healthy. Combined with her own immunity, it may work." Dr. Kinyoun looked hard at Addison and seemed about to say something but didn't. Addison was aware that he'd dropped his professional detachment, but he didn't care if

Kinyoun suspected him of a more personal attachment to Esther. It was true, he thought, more true than Kinyoun could imagine.

Addison breathed a sign of relief. Now to get the serum back to the hospital and inject Esther. She hadn't regained consciousness after their desperate ride to the hospital. He could tell from the faces of the nurses what he must have looked like when he carried her into the ward. He didn't care. His only concern was Esther.

After administering the serum by injection, he sat down by her bedside to wait. It would take a few days for the serum to take hold, if it would even work. He put aside those troubling thoughts. He waved away the infectious-ward nurse and performed the homely nursing chores himself. It was the least he could do. It was his fault she'd contracted the plague. If she died, that would also be his fault. He sponged her forehead and, for the first time in years, he prayed.

Chapter Seventeen

Kerry had just finished distributing several jars of whiskey to her two confederates out in alley behind the Palace and was absorbed in making notes for Irish Mike. He might have been a criminal, but he was still a businessman and insisted on records. A rough hand clapped on her shoulder and spun her around so fast she nearly lost her balance.

She was face-to-face with a hard-expressioned man about her age wearing a Palace Hotel's bellman's uniform. It was Rodney and he looked furious.

"So," he said, giving her a shove. "It's true then."

Kerry recovered from her surprise and, though she was afraid, pulled her face into a scowl to hide it. "What's your trouble, Rodney, that you had to sneak up on me like that?"

His face, as narrow and crafty as a rat's, set into an angry mask. "I know what you're up to, you—I don't know what the hell you are, man or woman—but I know you're a sneak."

"You're a fine one to talk. I know all about you and the whores. So we're quits, yeah?'

"So we're even in one way. But I've got a way to make you sorry if you don't cut me in on your takings."

"What's that, then?" Kerry thought he'd never rat her out because she had the goods on him as well but still...

Rodney laughed. "I'm not telling you that, you scum. Just be sure it's true. You need to give me at least a nickel's cut for each bottle of the juice you sell."

"No." Kerry was ready and ducked out of the way when he tried to hit her. He was clumsy, and she came in under his arm and punched him in the balls.

He doubled over, moaning. Between gasps, he spoke in jerky phrases, "You'll be sorry—ugh—if you don't come through."

"Go ahead." She taunted him. "You say anything, I'll let Miller know about you too, and you'll be out on your ass just the same as me." Miller was the hotel manager and the boss of all the bellboys.

"You—"gasp—"don't know what"—gasp—"you're talking about."

Kerry picked up her burlap sack and her pencil and paper and left Rodney in the alley. She had no idea what would happen next, but she was determined she'd take him down with her.

Beth and Scott sat at their lab table and watched Mr. Hardesty pass around the lab practical-exam books he'd finished grading. When he reached their bench, he handed their books over and said, "Well done." That was a rare bit of praise from the taciturn anatomy instructor.

Beth opened hers and saw a red letter "A" on the first page. Scott, grinning, showed his book to her. He'd gotten an A minus. They shook hands.

Mr. Hardesty said, "Now that this course is done, you'll be moving on to physiology and learning about the function of the organs you've spent the last three months dissecting. For those of you who do well on your first courses, you might consider sitting for the exam for the Carruthers Prize, which is given to a promising first-year student. It's quite a difficult test, and I would encourage only those students who are superior in anatomy work to try it, but the prize is full tuition for your second year's study."

Beth and Scott looked at each other. She and Scott were, no doubt, thinking the same thing. They both would try for it. It would be a great relief if Beth could cover some of her tuition. She couldn't wait to tell Kerry of this possibility. It would perhaps cheer her up. She'd gone quiet again since their Sunday holiday, and they'd returned to their usual life of rarely seeing each other.

Beth wondered what would happen during Thanksgiving break. Kerry would generally work at the Palace's gala banquet. Maybe it was a blessing, though, that she was on the outs with that chef and could actually be home with Beth at Mrs. Thompson's and could cook a dinner for them. Beth cheered herself with that thought. It would be wonderful to share that with Kerry before returning to full-time classes.

❖

Addison left Esther's bedside for only a few hours at a time, and he instructed the nurse on duty to wake him immediately if there was any change. Four days had passed since he'd administered the Yersin serum. Her condition hadn't worsened but it hadn't improved. The nurses bathed her in alcohol every two hours. She lay unmoving, pale and still. She was still alive because he listened for the faint beat of her heart every hour. Her fever fell to one hundred and one, for which he was thankful. He hoped that it indicated she would recover. He sat, unmoving, with his head in his hands. He heard the nurses whispering, but he was beyond caring. She had to live; that was the only thing that mattered.

On the afternoon of the fourth day, he had stumbled onto the ward, unshaven and haggard, and sat down, bent his head, and said his prayer for the thousandth time. He sensed a faint movement against his arm and opened his eyes. Hers were open too, just barely.

"Esther, it's me. Don't try to talk. Just nod if you can hear me." She did so. He squeezed her hand, and she closed her eyes again and he took her temperature. It was ninety-eight. The fever had broken and she'd awakened from the coma. He was weak with relief. Finally, after giving many orders to the nurses, he went home and slept for fourteen hours.

When he returned the next day, Nurse Shaw reported that she'd taken some water and some broth. She'd even produced a little urine so she wasn't completely dehydrated. The nurse nodded gratefully when Addison thanked her and squeezed her hand. Then he issued more orders. It was time to disengage a bit, but he was reluctant to do so. She would be recovering, and he had to return to behaving strictly as a doctor.

He began to spend time on his other duties and to see his patients. He was happy but apprehensive when Nurse Shaw came to tell him Esther had asked to see him. He was certain his feelings would show on his face, and he didn't want to trouble her.

She was sitting up and her hair had been combed, though it was oily with lack of washing. Her expression was unreadable. He seated himself a decent distance away and favored her with the avuncular smile of a physician pleased with his patient's recovery. Though he had far more in his mind, he wasn't quite ready to reveal all of his feelings.

"So. Doctor. You're back among the living. I was quite worried that you didn't respond immediately to the antiserum."

"I don't remember much. How long was I unconscious?" She looked at him closely.

"Four and a half days."

"I see. Well, I have asked to be released to return to my home, and they said you would have to make that determination."

"I, er, I wouldn't think you ready to be on your own just yet. You have a long recovery ahead of you."

"But you need this bed. What shall we do?" She'd gotten back some of her old fire and decisiveness, that was clear.

Addison was at a loss. She'd have to engage a private nurse, and that would be hard to do on the salary of a city-hospital physician.

"Perhaps, you could stay at my house. Mrs. Evans could keep you fed, and I'll see to your medical needs."

She seemed about to say no but didn't. She nodded yes and lay back on the pillow, seemingly exhausted.

❖

For the next month, Addison spent time with Esther both before and after he left for the hospital every day. She was on the mend and grew daily more like herself, which meant she was growing more restive. To Addison's surprise Mrs. Evans made very little complaint about her extra duties and even spoke approvingly of Esther's patience and lack of demands.

Addison came home one day to find Mrs. Evans in Esther's room. She sat near the bed, and they were engaged in an animated conversation. He stopped in the doorway when he heard his name mentioned, and they looked at him guiltily when he cleared his throat.

After Mrs. Evans made her exit, he said, "It's good to see you looking so well." It was true. Esther was in bed, propped up by pillows, wearing a clean nightgown, and her hair had been recently washed. She looked alert and impatient.

"I'm nearly ready to resume my normal duties, but I suppose I have to rely on you to give the word for my release." She didn't sound too irked. In fact, she spoke with an undercurrent of laughter in her voice.

"I'll call in one of the other physicians to examine you, if you believe you're ready."

Esther looked at him silently for a long moment. "I've had a great deal of time to think these past few weeks. Certain memories have occurred, and I would appreciate you either confirming or denying them. Mrs. Evans has also apprised me of your activities during the acute stage of my illness. She avers that you were at the hospital almost the entire time. Is that true?"

He was found out, it seemed. "Yes. It's true. With such a dangerous illness as pneumonic plague and the uncertainty of treatment, I thought it necessary to monitor your condition closely." He sounded like a pompous ass, but he was trying to disguise his true feelings.

"I see. And does the duty of a doctor extend to sitting by his patient's bedside, praying?"

So she'd been aware at times of his presence. He didn't know if this was joyful or embarrassing news. Either way, he was exposed. "I may have once or twice."

"Addison, why must you lie in such a ridiculous way? The nurses confirmed what I had sensed dimly, and Mrs. Evans added a bit more detail."

"I was extremely worried, that's true." He could admit to that much. As for the rest of it, he couldn't. There would be no point in admitting he was in love with Esther, as his marital status was unchanged. He would gain nothing by revealing how he felt about her.

She was even lovelier, a bit ethereal with all the weight she'd lost during her illness. More delicate, fragile in a way she'd never been before. And he was as enamored of her as a recovering patient as he was of the no-nonsense, assertive, but compassionate doctor.

"I. I am very fond of—"

"Addison…" Her tone was both dangerous and sad, an odd combination. Her eyes flashed, then filled with tears.

"I love you," he said, at last. It was a relief to speak the truth. "By God, I do. But what good is that. I—"

"I am in love with you too, and it's good to hear I'm not alone in my feelings."

"You are most assuredly not, but Esther, my dear, what am I to do—"

"Oh, damn, there you go again. Moaning and whining about your wife and being married. It's tiresome. I've done everything I could to make you understand that I want you and that I don't care if you're married. Must I be explicit and simply tear off my clothes and throw myself at your feet? Why must you make me feel like a fallen woman? I can't stand it." She began to weep a little, which astonished and ashamed him.

He was about to say something, but he stopped. He wanted to be honorable; he wanted to honor *her*. But what was honorable about denying the truth? If she wasn't asking for marriage but just for love, where was the harm? He wanted her so much. He wrapped her in his arms and she pressed close to him. He found her lips, closed his eyes, and they kissed, tenderly and then with increasing passion. Her hands entwined in his hair, and that simple gesture affected him more profoundly than anything he'd ever shared with Laura. He stopped their kisses to take a breath, but before their lips met again, he heard her whisper, "Yes." It was an answer to his unasked question, an affirmation of their mutual desire.

"Not here or now," he said, stuttering a bit.

"No, I'll return to my home."

He looked at her for a long time and saw her looking back at him, challenging, questioning. He was tired of denying his feelings, tired of being a moralistic prig. "I'll see you after I finish my work at the hospital. Shall I bring some supper with me?"

She nodded.

"We'll take you back to your home, and then after a few days, ahem—" He was abashed but needn't be. She'd told him clearly what she wanted.

She glowed, smiling. He kissed her again, then kissed her hand and left, his steps and his heart light.

Kerry spent the next several days looking over her shoulder, wondering what would come of Rodney's threats, if anything. She half believed it was all empty talk, but she was still tense and anxious. This was a further burden to carry, along with the secrets she was keeping from Beth. After their day together, Beth had gone quiet and only mumbled about having to study. They returned to their separate lives, only seeing each other asleep, and Kerry despaired of them surviving the four years it would take for Beth to complete medical school. She had no idea how she would manage to keep up a front with Beth, fulfill the duties of her actual job, and continue to run her clandestine moonshine business. The only things keeping her going were the two reasons for all of it: Beth's school and their future home.

When she and Beth had first taken up residence at Mrs. Thompson's, they'd talked about their plans, and Kerry recalled what she'd said.

"We're going to have a home of our own if I have to work myself into the grave."

"Kerry, dearest, surely it isn't worth your destroying your health. We're fine wherever we are, as long as we're together. Be that at Addison's house, here, or elsewhere."

"You don't quite understand, Bethy, so I'll try to explain. I grew up in a whorehouse, and then I went to live with Addison, but his wife never made me feel welcome. I want my own home, with you in it, of course. But mine, ours. It's my dream."

"I see, love. Well, we must work toward that, and it could take some time."

Then came the opportunity for Beth to be a doctor and Kerry had realized how much she wanted it. The dream of the house plus Beth's dream of her future had collided. Kerry saw no other path than the one she was on that would take care of both dreams: hers and Beth's. She hadn't, however, reckoned the price would be so high.

She snuck in one of the back service doors of the Palace Hotel and into the cellar. Since it was pouring rain that night, she'd ordered her two helpers to meet her there to get their fresh batch of whiskey jars. She'd had to walk in the rain from Irish Mike's saloon on Pacific the nine blocks to the Palace with a heavy burlap bag of whiskey on her back. She put her burden down gently and stretched, trying to ease the aches and pains. This was what an old woman must feel like after a lifetime of labor.

She sat down on the floor, hoping John and Bob wouldn't be late. She'd gone from working a busy dinner service to this errand, and she wanted to be done and then go home and sleep. Finally, she could trust them to work without her supervision. It was autumn and the hotel was full and the restaurant was busy every night and she was out of energy.

She woke when someone roughly shook her shoulder. In the dark, she could just make out the outline of a bellboy's pillbox hat.

"What? John? That you?" She tried to wake up. She was foggy.

"Kerry. It's Bob."

"Bob. Where's John?"

"He wouldn't come. He's ascared Rodney's going to thrash him. Rodney's on to you. Bob was almost incoherent with fear.

"Never mind him. He's just a blowhard. Go find John and get him down here. Time's getting short. It's Saturday night and the hotel's full of gentlemen in need of booze."

"But Kerry, Rodney's going to tell someone. He told me we're all going to get fired."

"Bob, get ahold of yourself. He's just making threats. He's—"

Suddenly, after the sound of thumps and a deep voice threatening a more fearful one, a lamp shone in Kerry's eyes. She blinked, temporarily blinded. A body crashed down before she could react.

It was John, and his weight knocked the wind out of her. He rolled away and curled into a ball, crying. Kerry, struggling to get her breath back and see who was holding the lamp, heard Rodney's voice before she could see him.

"This little snot told me everything." In the glow, Rodney looked malevolent, his sharp facial features shadowed.

Kerry struggled to calm herself. She couldn't look or sound like she was afraid, or Rodney would pounce. She forced her voice into a low growl. "What do you want, Rodney? You got no reason to bother these boys. Your problem's with me."

'Damn right it is, but these twerps are helping you. You didn't hear me so good the last time we talked. If you don't cut me in, I'm going to rough these two up."

"You're a no-account, dirty coward."

"Don't listen to him, Kerry. He's got nothing on you. We'll never back him up."

Kerry was surprised at John's bravery. Rodney had a hand on his neck and shook him roughly. John retaliated by kicking him in the shins and spitting on him. Rodney groaned and let him go. Kerry stood up and punched him in the stomach.

"You can't break me so give up. Leave John and Bob alone. If you say a word to anyone, I'll tell 'em what you're up to."

Rodney was bent over and coughing. Between gasps, he managed to say, "You won't get away with this. I'll show you." She ran back up the stairs and out to the alley where the two bellboys waited.

"We're going on as usual. Don't pay Rodney any mind. If he comes after you, tell me and I'll deal with him."

They nodded and left with their allotment of moonshine to sell. Kerry hoped Rodney had learned his lesson. She hadn't backed down and had shown confidence in John and Bob. But she really had no idea what he would do next.

It was long past midnight as she huddled on the seat on the cable car while it rumbled up California Street. She was exhausted and wrung out from the fight with Rodney and the worry about keeping her clandestine business going. She turned up the collar of her jacket. It was only October, but the nights had started to turn cold. She thought of Beth again, and that gave her even more heartache. She was discouraged and sick at heart but couldn't talk to Beth about her troubles because the news that Kerry had gone back to her Barbary Coast ways would devastate her.

She had no idea how she'd be able to keep this up. She hoped to make enough money that she could stop. If Irish Mike was amenable to losing the income, that is. No telling what he would say if she quit. Kerry shivered and shoved that thought from her mind. She had enough to think about as it was.

For the fifth or sixth time, Beth looked through her notes. She'd have to throw them out before she entered the exam room. If she could win the Carruthers Prize, Kerry wouldn't have to worry about her second-year tuition. She hadn't told Kerry what she planned to do, partially because she didn't want to say anything before she knew the outcome, but mostly because they hadn't spoken in some time.

It was a constant source of grief to her to find so much distance between them, but she saw no way around it. They had their separate obligations and that was that. The four years of medical school stretched before Beth like a long walk through an unforgiving desert. She sighed and straightened out her papers, trying to concentrate on the task at hand. She had to be clear and focused. She stared at her neat handwriting but the words were meaningless.

The proctor opened the door and motioned for the students to enter. Beth threw her notes into the waste bin and followed the crowd. A couple of the men caught her eye and they exchanged encouraging smiles. For some reason, this heartened her. She thought they all disliked her except for Scott. Clearly that wasn't the case. She took her seat, lined up her pencils just so, and steeled herself as the proctor passed out the exam materials.

Chapter Eighteen

Addison woke up early and watched Esther sleep for a few moments. He thought about the difference between her sleeping self and her awake self. Asleep she was peaceful, serene, the exact opposite of her daytime personality when she swept through the hospital wards, moving quickly from one task to the next.

She was still recovering, and he wanted her to sleep as much as she could, though he partly wanted to awaken her. He kissed her shoulder and got out of bed and dressed quietly to prepare to go the hospital.

He would go about his duties with a thankful heart. The most mundane of tasks was a joy to perform. The patients were far more compliant and cooperative than he ever remembered them being. The nurses were more efficient and uncomplaining. In short, his world was suffused with a golden glow of happiness, and nothing and no one was going to dim the glow. He marveled that he'd waited so long to agree to enter into an intimate relationship with Esther. His endless reservations and rationales for not doing so seemed especially silly.

She was a source of bottomless affection, both physical and emotional. She gave herself so freely and so thoroughly and in so many ways, it stunned him. He contrasted how he felt with Esther to the sterility, both literal and figurative, of his marriage to Laura. Why had he been so amenable to consigning himself to a lifelong prison?

He was a fool when it came to women, that was obvious. He'd married Laura because he'd convinced himself he loved her. She'd appeared to be the right sort of woman at the time. She was conventionally pretty, she was well spoken, and she was certainly cognizant of the realities of life as a doctor's wife since her father was a physician. Ah, Dr. Matheson had done everything but outright offer him money to marry Laura. It had seemed like the right thing to do at the time. He'd needed a wife, a nice woman from a good family, and Laura fit the bill. Laura had offered many proper characteristics, but none had really added up to a woman he could truly love. Other than sharing a common gender, Esther and Laura might as well have been from different planets.

Addison finished his morning routine, went to retrieve his carriage, and clucked his horses into a trot. He'd spend a productive day at the hospital and then return to Esther's home with some supper for them both and an evening of pleasant and stimulating medical conversation followed by tender relations. He had no idea sex could be something more than a routine release of tension. Esther excelled as a lover. His body ached in a pleasant manner with sense memory, though an unwelcome thought about where and how she'd acquired her experience surfaced in his mind. He pushed it down immediately.

They hadn't said a word to each other about what the future would bring other than Esther expressing her wish to return to the hospital and to work soon. She wanted to resume doctoring, but he was in no hurry for their situation to change. It would have to, at some point, but he wanted to delay it as long as possible.

Kerry walked from the California Street cable-car stop up Market to the Palace Hotel in the rain. The foul weather suited her mood. The night before, Beth had tried to seduce her. When she should have been ready for lovemaking, she found she couldn't face it. She couldn't tolerate the intimacy with Beth while she was concealing so much. She hadn't thought about what sort of effect her lies would have on their lives. Something was amiss, and Beth's sad and concerned face made Kerry feel worse, but she still couldn't face telling her the truth. She pulled her gray newsboy's cap down as the rain blew into her face. Market Street was lined with buildings, and the winter rainstorms blew down the street, buffeting the hapless pedestrians.

Kerry never bothered with an umbrella; the wind would make short work of it anyhow.

She made her way down New Montgomery and around to the employees' entrance in the alley behind the hotel. When she got to the staff room, she pulled off her wet overcoat and cap and hung them on a peg, then found her cook's coat and pulled it on. As she was buttoning it up, Davey came in.

"What's the matter?' she asked when she saw his distraught expression. Davey's face was an open book, and she always knew what he was thinking.

"You have to go speak to Chef right away. I heard Fermel talking to that bellboy, Rodney, and it was about you."

"What was he saying?" Kerry's heart nearly stopped beating and her stomach churned.

"I don't rightly know, but Fermel looked like he was about to explode. He hates you and—"

"I know, I know." Kerry's dismay made her speak harshly. "Where's Chef?"

"Who knows? He could be upstairs in the hotel manager's office. Thanksgiving's coming soon. We'll be creating a banquet."

Kerry didn't say another word but left the kitchen and walked rapidly to the lobby and found Chef's office. Her heart was pounding as she ran through her mind exactly what she was going to say to Chef. She would remind him that she was his best and most reliable line cook. He needed her in the kitchen, especially for the upcoming holidays. She wouldn't mention to him that she was also looking forward to selling more moonshine to the increasing number of guests who would be in a festive and celebratory mood.

She ran smack into Chef Henri as he stood waiting for the elevator. "Chef. I was looking for you. May we speak?"

Chef Henri, rotund and mustachioed, walked into the elevator without acknowledging her. They rode in silence back to the first floor. She didn't know what else to do, so she followed him to his tiny cramped office near the pantry closet.

He slammed the door of the office behind them and sat down heavily in his chair but didn't invite her to take a seat. He put his head in his hands and sighed. Kerry waited. Chef was emotional and given to exaggerated words and gestures. He spoke, not to her but to the top of this desk.

"Mon Dieu, why must I be plagued by these silly problems?" He looked up and his expression was stony. "You're fired."

Kerry's blood froze and her stomach churned. "But—"

Chef waved his hand for her to be silent. Kerry closed her mouth, struggling with her emotions and trying to think of what to say.

"M. Fermel says he has discovered you are selling the—what do you say—moonshine, to the guests. That cannot be done. The hotel, she must make money on the spirits it sells. Why would you do such a thing? Kerr-ie? It is *incroyable!*" He meant unbelievable.

"How does M. Fermel know this?" she asked finally. She tried to keep her features set and to not look guilty or ashamed. She wanted to brazen it out.

"Never mind. He knows!"

"The person who said this is not reliable. He's also a sneak and a pimp."

Chef stared at her for a very long time. "So it is not true?"

Kerry wilted under his scrutiny. "No, it is true. But—"

"Then there is nothing more to be said here."

"But Chef. I promise I'll stop. I was just trying to make some extra money."

"By robbing your employer?"

"No, not exactly. I only wanted—" She stumbled, all bluster deserting her.

"Yes, that is what happened. You are a vile person. In the end, you're an untrustworthy underhanded...woman! Now get out of my sight." He gave the word "woman" an extra twist, as though it were a curse.

Kerry didn't know what else to do, so she left and returned to the kitchen. In a panic, she pulled Davey outside. As they went out the door, the other cooks stared at them curiously and whispered.

"Chef has sacked me." She told him why.

His face fell. "Oh, no. Why'd you go and do something like that for? That was dumb."

"No, it wasn't, but I wasn't supposed to get caught. It was Rodney. If only he'd kept his mouth shut. Can't you convince Chef to take me back?'

"Don't reckon I can. He's got Fermel kissing his butt, and he doesn't care anything about us so long as the kitchen runs like a clock."

Kerry raised her eyebrows in a wordless question.

Davey shuddered and backed away from her a little like she had a disease. "No, no, we can't do nothing like that again." He meant their conspiracy to undermine and get rid of the previous sous chef.

Kerry dropped her hands to her sides and her head to her chest. She was done for. She collected her coat and left the Palace and stumbled up Market Street, her mind running a mile a minute.

She had no job of either the legitimate or the criminal kind. And she'd have to go tell Irish Mike the truth as well. But the worst wasn't facing Irish Mike, but confessing to Beth all she'd done and what the results of it were. Whatever was she going to tell her? They'd have no money and she'd have to leave school.

She'd failed. She'd let herself down, but she'd let Beth down too. Perversely, she longed to go lie down in Beth's arms and tell her everything and be comforted by her. That would be the only thing that could make her feel even halfway good. She boarded the California Street cable car and headed home, unsure what exactly she would say and how she would say it.

❖

"I think I shall return home by myself today," Esther told Addison as they prepared for rounds in the infectious ward. She had a pile of charts clutched to her chest and her old air of purpose and certainty. He'd been dreading this moment. She would withdraw and things would go back to the way they had been.

"You will join me at home later?" he asked, hopefully.

"Ah, no. I've many chores I've neglected at my house." Esther smiled brightly.

He leaned close to her ear. "I'll miss you profoundly. I'll be all alone."

She tilted her head up to meet his eyes and became flirtatious. "Mrs. Evans takes good care of you."

He sighed theatrically. "It's not at all the same."

"Addison, my dear. Absence makes the heart, well, you know the rest."

"I've heard it but I don't believe it. Not a word of it." He grew serious then. "My dear. We shall have to make a decision about our future. Soon."

She frowned and slapped the charts on his desk, abruptly. "Please, Addison. Not yet. I'm so enjoying our connection. Do not, I beg you, start trying to plan and control and make choices for us."

He was baffled and somewhat affronted. He'd hoped the change in their relationship would somehow make her more pliable. That was clearly not to be. "No. Of course not. I only wanted to—" He wanted to ask her to come and live at his house so they could be together more.

She put her fingers on his mouth, and he was just able to restrain himself from grabbing her hand and kissing her palm desperately.

She fixed him with her dark eyes. "Shh. I know what you want, my dear. Just be patient." And her look grew warm then, and it stimulated his nerves and made *him* feel warm.

"Very well then. As you say, madam. What do you say we see to our patients?"

"Oh, yes, those people whom we are paid to care for. Let's turn our attention to them, shall we? I suppose it's well we've seen no more plague cases. In the autumn in New York we often see an uptick in influenza cases. Is that also true here in the West?"

"Ah, somewhat, but not as severe. I believe our mild winters are helpful. The children return to school so there are respiratory illnesses, naturally, but we can cope."

She tilted her head. "I suppose I should be happy about that, but to tell you the truth, it's somewhat boring."

"Well then, Esther, perhaps we could drum up some smallpox or cholera for you. Of course your vaccine crusade has probably reduced the incidence of smallpox. And since I haven't heard from Dr. Kinyoun regarding any new plague cases, I suppose we'll have to search elsewhere to get more business for the hospital." He raised his eyebrows. It was enjoyable to flirt in a medical fashion with Esther. It was enjoyable to do *everything* with Esther. He experienced the joy of having a true partner in all ways, not like Laura. Then he berated himself for even thinking of her. He wanted to be free of her in all ways, but he especially wished she would stop invading his thoughts.

At the end of the day, Addison dropped off his carriage at the stable and took a moment to examine one of his horse's hooves with the stable hand. His filly had gotten a stone in her shoe, and the stable hand promised to see to it before he left that night.

Addison walked the two blocks to his house, his mind wandering to his previous few nights with Esther and enjoying the anticipation of seeing her again the next day. He was a little tired, but pleasantly so, the result of shortage of sleep. Dear Esther certainly would herself deserve a long, unbroken night of sleep. He opened the front door and stood in the entryway as he unwound his muffler and hung his hat on the coatrack.

"Addison?" The familiar voice out of the blue made him jump. He turned around, and there in his hallway stood Laura, his wife, smiling at him hopefully.

❖

Beth heard a voice nearby calling her name, but it took a moment for her to realize it was Scott and he'd jogged her elbow.

"Miss Beth? Where have you gone? You're here beside me in physiology lab, but it seems your mind is far, far away. I would hope in a much more attractive place than here."

She turned to look at him. His green eyes were wide and he looked at her gravely. "Oh. Scott. Sorry, I was daydreaming."

"From your expression, I can't think it was a pleasant daydream or one that would be more absorbing than the experiment we're undertaking at the moment."

"No, it's not. Let me turn my attention where it should be. Am I to determine your blood type?"

"Well, one of us must be the donor, so it might as well be me." Scott held up his finger, and Beth nicked it with a scalpel and squeezed three drops onto a microscope slide. She added the antisera for the various blood types. They waited for a few moments for the reaction to take place, then looked together at the slide.

"Well. You're type O, universal donor."

"What a relief! It's your turn, Miss Beth."

Beth watched him perform the same process with her. She hadn't spoken with Kerry in two weeks and wanted to find out what their holidays would be like. She didn't want to be sharing her Thanksgiving dinner alone with Mrs. Thompson, if that were even possible. Mrs. Thompson usually went away to her sister's home for the holiday. Should she talk with Addison? She also wanted to speak to Esther. It would be ideal if they could enjoy the feast with Addison and Esther, provided Kerry didn't have to work. She most likely would, as usual. Perhaps they could plan something else, together, like they used to. As they were supposed to.

She was adrift without her anchor. Her heart ached and she couldn't share any of it with Scott. What would he think? He would question her attachment to Kerry. He would fix her with that knowing, severe look that men used and become condescending and dismissive. He'd never been other than friendly and companionable, but she feared the moment she exposed herself he would change. She hadn't felt so completely alone since her childhood experience with the Reverend Svenhard.

"Miss Beth!" He'd nearly shouted, which startled her back into the present.

"You've put your elbow onto our slide." He spoke with a certain amount of reproof, but with more concern than censure.

"Scott. Forgive me. Here, you may prick my finger again."

"We'll redo the test on your blood, but at the end of laboratory period, would you please come down to the students' break room with me for a coffee?"

"Very well."

Once they were settled with their drinks, he looked at her once again with an air of exasperation. "Whatever is ailing you, Miss Beth? I've never seen you so distracted. Tell your Uncle Scott what the matter is."

"Oh, Scott, don't we have to be in class again soon?"

He pulled out his watch and looked at it. "We've an hour until microbiology lecture. Proceed." He put his hands together on his waistcoat and waited. When Scott made up his mind about something, he wouldn't be put off. She couldn't think what to say. She'd have to make something up.

"I've heard that my grandfather is ill. I'm worried about him." Lying to Scott was horrible and he would surely be unconvinced; she wasn't a competent liar.

"Do tell. Where is this grandfather you've never mentioned?" His expression said he didn't believe her.

"Er, in San Jose. Cancer."

"Is that a fact? What are his symptoms?"

"Good grief, Scott. How should I know? Why are you so interested?" Her sense that she wasn't sounding especially convincing annoyed her.

"Why wouldn't you know? You saw him? You're going to be a doctor, am I correct?

What better way to practice than with your relatives?"

"I suppose. He's old." She sounded petulant and hated it but was unable to think of anything to say.

"Miss Beth. I don't know why you're fabricating this silly story to cover up whatever is truly troubling you, but I'll not press you. It would be impolite, and my dear mother would box my ears if she caught me being so rude to a young lady."

Scott's Southern manners were going to save her, but she was ashamed she was misleading him. She burst out, "I'm sorry, Scott. I can't explain. I'll attempt to pull myself together and pay attention."

He looked slightly mollified but still doubtful. "I should hope so. We're going to have to study for our finals together, and I can't afford to have a study partner who's not thoroughly committed and attentive."

"I know, Scott. I promise you I'll be better."

His face softened and he said, "I have perfect trust in you. But, Miss Beth, if you ever have trouble, I hope you know I want to help if I can."

His tenderness nearly caused her to burst into tears. She could just manage to say, "Thank you." They spent their time until their next lecture in pleasant gossip about their professors and classmates.

❖

Kerry took off her clothes and crawled into bed, wondering when Beth might arrive at home. She had no idea. In the old days when Beth was at the Presidio Hospital, her homecoming was quite predictable. Only rarely did she have to stay late for an emergency. Kerry had been home so little in the past months she simply had no clue what Beth's school schedule was like.

She speculated how their conversation would go. How would Beth respond? She'd be upset, disappointed, fearful. Well, it would be Kerry's task, no matter how unsure she was herself, to reassure her, except Kerry hadn't the faintest idea what she was going to do next. She would have to find another job, that was certain. She didn't know how she would make enough money to support them, so she was back to the original dilemma. Her stomach and her head hurt. She pulled the covers over her head.

❖

"Laura." Addison was so astounded, he could barely speak.

She kissed his cheek and beamed at him, which infuriated him. "Hello, my darling, I hope you can forgive me for arriving so unexpectedly."

"What are you doing here?" Addison couldn't imagine why Laura would be back. Their parting a year and half previously had been fraught with hostility and recrimination.

"I'm in the area to see my cousin in Petaluma, so I thought I might visit you. We're married, after all." Some of her old venom came through, and, oddly, it made him feel better. A sweet, warm, winning Laura would be too jarring to his psyche.

"Your cousin."

"Yes, you remember, don't you? Amy married that chicken farmer and—"

"Enough."

She stopped speaking and looked at him, appearing hurt. "Addison, when I went back to Kansas City, I was most unhappy. You and I weren't getting along. I've had some time to think, and I'm come to the conclusion that I acted too hastily. I didn't write to say I was coming because I didn't want you tell me not to."

"But you decided you would come uninvited anyway."

Laura very obviously was trying to control her temper, something he hadn't seen her do for the five years they'd been married. She was after something.

"Addison, please don't be angry. I thought if we could see each other and perhaps talk, and after the passage of time, we could be reconciled—"

"How did you get here?" he asked, abruptly.

"I, er, hired a cart downtown at the Ferry Building."

"Ah. I see. Well, I'd be happy to take you right back to the Ferry Building."

"Addison—"

"We've nothing to say to one another. There'll be no reconciliation, no reunion, whatever it was you envisioned. You will take the ferry over to Tiburon and go back to your cousin Amy's home. That's that."

"No, Addison, that is *not* 'that.' I haven't come all the way from Kansas City to be summarily sent back. We're married, in case you've forgotten."

"I'm aware that we're married. It was you who originally suggested that you return home to your parents. But I admit I've grown rather used to your absence and also to enjoying it. Whatever has prompted you to come back?"

"My parents urged me, especially my father."

Addison recalled Dr. Matheson's powers of persuasion. That was how he'd ended up marrying Laura in the first place. Dr. Matheson was convinced he was always right. When it came to medicine, that might be true, but Addison thought grimly that it wasn't a guarantee he was correct when it came to human relations. It was maddening to think that Laura's father was attempting to compound his original mistake by engineering their marital rapprochement.

"Laura, come in and sit down." The sudden change in tone confused her, he saw. That was good.

He sat next to her on the sofa and took her hands in his and looked into her face intently. When they were courting, that gesture had made her become dewy and compliant. If nothing else, it now got her attention.

"Laura, I understand what you've pinned your hopes on, but it's not to be. The passage of time has had the opposite effect on me. I've gone on with my life without you, and I would prefer to continue my life as it is. I think it's best if you return to Missouri and forget about me."

Laura put her hand over his so that both their hands were clasped together. "I could not! I cannot, don't you see? I'm sorry for all the trouble I caused and hope you can forgive me. I wanted to give you some time to yourself. I wanted you to start to miss me. I want to start anew."

This plea for forgiveness had a familiar ring to it. After her successful campaign to eject Kerry and Beth from Addison's house she'd been much more pleasant to live with. But Addison's feelings had changed, and he'd let her become aware of that. She in turn had reverted to vindictiveness directed toward him instead of toward Kerry and Beth. He'd responded with anger and their parting was acrimonious.

"No, you're mistaken, Laura, there is no 'starting anew' as you wish. My heart is no longer available."

She drew back then and stared at him. "Your heart?"

"Yes. I've fallen in love with someone else."

"Who?" Her manner had switched entirely from sweetly beseeching to angry dismay. The old Laura was evident.

"That's not relevant."

"Yes, it is. Does this woman—" She made the word sound like "demon"—know you're married?"

"Yes, she does. It doesn't matter to her."

"Well, it matters to me, Addison Grant. It matters to me."

"Laura, it's over between us. If you wish, you have grounds for divorce. Abandonment should do nicely." He didn't add that she had technically abandoned *him*. It wouldn't do any good to further enrage her. He hoped she was angry enough, but not too angry. He was quite sure she was capable of doing him great harm.

"I wouldn't give you the satisfaction." She was angry and growing angrier. Perversely, her reaction made him calmer.

"As you wish." He refused to tell her Esther had no interest in marriage. He didn't want Esther's name to play any part in this situation.

"You cannot think this isn't going to have consequences!"

"I'm certain it will. I'm prepared to face them. I believe our conversation is over. May I take you somewhere?"

She compressed her lips together in a fashion all too familiar to him and spoke between her teeth. "The Edward Drake Hotel."

They rode downtown in complete silence, but Addison was sure he could hear her thinking, turning over in her mind how she could get even with him. He hoped he and Esther would be able to weather the storm.

CHAPTER NINETEEN

Beth climbed the stairs slowly. It was early evening but had been a long day. All her days lasted forever, her constant state of anxiety lengthening them. She was weary and wondered if she had the energy to even prepare anything to eat. Kerry was no longer cooking any meals where there would be something left over to reheat. She often just ate bread and cheese or whatever was available unless Mrs. Thompson invited her to dine with her. Mrs. Thompson, in fact, was looking at her in a concerned manner, but to Beth's relief, she didn't ask any prying questions. If she did, Beth wasn't sure she would be able to keep from breaking into a tearful confession of her woe.

She opened the bedroom door and nearly fainted. Kerry was asleep in bed. She approached slowly, a dim gas lamp in her hand that made Kerry look ghostly. In the shadows, her cheekbones were dark and hollow, her brow furrowed. Although she was asleep, it didn't appear to be a restful slumber. Beth touched her shoulder and she opened her eyes.

"Bethy." That was it. Just her name, spoken in a dull voice. No smile, no hello.

"Kerry, dearest, I'm overjoyed to see you but curious as to why you're home at this hour. Are you ill?" That would be quite unusual. Kerry was never sick; she was the epitome of health and vigor.

"No, I'm not ill." Kerry flipped the covers off and put her feet on the floor. She bent over and stared at her feet. "Beth. Love. Sit here by me on the bed."

"Very well." Beth removed her shoes and plumped up her pillow in order to lean against it. Perhaps she was going to hear, finally, what was ailing Kerry and making her behave so strangely. They could clear the air, talk it out, and all could return to normal. Then she would be able to concentrate on her studies.

Kerry slipped on a shirt to ward off the chill in the room but tucked her legs back under the covers. Beth turned and looked at her intently. Kerry didn't meet her eyes but tilted her head back and stared at the ceiling and sighed. "Beth. Something's happened. Something bad." She seemed to have difficulty speaking.

Beth thought it best to ask no questions but to let her explain in her own time and in her own way, but Kerry's hesitation worried her.

"I was let go by the Palace today. Chef told me to leave and not come back."

Beth's heart stopped and her whole body tensed.

Kerry said no more.

Beth was so dismayed she blurted out, "What happened?"

"Uh." Kerry rolled her head on her neck, obviously trying to stay calm. "I was caught doing something I shouldn't have been doing."

"What was that?" Beth was dumbfounded, but she grew angry at Kerry's lack of detail. To Beth, her demeanor resembled that of a thief who'd been caught and was mildly but not completely remorseful. The implications of what she'd said were slowly unfolding in Beth's mind, and her distress grew.

"I was selling moonshine to the hotel guests under the table." She looked at Beth then, her eyes sad and her face still.

"How? Whatever—? Why?" Taken aback and enraged, Beth couldn't speak in sentences.

"We needed the money," Kerry said, as though that was an obvious reason.

Beth realized how naive she'd been, which made her feel silly and more infuriated at Kerry and also at herself. "We needed money? I thought you told me you were getting extra shifts and cleaning the kitchen at night."

"I wasn't cleaning the kitchen. I was at the hotel moving the bottles of 'shine.'"

"You lied to me," Beth said, the enormity of this fact slowly dawning on her and adding to her growing sense of devastation, both mental and emotional.

"Yes. I did. But I had to." Kerry's tone was perilously close to whining, and that grated on Beth's ears.

"You lied," Beth repeated, flatly. "How could you lie to me?" She couldn't keep the tears at bay any longer.

"Beth, I'm sorry. I'm so, so sorry. I thought it was the only way." Kerry tried to embrace her but she moved away. Beth couldn't stand any touching, not at that moment.

"So *this* is why you've been acting so strangely, why you're so tired all the time." Beth stood up and began to pace. As she moved around their small bedroom, she tried vainly to keep her feelings from erupting like a volcano. From behind her, she could hear Kerry speak in a small, fearful voice.

"I couldn't think what to tell you. I felt badly and—"

"You felt badly? What does that mean?" Beth was close to shouting. She couldn't recall ever being so angry. She looked at the woman she loved and couldn't reconcile love with what she was feeling. She couldn't connect what she was hearing to the person she thought she knew, the woman who'd promised her two years before that her criminal days were over.

"Beth, you have to believe me. I didn't want to lie, but I didn't want you be upset."

"You didn't want me to be up—That's ridiculous. Am I not upset now?" Her voice cracked.

"I know you're terribly hurt, and you have a right to be. I hope you—"

"You promised me that you were never going back to the Barbary Coast. Do you remember when we talked on New Year's Day at the turn of the century? Do you remember what you said?"

"Yes. And it nearly killed—"

"No. No more excuses. I don't want to hear any more reasons why you did what you did and then lied to me about it."

"Beth, if you could just give me a chance to explain."

Beth stood, clenching her fists and tapping her foot. She was of two minds. On the one hand, her anger was so enormous she wanted to throw something. She also struggled with her love for Kerry and wanting to trust her.

"All right. All right." Beth inhaled as much air as she could and tried to calm herself. She looked around and fetched a chair and sat down. Kerry peered at her from the bed, appearing hurt, no doubt because of the physical distance she'd put between them. That was necessary for Beth to maintain her strength. She didn't want any pity or softness to distract her from her fury.

"I needed to make money. We couldn't afford to send you to medical school and still save for our house without more money."

"That's the reason? *That's* why you turned to crime?"

"Yes." Kerry's voice was dull with grief and remorse, but Beth was unmoved. The betrayal was too great. It was unbearable to hear of the act itself, followed by the deception, both carried out by the woman she thought she knew and whom she loved. It was unsupportable. She knew what it meant to "see red." Her vision was wavering both from emotion and the tears that flooded her eyes.

"I want you to leave. Now."

Kerry's eyes widened. She paled and started to cry. "You-you want me to leave?"

"Yes. I do. Please go."

Without another word, Kerry got up and put her clothes on. She left the room and returned with a worn suitcase she'd no doubt fetched from the cellar. During her absence, Beth nearly changed her mind, but in the end she held strong. She watched dispassionately as Kerry packed some clothing and then turned to her. "When you're ready to have me back," Kerry said, "I'll probably be at the Grey Dog Saloon."

That news sent a fresh wave of outrage though Beth's mind. "You're truly going back to the Barbary Coast. I see. I'll send word if and when I'm able to consider seeing you again." Beth was proud she spoke in a cold, flat voice. It masked the turmoil within her.

Without another word, Kerry lifted her suitcase and left the bedroom. Beth heard her footsteps on the stairs and the sound of the front door opening and then closing with a bang.

❖

Kerry stood in front of Mrs. Thompson's house and looked to the left up Divisadero Street, then to the right toward the intersection of Washington Street. She turned and stared at the house itself as though it contained some sort of answer within its dark, silent bulk. In their room on the second floor, she saw the light and the shadows. Beth was moving about their bedroom, hopefully thinking of her. Perhaps she was wondering what to do, regretting that she'd summarily dismissed her.

She'd never seen Beth like that—cold, beyond angry, and not willing to listen to her, let alone touch her. Kerry prided herself on fearing nothing, but she was very afraid. She was adrift, a small boat on the ocean without sail or rudder. The night was somewhat chilly, but her coat should have protected her. It didn't feel that way, though, for she was freezing. She turned her collar up and pulled her cap low on her forehead and began to walk, heading for the California Street cable-car stop. She would be heading back to the place she thought she'd left for good. Obviously, she hadn't.

As she walked, she turned their conversation over in her mind. It had been a relief to confess, but she'd been stupid to think Beth would welcome her back. It wasn't as though she was cruel, far from it, but she had a strong sense of morality and of rightness. Worse than that, Beth's image of her had been shattered.

I love you. Therefore you must be good. She'd said that a long time ago. Well, if Beth no longer thought she was good, she might not love her anymore. Kerry couldn't entertain that thought. If it were true, she would be devastated. She had no idea if it was true or not, and she had no clue as to how to change Beth's mind if it *was* true. She wasn't religious, but during her teenage years living with Addison and Laura, she'd been forced to say grace at meals and attend church a few times. She had no idea if she believed in God, but if there was a God, she thought she might as well ask for His help because she surely needed it. She trudged on toward the cable-car stop, and as she walked, she prayed.

In due time she was in front of the Grey Dog Saloon, screwing up her courage to walk through the door.

❖

Beth paced back and forth, wringing her hands. As soon as she heard Kerry leave, she thought about running after her, to bring her back. To do what? To say what? She had no idea. She was used to being sure, used to knowing what step she had to take, what she had to do to meet the next challenge, whatever it was. She'd been through a war, for God's sake. She'd had to care for desperately ill soldiers under horrible conditions. She was proving herself as a first-year medical student. She'd always been positive and determined, but now she was none of those things. She was helpless, confused, and uncertain.

Her world had been turned upside down and inside out. She took some grim satisfaction, she supposed, in knowing she hadn't been mistaken about Kerry's odd behavior. Though the reasons for it were now clear, she wasn't comforted. She had no idea what to do. Anger, bewilderment, grief, horror flowed through her one after the other and then repeated the process. Her mind whirled. She wasn't in control of her thoughts, which veered every which way as she marched around the small room. She went to the bureau and tried splashing a little water on her face and hands, but that didn't soothe her. She couldn't find any respite from this pain. She stood in front of the mirror staring at her ravaged face, her eyes red-rimmed and teary, her hair coming loose from its tie. She thought of another abrupt departure by Kerry. That time, she hadn't ordered it, but she'd caused it.

She heard the front door open and shut, and her heart leaped. Kerry had come home. She ran out of the room and downstairs, but all she saw was Mrs. Thompson removing her coat.

She stopped halfway down the stairs, and Mrs. Thompson looked up at her. "Hello, dear. Have you had supper yet? I'm famished."

The mundane question didn't register right away because Beth was occupied regretting that Mrs. Thompson wasn't Kerry and then with trying to assemble a normal façade. She smoothed her hair back and followed Mrs. Thompson into the kitchen. "No. I haven't eaten yet."

"Well, sit then and let's see what we can come up with."

Beth sat and numbly watched Mrs. Thompson assemble a simple meal of soup and corn bread. They sat together and Beth tried to eat, but the smell of the food threatened to nauseate her.

"Are you unwell, Beth?" Mrs. Thompson looked at her sharply.

"Ah, no. Just not hungry."

"That's odd, seeing as you been up at the school all day, trying to learn to be a doctor. You ain't caught nothing from someone, have you?" Mrs. Thompson was sure that medical students spent their days awash in unspeakable contagion.

"No. We aren't allowed to see patients yet. It's all lectures and laboratory."

"Still, you got to eat. What's the matter?" Mrs. Thompson was staring at her and Beth shifted uncomfortably.

"Mmm. Kerry and I had an, an argument." She was chagrinned that she was stuttering.

Mrs. Thompson went back to eating her soup and was silent. After a few moments, she said, "You best let it go for a bit. After some cooling off, most folks can come back together and clear the air. Then things'll settle down." She kept right on eating and said no more.

Beth suddenly realized that perhaps Mrs. Thompson wasn't quite so oblivious as she seemed. Her advice was sound, too.

"Come, my dear, eat your soup. You'll be no good for anything if you starve yourself."

Beth picked up her spoon and breathed deeply through her nose. Her stomach settled and she started to eat the soup, which tasted good. She *was* hungry. It'd been hours since her midday break, and she hadn't had time to eat much then.

She was too weary and troubled to study, so she went to bed and tried to fall asleep. It was futile. She kept hearing Kerry's voice in her head, telling her what she'd done and how she'd deceived her. It was torture. She tossed and turned. She fell asleep only to be abruptly awakened by the alarm announcing it was time to get ready to go up to the Medical Department on Parnassus and start another day.

❖

Kerry lay in bed with her elbow over eyes. Images danced in the darkness. Formless, disturbing images. She was attempting, without success, to sleep. She couldn't believe she was once again back at the Grey Dog. She'd made Leo promise to not tell anyone. She was miserable. She remembered the look on Beth's face when she'd confessed and the way she looked when she'd ordered Kerry to leave.

Leo had welcomed her in without asking many questions beyond simple inquiries if she was hungry and tired. He seemed distant and not like himself at all, and she thought it was just as well. She didn't want to discuss her situation. It wasn't his business. She and Beth had to solve it themselves, although she couldn't see how. She still had to face Irish Mike as well, and find another job. It was completely overwhelming. She gave up trying to sleep and went downstairs.

She wondered if Leo had any drink and went to the kitchen, trying to search quietly. She wracked her brain trying to remember where he stored his whiskey. He rarely drank it, but there had to be some. She found it in the back of a lower cupboard behind some cooking pots.

It burned the back of her throat but she liked it, remembering the whiskey Leo had given her after her father was murdered. The effect was almost immediate. Her mind whirled but gradually slowed down. She downed about a quarter of the bottle and was sufficiently numbed finally. She stumbled back upstairs and threw herself on the bed and passed out, mumbling Beth's name.

❖

"I don't understand. Why has she come back to San Francisco?" Esther asked.

"That, my dear, is the question. I'm afraid she means to do me harm. Possibly to harm both of us."

"Both of us? She knows about me?" Esther's black eyes flashed in that familiar way.

It unnerved Addison. "I wanted to discourage her." His voice contained an unbecoming tone of pleading, but he didn't want Esther as well as Laura angry with him. That would be too much. Esther should be on his side.

"Addison. If there's one thing a woman hates, it's another woman who's got the attention of her man. Even if she doesn't want her man anymore. But it sounds like Laura does want you to take her back. Does she?"

Esther asked the question in a level tone, but Addison wasn't deceived. "Oh. I don't believe so, not really unless it's now out of spite since she knows about you. As for me, I want no part of her."

Esther seemed to relax upon hearing that, but she merely nodded. "Well, done is done. Don't worry. I'm not angry with you, but what, in your opinion, may be her reaction? You don't think she still loves you?"

"I'm not sure she ever did, not in the way you and I think of love. But she could still be jealous, as you say. That's very likely. She's not a woman who takes things in stride." He shivered. Laura was a termagant when she was crossed.

Esther shrugged. "We can't do anything until she makes her intentions known. We may as well turn our attention to work."

Addison had to chuckle at Esther's touching faith in the ability of the practice of medicine to solve just about anything. "You're right, as always, love. I happen to have a patient who—" The sound of a throat clearing at the door made them both look around. It was Laura, and this time her smile was cruel and triumphant.

"I see you have found your paramour at work. How convenient. It will come as a shock to the head of hospital, won't it, to find two of his staff involved in an illicit affair."

Addison stood up and started toward Laura, but Esther put a hand on his arm. "Wait a moment, Addison. Let's invite Laura in to discuss this."

Esther turned toward Laura, drew herself erect, and put her hand forward. "I'm very pleased to meet you. I've heard so much about you. Won't you come in and have a seat?"

Her gesture had quite an effect on Laura. She lost some of her confidence and was rendered speechless. Addison was again surprised at Esther's effortless command of a situation. He sat behind his desk as Laura, her face still set in surprise, took the chair next to Esther's. Esther quietly closed the door and sat down.

She appeared unruffled and calm. She folded her hands on her lap and faced Laura. "Now then. Let's have a civilized conversation, shall we?"

❖

Kerry dragged herself over to the Palace Hotel and managed to find Teddy. "You oughtn't to be here. You're going to get me in trouble. Jeez, Kerry."

"Shut up. I don't have time for your nonsense. Just get a message to Davey for me."

"He ain't supposed to talk to you neither!"

"You're such a yellow belly, Ted. They can't stop people from talking. Just tell him to meet me after dinner service, down by Rincon Hill, bay side, just a half mile from the water. Look for the fire."

"Say that again."

Teddy wasn't fast on his feet, so she patiently repeated the instructions. She'd gotten Irish Mike to let her go back to tending the still because one of his boys had let the fire go out, ruined a whole batch of mash, and been dismissed. She couldn't make as much money, but it would have to do. She had two problems: getting back both Beth and her job at the Palace. She planned to try to get rehired before the big banquet next week for Thanksgiving, but she was going to have to persuade Davey to help her again. It was a long shot, but it was worth.it.

In the meantime, she'd have to let Beth have her time, and maybe she'd start to miss her. She also needed some advice, but she wasn't too sure who to ask. Addison was the only one she could think of. She still had some lingering unease about their relationship, but it was mostly because of how she'd acted after she and Beth moved from his house. He didn't appear to harbor a single bad feeling about her, even though she'd caused him to lose his wife. He hadn't seemed to be heartbroken about that, in the least.

She was ashamed of having to go tell him this entire sordid story *and* beg him for help. She was desperate, though, and hoped he could help her figure a way to reconcile with Beth. He was the key. He knew them both well, especially her. He knew all about the Barbary Coast and her dad, Lucky Jack. He was also close to Beth. He could provide the counsel she needed. She was clearly not able to solve this on her own, and that realization was at least as painful as the rest of her troubles.

She went over to the still early, glad that the one remaining tender was the smarter and less hostile of the two thugs who had the job. He might still catch on that she was really a girl, and then there'd be hell to pay. Well, that was just going to be how it was. She needed to do something, anything, until she figured things out about work.

And she had to repair things with Beth. She was terrified that they'd really reached a point of no return because of her. She prayed some more and prayed that, somehow, Addison would have the right advice for her too. Her head ached from all the thinking and the praying and the memories of their fight.

She barely said a thing to Sam but settled on the log, pulled her cap down, and poked at the still's fire obsessively to keep it burning bright and hot. Of all the mistakes she'd made, the one that rose up in her head and made it ache the most was the thought that Beth would have to leave school and never be a doctor. She'd blame Kerry, and rightly so. Kerry didn't know if Beth would forgive her for that, let alone every other terrible thing she'd done. She had no idea if things could be put right, but she had to try. Beth was her love, her life. She couldn't lose her, because then she'd have to die or have someone kill her, because she couldn't bear the idea of living without Beth.

She cursed her stupidity over and over but still wondered what she could have done differently to make things work. It was an insoluble problem, as far as she could see. She got up and put more wood on the fire and watched the steady drip of the distilled corn liquor into the pail.

Chapter Twenty

Beth sat in the physiology laboratory with Scott and all their notes and drawings spread out on the bench before them. They were quizzing one another. It was two days before Thanksgiving, and the Monday after would be their final examinations, after which their winter break would start and they would be free until January. Beth stared dully at Scott's meticulous drawings and her obsessively recorded notes. She had no motivation for the work they had to do, and it was almost impossible to concentrate. Scott kept stealing looks at her as she gave dispirited and sometimes incorrect answers to the questions he posed.

After a string of questions to which she only responded, "I don't remember," he threw a sheaf of notes onto the bench in front of her and said, sternly, "Miss Beth, where's your mind? I can't fathom where it's gone, but it's not focused upon the inner workings of the human body. Need I remind you, we both must know a great deal about that subject, as well as others, and be able to confidently answer questions both theoretical and practical in less than one week. Need I further remind you that our continued matriculation at this august institution of higher learning depends upon those answers? Whatever is the trouble, and how may I help you repair it so that we may proceed?"

He stopped talking, his green eyes glittering and fixed upon her face. He would not be put off this time. She struggled with her inborn reluctance to discuss personal things. He was right, of course. She had to pull herself together, for her own sake as well as his. She tried to frame her sentences so she could be honest without being too revealing.

"I had a falling out with a very close friend of mine two days ago. I'm still distressed by it."

"Oh?" Scott said, with his eyebrows raised, an obvious command for her to continue.

"She, well, I, I mean, we had an agreement and she, er, she didn't follow through, and I'm very upset by that." She sounded silly to herself, and she wasn't telling him anything remotely comprehensible. If he was going to help, he would have to understand. She wanted to talk about it, desperately.

She had no idea if she could trust him. She thought she could, but she wasn't sure. Hers and Kerry's relationship was unusual and could subject them to derision, or worse. She remembered what had occurred with Addison's wife Laura. Scott always seemed kind and gentle. He was unlike any man she'd ever met, except Addison. She thought Addison one of a kind.

Scott was looking at her, his brows furrowed. He bounced his knee up and down, a nervous habit. She wondered why he'd become uneasy.

"Miss Beth. Could you be a little more forthcoming? I can't guess what sort of trouble you're having."

"Well. We're very close, or I, uh, thought we were, and I thought she was doing something but found out she was actually doing something else, and she lied to me about it."

"Did this deception perhaps involve another woman?" He asked the question casually, as though asking about an everyday matter. Her head had been bowed and she'd been speaking to the surface of their lab bench, but now she brought it up sharply and met his eye. His knee bounced faster as he waited for her reply.

"No. It didn't. Why would you ask that?"

"Oh. I have a lot of women friends back home, and they were always in the midst of some intrigue with one another. Or someone was always having a falling-out with some other girl. And jealous? My lord." He laughed.

Beth was intrigued and confused. "No, it wasn't anything like that." Finally she told him the details of their disagreement, still without owning to anything more explicit about their relationship.

Scott was quiet for a time and finally said, "I see. I've had a hard time with a friend somewhat like that. Luke Stratton just about broke my heart. My word, he was a handsome devil, but he was treacherous."

Scott's look was dreamy, and Beth suddenly understood what he was getting at. He, like her, loved his own gender; he wasn't a man for women. It occurred to her suddenly that he'd never once mentioned that he was engaged or had a sweetheart. He spoke at length about his mother, his aunts, various female acquaintances and friends. But he never mentioned any women in romantic terms.

He continued to speak. "So you're in a pickle. Your 'friend,'" he put undue emphasis on the word, "has been busy behind your back. But it seems to me her heart was in the right place. She was just, er, in error in her methods."

"I suppose." Beth brooded. She was still no better off than she'd been ten minutes previously, but she was slightly relieved to have told the story to someone. "Did you know about me? How did you guess?" She was genuinely curious.

"I suspected. Even the most ardent student like yourself would still not fail to express some interest at being surrounded by eligible young men. Such as me." He grinned.

"You're not exactly eligible."

"Indeed, I'm not, but to many a young lady, I often appear to be. A little kindness, attention, and flattery go quite a ways, I assure you. They become enamored of me in no time. But you didn't have the typical response to me, and you never once mentioned any suitors. When I suggested that your connection to Dr. Grant was romantic, you nearly took my head off. You have a forthright air about you. It was a lucky guess. But have no fear. Your secret's safe with me." He beamed even more widely. "In fact, a number of our classmates have tried to express some subtle interest in you, and I've just as subtly let them believe we've become quite, er, close."

It was a nearly perfect solution. Beth was impressed and relieved to discover this fact about Scott, but she still had her dilemma with Kerry. She told Scott much more about them. He was attentive and sympathetic but demurred when she asked him for advice.

"Do you love her?"

"More than my life."

"Then you need to find out how to recover from this."

"I also need to find out how am I to continue my studies. I hate to be selfish but—"

"Miss Beth. You have no reason to feel badly about wanting something like that. Perhaps you'll win the Carruthers Prize."

"I may, but I hate to have to rely upon something that may not happen."

"But it may. This school year is paid up, isn't it?'

"Oh, yes. I don't know about our rent. I'll have to ask Mrs. Thompson."

"Well, things may not be as bad as you think, at least in practical terms." Scott gave her a meaningful look, and she finally managed to smile back.

"I may need to speak to another friend. Another woman," she told him, the thought having just occurred to her. She ought to speak to Marjorie. That is, if Marjorie would even speak to her.

They went back to their exam-cramming, but she felt she'd finally taken a full breath for the first time in days.

❖

Addison sat behind his desk, bemused by the absurdity of the situation. His wife and his mistress sat across from him in chairs next to one another. He decided he was just going to keep quiet and let this confrontation unwind itself without his active participation, if at all possible.

Esther's smile was tight and grim as she turned toward Laura, who still seemed a bit in shock. She probably had never envisioned being presented with this circumstance, much less with the actual woman in question. She was still trying to recover her voice, and Esther pressed her advantage.

"Mrs. Grant, I hope you'll allow me to be candid."

Laura nodded, her gaze fixed on Esther as though she was a ghost whom she doubted the existence of but couldn't argue with the evidence of her senses.

"Please don't be offended."

Addison thought, *Little chance of that.*

Laura's face changed to the combination of injured virtue and absolute fury Addison remembered so well. "You." She started to speak, but Esther held up her hand and Laura, astonishingly, stopped.

Esther continued, smoothly. "I'm sure none of us would be served by an unpleasant scene."

"I hope you understand that I will never dissolve this marriage. Whom God has joined let no man put asunder." She intoned the last sentence with all the pomp of a clergyman.

"Hmm. Interesting. In the first place, I am not in the market for marriage, so Addison's marital status is of no matter to me. Secondly, I believe that you decamping your home for Kansas City constitutes desertion. Addison would be able to divorce *you*, I expect, although he's too much of a gentleman to suggest that. She glanced at him, and he gave the tiniest nod.

"Well, then. I will have to report this to the director of the hospital."

"It will be old news to him," Esther said.

Laura flinched.

"I confided in him early on, before tongues began to wag, and informed him of your absence from San Francisco."

This was a surprise to Addison and he started to protest but thought better of it.

"You'll be shamed! You'll lose all social standing."

"When one doesn't care for social standing or for the dubious opinions of the uninformed, then there is little fear of losing what *you* consider so precious."

Laura was so angry she stuttered. Addison kept his face straight, but he enjoyed her discomfiture. Perhaps divorce *was* possible, if Laura would agree to it. He hadn't thought it possible before this moment. Before Esther.

"My dear Laura," he said, and both women turned to look at him. "I'm in love with Dr. Strauss. I don't love you. Isn't it better you cut your losses, allow us to obtain an amicable divorce than to persist in trying to change that over which you have no control? You may feel free to blame me for our breach, if that soothes your bruised ego. You will then be free to tell the eligible bachelors of Kansas City as many lies as you wish and marry the wealthiest one you can trap. We both can count ourselves lucky." Esther's admiring smile heartened him. Taking action was not only a relief. It was positively exhilarating.

Laura started to say something else, rising from her chair like a frog puffing itself up, but her shoulders fell and she was silent.

Addison pitied her. He caught Esther's eye.

She said, "It's a good decision, Mrs. Grant. We wish you the best."

Addison added, "Please engage an attorney to send me all the proper paperwork and make our appearance before a judge. We can complete this matter as soon as possible, and you may return to Missouri. Please give my best to your parents. I'm sure they'll come to see the wisdom of it when you tell them how I've betrayed you."

After Laura left, Esther came behind the desk and sat on Addison's lap and kissed him soundly. "That is that, love. Now. Please don't think I'm ready to marry."

"I have no plans to ask you that, but I would be made very happy if you would consent to share my home."

She moved restlessly in his lap and sighed. "I'll think on it." She kissed him.

He returned her kiss and touched her cheek and hair and tried not to feel impatient and anxious that she wouldn't agree to his request right away.

"I'm certain there will never be anything I'll be able to talk you into for which you aren't entirely ready."

"Excellent insight, Doctor. I'm certain we can maintain harmony as long as you remember that." Her dark eyes sparkled mischievously.

Kerry waited for Davey. She'd stationed herself a ways from the door so she couldn't be seen. She watched dogs nosing in the garbage in the alley. She coughed and pulled her collar up. It was overcast and damp.

As always, when she had a moment, her thoughts turned to Beth. She was going to get some money from Irish Mike later in the day, and she would be able to get something to eat and make the trip out to the City and County Hospital to see Addison. She was tired of sitting up all night and then sleeping at the Grey Dog Saloon. Leo had taken her in without a question, but she couldn't stay around there for long. Too many memories. Sally, her old sweetheart, had disappeared, but her daughter, little Minny, as Kerry always thought of her, was still there. Her anger at Kerry's departure was as fresh as ever, and Kerry didn't want to see Minny's accusing glares. After her argument with Beth, that would be the last straw.

Davey appeared and sat down next to her with his back against the wall, handing her a leg of mutton. She couldn't keep him out of the kitchen for very long so she ate quickly.

He stared at her for a long time until finally, he said, "You're in a lot of trouble."

She spoke rapidly between bites. "I know. Thanks for the meat. Thanksgiving banquet is three days away. I want to know if anyone's been mucking up, if Chef or Fermel is mad at any of the other cooks. They need everyone for that day."

Davey shook his head. "Yeah. Nobody's in particular trouble. What're you thinking, Kerry?"

"I'm thinking if I'm at the restaurant and something happens, I can step in and help and get my job back."

Davey snorted. "That's a real long shot. Fermel really hates you. Chef? Well, Chef is Chef."

"Yeah, but Fermel's got himself to think about. If the restaurant fails, Chef will blame him. And Chef—you know what he's like. He'll say one thing one day and the opposite the next."

Davey grinned. He knew of Chef's capricious ways as well as Kerry did. "All right. You show up at six a.m. and we'll see what's what." They stood up and shook hands.

❖

It felt odd, staring once again at the entrance of the City and County Hospital and wondering what her reception would be. Kerry had swallowed her pride and concluded her only hope of ever winning Beth back was to get advice from Addison.

She asked for him at the desk, and the same old grim-faced nurse there gave her a look of disdain before dispatching a junior to find Dr. Grant. He appeared some fifteen minutes later, appearing flummoxed.

"Kerry. Whatever is the matter?"

The stress of the last few days caught up with her, and she started crying. "Can I talk to you?" She managed to squeeze the words out between gasps. This was embarrassing. She thought she was tougher than this.

Addison put an arm around her and led her away from the desk and the curious stares of the nurses. "Yes, of course. I'm engaged, but you can wait in my office."

She sat down in one of his chairs and again relived the day some seven years previously when she had made her way to the hospital and to a man she scarcely remembered.

Before long he returned carrying two cups of tea. He handed one to her and seated himself, not behind his desk but in the chair next to her.

She sipped the tea. The steam from it soothed her somewhat and she calmed. Shame at her own weakness rose in her mind, but she fought to tamp it down. Addison drank his tea and waited patiently for her to speak. His thick brown hair needed cutting and he looked tired, but aside from all that, he seemed unusually serene.

She swallowed and gathered her resolve and told him the story, not omitting any detail. He listened without comment, and she waited for the censure she was sure was coming.

"You behaved most recklessly, and the consequences of your behavior, well, you can see clearly what they are." He didn't seem angry or disgusted, just thoughtful and sad.

"I was wrong but I had reasons. You understand, don't you?"

He cocked his head to one side, and the corners of his mouth crinkled in a near grin.

"Kerry. I'm not discounting your motives. I'm only concerned that you see how misguided you were."

"I wasn't! I had to find a way to help Beth. I—"

Addison held up his hand. "You're saying 'I' a great deal. With you and Beth, isn't 'we' more important? You also, I fear, carry the same conviction that your father Jack had and, I venture, many others who aren't necessarily criminal, that the end justifies the means."

"What do you mean by that?" Kerry had never heard that phrase.

"I mean that you believe as long as your goal is honorable and for the good, then any wrong you do, anyone you hurt is dwarfed by the rightness of your aim."

"Huh." That was all Kerry could think of to say to Addison's explanation as she allowed it to slowly sink in.

"So." She spoke in hesitation, not willing to admit she might have erred in her quest to obtain financial security for herself and Beth. Even though she saw that, in the end, it was truly all for naught. She had no source of income and she didn't have Beth either.

She paused. "It wasn't right for me to try and make money illegally and not tell Beth about it."

"Correct. You were dishonest in several different ways, and it got you exactly nothing."

"Yes. Nothing." Kerry absorbed that idea. As long as she was confessing, she might as well tell Addison the rest of it.

"I'm devastated. I told Beth I was done with the Barbary Coast and its ways, but I broke my promise to her. I wasn't done. I hadn't changed. I was exactly the same."

"Not precisely. You see how wrong you were. When Jack first asked me to be your guardian, the thing he emphasized the most was that he wanted you taken away from the Barbary Coast and into a better life."

"I know that. I've disappointed everyone. You, Beth, and Jack, if he can see from wherever he is."

"It's yourself you've let down the worst, you know." Addison was looking at her intently, seeming to want her to say more.

"But Beth—"

"First, you. Beth got a shock. You must see that. Her whole world was made topsy-turvy in an instant. She's angry but she loves you. I believe, given what I understand of her feelings, that she wouldn't turn you away should you approach her with the right spirit."

That was the biggest problem. How would she be able to get Beth to even speak to her?

"By the right spirit, I mean you must apologize, thoroughly and unreservedly. No temporizing, no rationalizing, no excuses. That's first. Then you must pledge to change. But before all that, it must be clear in your mind and you have to forgive yourself before she'll forgive you."

"I see, or at least I think I see."

Addison nodded and patted her shoulder. "Then you must work together to repair the damage you've caused."

"I think I can get my post at the Palace back, if the circumstances favor me."

"Very well. But be prepared to think of other avenues. As for Beth's medical-school tuition, there are possibilities we can explore. I wish you'd come to me first, but no matter. You're here now. I'm prepared to help you and Beth."

"I can't express how grateful I am, Addison. I'm already in your debt and I'll be even more so—"

"Tut, don't be concerned. I promised Jack I would look after you, and I will."

❖

Beth took a chance that not only would Marjorie be available but that she would welcome a chance to speak to her. As a further temptation, Beth had brought a meat pie to share. She thought of the expense as she bought it but dismissed her misgivings. It was vital that Marjorie agree to see her, and bringing something tasty to eat could only help.

She looked around the Presidio General Hospital, remembering her time there and missing it a little, but not as much as she would have thought. When Marjorie appeared, she looked surprised but not angry.

"Hello, Marjorie. Forgive me for summoning you without warning. I think your midday break will start soon, and I desperately need to speak with you." She drew the pie out of her satchel. "I've brought something to share with you."

Marjorie looked down at the pie then back up at Beth, her expression unreadable. "Beth. I scarcely expected to see you back here." Not friendly but not hostile either, just matter-of-fact. Just Marjorie.

"I hesitated, but I truly need your counsel. We were friends, and I hope we still are." She ended her sentence with a hopeful question in her voice.

Marjorie said to the charge nurse, "I'll be on the pavilion but don't summon me unless it's an emergency. I'll be taking my dinner break."

Beth sat in the corner farthest away from the convalescent soldiers who lounged about taking the air. It was another mild day, and while she waited, she looked out toward the Marin Headlands, where she could see the white of the waves crashing against the rocks. Marjorie brought some bread and coffee, and they settled themselves with plates at a nearby table.

Finally, Marjorie took a bite of the pie and said, "This is wonderful. Thank you for sharing it. What brings you all the way up here in the midst of your studies? I can't fathom why you would take the time."

Beth drew a deep breath and stared into her coffee cup for a moment before answering.

"I'm preparing for final examinations for the term, and yes, they keep us quite busy."

Marjorie didn't ask for any further details on medical school. So be it. That wasn't what she'd come to discuss.

She sighed and then began speaking again. "Kerry and I are in some trouble." She sketched the story for Marjorie, whose face grew grimmer with each detail. Beth stopped talking and waited for what Marjorie would say.

Marjorie broke off a piece of bread and buttered it slowly. She seemed about to take a bite but instead put it back on her plate. She drummed her fingers on the small wooden table between them. Her face took on an unusually dreamy aspect, and she stared off into the middle distance. Beth became impatient but held her tongue.

"Florence is most displeased with me at this time. She has refused to see me until I have left my mother's house and taken up residence with her."

Beth wasn't shocked to hear of Florence's ultimatum. This had always been a sore subject between the two of them, with Florence pleading and Marjorie always putting her off. It had always been the same since Beth had first met them while nursing in the Philippines war. Part of her was deeply curious about their situation, and the other part resented Marjorie for not focusing on *her* trouble like a true friend would. She fought to not burst out with an angry remonstrance.

"I've always dictated the terms of our connection, and Florence, though she complains, has always gone along. Until now. If I do not make a choice, I may well lose her altogether."

Marjorie, as she said this, turned to look at Beth closely.

"After you left the hospital, I was angry with you for a long time because you didn't behave as I thought you should. You didn't listen to me. I think you and Florence could unite in your resentment of me and my dictatorial ways."

Beth was astounded. Marjorie never spoke of herself or her feelings in such stark terms.

"I see that in spite of my best efforts to push you away, you're still my friend, and a friend in need who saw fit to come to me for help."

"You're the only one who would really understand. I love Kerry, but I'm in a quandary."

"Yes, you are. As am I. I love Florence but I love my mother."

"Yes. You love both of them beyond reason."

"And you love Kerry the same way."

"I do." Beth nearly choked with emotion. Saying it aloud was unbearable pain.

"You mustn't drive her away. I fear I've done that to Florence. You must try to understand why she did what she did. It seems as though she did it for you."

"Yes, but—"

"No, don't qualify it. She did it for you. But how was it you were not aware of the facts of your situation?"

Beth started to be angry at Marjorie for judging her, but she quashed her reaction and thought hard. Was it possible she *wanted* to be ignorant? To let Kerry take care of everything so she didn't have to be bothered? Kerry made it clear to her that was how *she* wanted it, but was it right for Beth to capitulate so easily?

"You play a part in this every bit as much as Kerry does. You were content to let Kerry take charge without asking a question."

Beth winced at hearing this accurate assessment. "I—" Beth stuttered. "She wouldn't share the details of our financial state with me."

"Elizabeth. I'm not saying you were wrong, but perhaps you're naive and too trusting."

That was too much. "Why shouldn't I trust her?"

"Well, you did, and it turned out she tried to take care of matters the wrong way."

"So I should have questioned her?"

"Yes, of course. You must both understand clearly your monetary picture. How could you leave that to her? If we wanted to slough off responsibility for ourselves, we could marry men and never have to think about anything again."

That made Beth smile. Thinking of either of them in marital chains was a ridiculous thought.

"I don't believe that you want Kerry to go away forever. I believe you're angry, and you have a right to be, but just see her and talk to her."

"I'll do that. We'll work something out, somehow. I needed so much to tell you this. I didn't know where to turn. I'm less distressed now."

"That's good to hear." Marjorie looked sad again and Beth wondered what she was thinking, if she was thinking of Florence.

"What about you? What will you do?"

"Ah, that *is* the question, isn't it?" Marjorie played with her napkin, folding and refolding it and staring at her hands. "I cannot leave my mother *or* Florence. I'm boxed in."

"But you just told me that I shouldn't let Kerry go."

"I did. But my situation is different, though I'm thinking about it." Her face grew hard and sardonic. "I should take my own advice. Shouldn't I?"

"I honestly don't know. I hope it turns out as you want it to. I'm so grateful we're still friends. I was worried."

"We are. I wish you only the best, Elizabeth."

CHAPTER TWENTY-ONE

At six o'clock in the morning on Thanksgiving Day, Kerry stood in the alley behind the Palace Hotel kitchen in the rain. She shivered and tried to pull her coat close around her, praying the rain wouldn't soak her through before she could get inside to the kitchen. She was waiting for Davey and he was late. When some other cook would come through, she would draw back into the shadows so she wouldn't be seen. So far, to her it looked as though all the cooks were showing up to work. There wouldn't be a chance for her to get in.

She had almost gone to Mrs. Thompson's the night before to find Beth, but she decided it would be prudent to present herself when she at least was gainfully employed. She'd told Irish Mike she was done with the moonshine business, and he'd shrugged. There'd be another willing helper sometime soon. Instead of staying up all night, she went to Addison's and slept, or tried to. It was almost impossible. Every time she closed her eyes, all she saw was Beth's face as she'd last seen it, enraged and sorrowful and reproving.

She jumped up and down, trying to stay warm. The rain was beginning to drip down the back of her coat. She heard a woman's voice and drew closer, struggling to hear. The woman stood at the back door of the kitchen. She wore plain clothes, but they were obviously clean and mended. What could she possibly want? Kerry hoped it wasn't a job as a cook.

After a few moments, Kerry heard Fermel's voice, harsh and impatient. She was just able to make out their conversation from her hiding place.

"Madam, what is it? I'm very busy here."

"I'm Davey's wife. I come to tell you." Kerry heard the fear in her voice.

"Tell me what?" Fermel asked. "Where's Davey? If he doesn't show up soon, he can forget showing up. He won't have a job."

"He sent me, mister. Please don't be mad. He's real sorry, but he's awfully sick. He got the measles. Caught it from our youngest. He's so bad, he can't get out of bed."

"Measles," Fermel repeated, uncomprehending.

Davey's wife wrung her hands. "He can't cook how he is. Please don't fire him. It's my fault."

"Hmph." Fermel's voice was a growl. "Very well. You've delivered your message. Now be gone."

The woman backed away, then turned around and walked into the alley. Kerry didn't hesitate. She dashed in front of the door where Fermel still stood, glaring at the hapless woman's back as she hurried away.

"Monsieur Fermel. I heard what she said. I'm here. I can help you."

"You." That was all he said.

Then he turned away, closing the door behind him, but not before Kerry got her foot on the sill and stopped him. "Monsieur Fermel, you need me. There will be one hundred and fifty for dinner at three o'clock today, and you're short at least one man, maybe two. There's not much time to waste."

He lowered his eyebrows in a hostile stare. "Bah. You're worthless." He wasn't going to admit he was wrong.

He was a prideful French dolt, but she didn't care what he thought or what he called her, as long as he put her to work. "Maybe, but I can cook." She waited. They must have stood staring at one another for a full minute. He backed away from the door and she followed him.

He threw her a cook's jacket and, as he walked away, he said, "You won't be paid unless Chef is agreeable and you're up to snuff. No slacking."

"I won't slack. Just tell me what you want me to do.' She threw off her wet overcoat and buttoned up the cook's jacket, slicked her damp hair back, and pulled her shoulders straight. She was ready.

Fermel turned around and pointed to the center station. "Roasts and sauces. I'm in charge, and I won't take any lip from you." Fermel knew she was an expert in grilling, not in the two items he'd assigned her to. He was going to try to make her fail. Well, he wouldn't succeed.

"Yes, sir." She threw in a salute for good measure.

❖

At midnight, dinner service was over and the cooks cleaned the kitchen, summoning their last bits of strength. Kerry made sure to do more than her share as Fermel was supervisor. She looked up to see Chef Henri standing in the doorway. Fermel went over to shake hands, and Kerry saw them both look her way and whisper. She couldn't hear what was being said, so she addressed herself to mopping the floor with her head down. Someone tapped her on her shoulder and she turned around. Fermel motioned her to follow him. In silence, they walked to Chef's office.

In the cramped room, Kerry struggled to keep her anxiety down. Being so close to Fermel was hard. Chef stared at them, chewing his mustaches. "I said you were not to come back begging for your job, yet you did. And you—" he turned to Fermel "—let her back into the kitchen because it served your purpose."

Fermel actually flinched. Oddly, he seemed embarrassed for an instant, but he recovered and said with his usual certainty, "Yes, Chef. It was an emergency. Davey Moore took sick. I had to step in and we needed another line cook." He drew himself up. "I did what was required to ensure the success of the night."

"Yes. And it was a success by all accounts." Chef started listing off all of the notable guests at the restaurant and how that would show off his success, and Fermel nodded and murmured his agreement. Clearly he was kowtowing to Chef so Chef wouldn't be angry with him. Kerry grew impatient with the two long-winded Frenchmen, but she held her tongue. It wasn't the time to be argumentative. She had to wait.

"You're not to be making any extra money on the side, is that clear?" Chef nearly shouted. It seemed all might turn out well, after all. He would try to save face by yelling at her, but she would get her job back.

Chef addressed Fermel as though Kerry wasn't in the room. "Fermel, is it agreeable to you that Kerr-ie returns to work full time?"

"I'm not sure. It is disruptive to have a woman in the kitchen." He hadn't really changed his mind. Kerry would have to think of something.

"Chef, I've not been cooperative with M. Fermel, and I apologize. I will recognize his authority and do as he tells me. With no reservation."

Fermel raised one eyebrow. "Yes," he said, finally. "If Kerr-ie will behave properly."

Back in the kitchen, Kerry said to Fermel, "I know you don't think I belong here and you are merely allowing me to cook because I *can* cook."

He looked at her and blinked, then looked away.

"Teach me how to make the wild-game dishes. I can learn quickly."

He finally met her eye, and for the first time, she saw just a hint of assent.

"Very well. Be back here Saturday at noon." That was that.

Kerry had to walk all the way home to Addison's house in the rain and in the dark, but she scarcely noticed. She had so much to think about. On the one hand, she was deeply relieved to have gotten her post back at the Palace, and on the other hand, she still had no idea how to win Beth back. Well, she would have to ask Addison's advice on how to approach her.

She wanted to go home right that moment and pound on the door to get Beth up and tell her the good news, but she'd learned to think her actions through just a little better. Their meeting would have to wait. Kerry wanted it to be the right time, and she wanted to have the right words, the ones that would convince Beth to take her back. It was a good thing she was exhausted when she finally arrived at Addison's house. She was too tired to be grieved by Beth's absence.

❖

The next day, Kerry woke up late and enjoyed the sensation of being able to lie in bed. The only thing missing, of course, was Beth. It was lonely and disorienting. She had a day and a half before she would be required to report for dinner. Should she try to talk to Beth today?

But she found she was reluctant. It was a terrifying prospect because she had no idea how she would be received. Would Beth be ready to listen to her, or would she shut the door in her face? At loose ends, she waited around Addison's house all day long. In the afternoon, she was distracted by helping Mrs. Evans cook dinner. Addison had been at the hospital on Thanksgiving Day so his feast was delayed.

It comforted Kerry to be able to cook in a small kitchen on a normal scale for herself and Addison. After some initial chilliness, Mrs. Evans became downright chatty and told Kerry all about the doctor and his friend, the lady doctor. Kerry was amused. So it was true, Addison had gotten sweet on Dr. Strauss. That was a good thing. Esther was an entirely different woman than Laura.

Addison returned that evening with Dr. Strauss, and they all sat down to eat the meal Kerry had helped Mrs. Evans prepare. She'd made chestnut stuffing for the turkey and candied yams and pumpkin pie. Addison and Esther couldn't stop praising her efforts, and she let their appreciation soothe her, though she was still desperately lonely for Beth and wanted to talk to Addison about it. Esther and Addison fell into a discussion about the plague that didn't interest her, but it made her think of Beth again, who would have been rapt.

"Kinyoun sent me a note and asked me to meet with him. I was hoping we'd be summoned for more investigations," Addison told Esther. She stopped eating and looked at him, clearly excited.

"And what did he say? Are we going to Chinatown again and look for more plague victims? Can we perform our duties without the police?"

Addison held up his hand and said, "Kinyoun wanted to tell me that in payment for his labors, the Governor of California had him removed from his post."

"Oh, no!"

"Yes. It seems that the governor, under pressure from business interests, does not want it known that there's plague in San Francisco, even if it's confined to the environs of Chinatown, if not to the Chinese population, as we know." Addison looked soberly at Esther, and some silent communication passed between them that Kerry didn't know how to interpret.

About halfway through the meal, Addison said, "I've told Esther about your difficulties."

Kerry tensed, feeling defensive and under scrutiny. She hadn't expected Addison to share her troubles with an outsider.

"I thought it might help for you to hear a feminine opinion. I'm sympathetic but scarcely an expert on women. Esther's educating me." He waved a drumstick. They both laughed and looked at each other lovingly.

Kerry blushed, but when she turned to face Esther and saw her compassionate expression, she relaxed a bit, though she was still shy.

"I guess you know about us," Kerry said. "Me and Beth, I mean."

"Addison has told me, yes. I understand you've had words and are in a bit of quandary."

There was a pause. That didn't even begin to describe Kerry's trouble. She thought Esther would say more, but she instead she took a small bite of turkey followed by a dainty sip of wine.

Finally she spoke. "I am acquainted with a good number of people in New York who are of your persuasion. They live mainly in Greenwich Village. I happened to mention them to one of the doctors at Bellevue, a doctor specializing in ills of the mind. He was most informative and told me all about the German Ulrichs, who attempted to get the German government to stop persecuting those whom he called homosexuals. My colleague at Bellevue saw a few such people who came to him. He's a psychiatrist and treats the ills of the mind. He allowed that his prescriptions didn't seem to have much of an effect on these patients. They went away feeling exactly the same as when they began. It was those patients who took me to their homes, where I met a great many others like them. That's also when I first became aware of the anarchists, whose leader, Miss Goldman, I became quite fond of." Esther stopped to take another drink. "I don't believe that this is something that can be changed. I suppose it's debatable as to whether it should be."

Kerry was fascinated to hear all of this, but she was skeptical that any of it would help herself and Beth.

Esther continued. "Miss Goldman believes there should be no regulation of intimate relations between people, and she is critical of the contempt with which people hold for those who love their own sex. One of her circle, a young woman named May, became enamored of me. I've never been so beautifully or ardently courted." Esther's eyes shone with what were clearly pleasant memories.

Kerry glanced at Addison, who had stopped eating and was intently listening to Esther, his chin on his hand.

"May told me about Sappho and the island of Lesbos, and how women are so different from men that we might as well form an entirely different species." She laughed.

"At times I agree with that assessment. At any rate, I never succumbed to May's entreaties to make love with her. I was tempted, but in the end, I'm far too fond of the male body."

Both Addison and Kerry were speechless. Addison's face had gone dark but he said nothing. Kerry had never heard anyone speak of such things except in derision. Other than Marjorie and Florence, she and Beth had never met any people like them. She'd never told Beth so, but she didn't much like either Marjorie or Florence. They seemed closed-minded and priggish. Florence was always in a state of anxiety, and Marjorie was cold and harsh with her. She decided she liked Esther's candid and forthright manner, but she was still unsure how this conversation would be helpful to her.

"I told you all of that by way of convincing you that I am, like Addison, sympathetic, but that I also have some knowledge of the emotions you speak of."

Kerry could only nod, silently.

Addison said, "My word, is there any end to the surprises you have in store for me, Esther?" He didn't sound like he was looking forward to any more.

"I had a life before we met, dear Addison, as did you."

And there Kerry noted the acerbic tone. Esther wasn't like Laura, but she wasn't to be trifled with either.

Esther favored Addison with a placating smile, but she turned back to Kerry and put a hand over hers.

"We women can seem to be inexplicable creatures, but that's not the case. You've committed a very grave error, as Addison tells me. Such a breach of trust would make anyone reluctant to ever believe the perpetrator of such an injury."

"I was so sure I was doing the right thing." Kerry hated the wail she heard in her voice but was unable to moderate it. She disliked sounding like a spoiled child who had not gotten her way.

"In the end, that may be your salvation. If you can convince Beth that your motives were pure even if your actions weren't, she will forgive you. I'm sure she is a loving and loyal girl and could be induced to forgive you. Ask her what you can do to make amends."

"I don't know if she will even consent to see me," Kerry said, fretfully.

Esther patted her arm. "Addison, perhaps you could be of service and ask Miss Hammond over to supper next week."

"Certainly, I believe that the final exams, if the schedule is still the same, will be over on Thursday. It would be a good time for her to celebrate the end of her first term at the Medical Department." He spoke with his customary geniality, but his eyes never left Esther.

"I think I shall invite myself over as well, and we can all make general conversation for a while. Then Addison and I will make our exit after dinner to allow the two of you some privacy."

Esther looked at Kerry meaningfully. A little glimmer of hope lit the dark of Kerry's soul as she nodded in assent.

Addison said, "That's settled. May I suggest we distract ourselves with a few rounds of card playing?"

To Kerry's great surprise, after a few hours of cards, Esther went upstairs with Addison. She'd never given a thought to the idea that a respectable unmarried woman could spend the night with her lover. This certainly added a lot more detail to her picture of Esther, who wasn't a bit like either Laura or the pretty waiter girls on the Barbary Coast.

❖

Later, when Esther and Addison were getting ready for bed, he said, "You might have told me beforehand."

She took his meaning. "My love, it's of no consequence to us. I didn't think you were one of those men who fly into a frenzy when he finds out his beloved isn't as pure as the driven snow."

Her sarcastic tone offended him, but he managed to keep his temper down. He was also hurt that she hadn't told him more about her life before they met.

"It isn't that, but that I was hearing of it for the first time when you told Kerry. I understand there were other men before me, but I didn't think there would be a woman." He was irritated with her and with himself and kept his head down sulkily.

Esther put her fingers under his chin to make him meet her eye. "I don't think it necessary to regale you with my adventures in detail, but I've clearly let you know you are not my first lover. And anyhow, I was trying to establish rapport with Kerry, and I believe that I succeeded. Surely you know that people who are different are extraordinarily sensitive about their differences and—"

"I understand that. I...I don't wish to be the kind of man you describe. That is loathsome to the utmost. It's the worst sort of male inanity and vanity."

She was smiling quite broadly. "I'm so happy to hear you say that. Come here." She opened her arms and he went to her. With her head on his chest, she spoke almost in a whisper.

"Without a doubt, you are the most loving, kindest, most wonderful man I've ever met. We're together, that is all that matters. The past is in the past, not in the present."

She hugged him tight and Addison relaxed, feeling reassured and loved. He kissed her hair and held her.

❖

"I believe we're nearly ready," Scott said. "I just want to review the workings of the digestive system one more time. Have you the notes from that lecture handy?"

Beth's concentration had flagged again. She'd been hoping for word from Kerry for a week but had heard nothing. She was just managing to hold off despair. In one way, it was well they had their final examinations to study for. It forced her to take her mind off Kerry for large swathes of time.

Nights were the worst. She lay in her bed that had been hers and Kerry's at Mrs. Thompson's and thought her heart would burst. She couldn't stop thinking of Kerry and their last conversation. The bed was wide and empty, and she would have welcomed Kerry home had she appeared at the door and asked to be let in. Marjorie's words had had a powerful influence on her.

Scott was unfailingly kind, but he was strict about their study commitments. "You're right," she told him. "We should look at that subject again and make sure we've got the sequence down perfectly and we know the parts of the digestive system." She located the notes and passed them over to him. "Please question me."

He did so, and then they left the student lounge and went outside for a few minutes. When they came back, he took his turn to be questioned by her until they were both satisfied that they had memorized the necessary facts.

As they packed up, Beth asked Scott what he would do to celebrate at the end of the examinations.

"Oh. Howard has asked a group of us to his parents' ranch in Sonoma. You?"

"I'm not sure."

"Well. I'd ask you along with me, but I'm afraid it's a stag occasion."

Beth nodded. It was another aspect of her chosen profession that she would often not be asked to be take part in the men's social events. It was both a relief and a disappointment.

In her bag, Beth had a letter from Addison asking her to supper on the evening of the last day of the school term, but she hadn't responded. He'd said nothing about Kerry, and she concluded that Kerry wasn't at Addison's house. Was she truly at the Grey Dog Saloon? She decided she could only ask Addison of her whereabouts. She had no interest in making a trip there to see for herself.

She wasn't feeling festive at all but supposed she would go because her nights without Kerry at Mrs. Thompson's were wretchedly lonely. She regretted telling Kerry to leave. In retrospect, the show of temper on her part was unusual. She wasn't impetuous or arbitrary, but she'd acted so that night. Well, now she was living with the consequences. She only wanted Kerry to come home so they could talk and be together again. As to the rest of it, her future at school, she couldn't think of that until later, after they'd reconciled. She penned an acceptance note to Addison and put it in the post the next day.

A few days later, on the last day of examinations, Beth was confident and ready. She pushed her heartache about Kerry's betrayal into the back of her mind, where it resided, quiet if not dead. Beth took a seat next to Scott, who gave her an encouraging smile. The ordeal was over in a few hours, and Beth was so tired, she considered not traveling to Addison's house, but it was only a few blocks from Mrs. Thompson's, less than a mile, and she truly wanted to celebrate the end of the school term. Maybe Addison could tell her where Kerry was.

She walked up Fillmore Street from the streetcar stop on California Street in the December dusk. Beth didn't mind the cold nights, but the short days were hard. She liked the daylight. She could see the lights on in Addison's house, and at his front door, the leaded glass of the window sparkled from the lamp in the entry hallway in a cheerful, welcoming way.

At her knock, Addison came to let her in and kissed her on the cheek. Behind him stood Esther, looking happy and beautiful. She wore an unusually decorative dress, a dark-green damask with lace that looked ravishing with her black hair and dusky coloring. Addison caught Esther's eye as he took Beth's wrap, and she recognized the look that passed between them. Beth hadn't thought of it before, but others' happiness, while welcome, could be painful as well. She smoothed her dress and hair and followed the two of them into the front parlor. The entire house reminded her of Kerry because it was here they'd first lived together and fallen in love. How could it have been nearly three years? How could they have gotten into such a predicament? Addison stood aside at the door to allow Esther and Beth to enter first.

There was Kerry sitting on the sofa. Beth's throat tightened and she became light-headed. Kerry's deep-brown eyes registered nothing as they fixed on Beth's face. Her expression didn't change, but she watched as Beth sat down next to her. Beth was stunned but relieved to see Kerry.

Kerry said in a hoarse, throaty whisper, "Hello, Bethy." When her voice roughened, it meant she was greatly moved or unreasonably angry, Beth couldn't tell which. In a dream, she responded automatically, "Kerry, dearest." It popped out of her mouth with no thought on her part.

Addison's voice dragged Beth back into the present. "Forgive me for not warning you. We thought it best to not say anything." He tilted his head toward Esther, who smiled in an encouraging manner.

"We thought bringing you together would be helpful. Please take this as a hopeful effort on our part. We had no wish to distress you, but to give you a chance to talk together. We hope you aren't vexed with us, but if you are, please accept our apologies." The two of them took chairs and began a conversation as though nothing was amiss. Beth looked at Kerry, who stared dumbly back at her.

"Beth, my dear," Addison said in his heartiest voice. "Please tell us about school and your examinations. I venture you are relieved to be through with them."

And Beth, without thinking, replied, "Oh yes. The last one was today. I believe I did well, but we won't hear of our results until January. I studied as hard as I could and for as long as I could with Scott, my classmate. He and I tried to challenge one another."

"Excellent idea." Addison beamed.

Esther said, "That's certainly the best way. It's both more effective and more fun to pursue studies with a classmate."

And they continued in this vein until Mrs. Evans appeared in the doorway. Kerry didn't say a single word until they were seated at the dining table and Addison informed them that Kerry had helped Mrs. Evans prepare their meal.

Mrs. Evans said, "More like the other way around. I was the one takin' orders from Kerry on how to do this and do that." She didn't sound too perturbed by this change. Kerry blushed, and Beth remembered how sweet and charming she looked when that happened.

Addison poured glasses of wine, large ones, for everyone and handed them around. "A toast to Beth's completion of her first semester at the Medical Department and to Kerry's cooking."

They all clinked glasses, and when Beth turned to Kerry, she saw a familiar light in her eyes, mixed with apprehension. Addison and Esther took charge of the conversation and prevented any uneasy gaps. Beth, to her astonishment, found she had calmed down.

Addison turned to Kerry and said, "Well, this new type of cooking you're learning at the Palace seems to be just the thing. I believe I could become very fond of game." They were consuming a roast *salmis* of pheasant.

Beth was confused so she asked a question of the group in general so as not to have to address it to Kerry. "Oh, am I to understand that Kerry is back in the Palace Restaurant?"

"Yes. I've been given my cook's post back," Kerry said, "and I am, ahem, learning some new dishes from the M. Fermel. This is the first time I've made this roast. I've been watching how M. Fermel prepares wild game birds

Beth remembered her bitter complaints about Fermel and understood that something momentous must have happened. "It's so tasty. I never would have guessed it would be." Beth turned a glance on Kerry, who smiled for the first time that evening.

"Beth, I really am curious about how the men in your class are behaving toward you. I remember at the beginning you saying how odd, awkward, and alternately jovial and hostile they were."

"They've gotten used to me, I think. I don't know them well except for Scott, who's my staunch friend."

Kerry's brows furrowed and her face set.

Oh dear, now what's wrong? Is she jealous? Beth recalled their unpleasant discussion about Scott at their picnic in Golden Gate Park. She would have to wait to find out, because Esther was talking about patients and women doctors again, and she wanted to listen.

She was greatly amused how Addison seemed to hang on Esther's every word. Chin in hand, he gazed at her fondly while she talked, and he didn't interrupt or contradict her. It was nice to see that they were happy.

How could she and Kerry ever repair the damage that had been done? She was torn between being still angry with Kerry and longing for her. She just wanted things to go back to the way they'd been. She had no idea if she was going to be able to attend another year of medical school and grew furious again. She was so caught up in her whirling thoughts she didn't hear when Esther asked her a question and jumped when Esther touched her arm.

"Beth. How have your instructors received you?"

"Oh. Mostly well, but they don't stop the men from making rude comments."

"Ah, that's the thing. I had to develop a thick skin."

"It's better now. They teased me at the beginning, playing pranks with our cadaver, but now they leave me alone because of Scott." *Let Kerry stew about that if that's what she wants. She was never home to talk to, so I went elsewhere for some human contact. Let her think what she likes.* With Kerry staring at her, she felt exposed and took a big gulp of wine. She'd scarcely touched her supper, and the alcohol went right to her head, making her dizzy.

"What sort of pranks?" Kerry asked through her teeth.

"Nothing I can decently discuss at a supper table!" Her voice sounded too loud to her, loud and raucous. Esther and Addison glanced at her curiously. She flushed and tried a bite of stewed turnip but nearly spit it out because it tasted so foul. She drank more wine to wash out the taste. The room was growing hazy, and her head was spinning along with her stomach. Oh no, this was terrible. She remembered suddenly that she was deeply tired. For the last week, her sleep had been brief and tortured because of all the studying. Esther and Addison were speaking, and Kerry was still staring at her.

"I—I have to—Excuse me!" Beth leaped from her chair and ran out the front door just in time to be able to vomit over the porch railing. She bent over, gasping for air, then vomited again. She felt a hand on her back. When she was able to get her breath, she looked and it was Esther, who put an arm around her and said, "Come with me." She let Esther lead her back into the house, upstairs, and into a bedroom she recognized as the same one she'd once shared with Kerry. She lay down, and Esther washed her face and patted her hair.

"Better? Will you need a basin?"

"No. I'm all right now." Beth tried to sit.

"Be still, Beth. No need to get up. Just rest. Here's some water."

Beth took the water. She was embarrassed and still dizzy. This was ridiculous. She lay on her side. Esther put a cool cloth on her forehead.

"You may have had a little too much wine, too little food, and, I suspect, too little rest in the last several days. That and all the anxiety of your exams have sickened you. Perhaps it was also a shock to see Kerry. It's no surprise you've taken ill. We'll see how your stomach is presently. I think some broth is called for, and no more of our rich supper."

Beth was beginning to feel better, but she was chagrined at making such a scene. Esther was kindness personified. She wondered, though, what Kerry was thinking. In her distress, she wanted Kerry at her side, never mind their estrangement. And yet she was still angry every time she thought of what had happened. It was impossible to tell where one feeling stopped and the other began.

Chapter Twenty-two

Is she all right? Should I go up?" Kerry was frantic with worry. She'd watched as Beth fled the dinner table.

Addison put a hand on her arm to keep her in her seat. "Perhaps in a moment. Let's see what Esther has to say. I made a mistake inviting her without telling her you would be here. I should have warned her." Addison looked contrite.

"Oh, it was a shock for certain, but she didn't run from the house screaming." Kerry wondered if she'd been the cause of Beth's distress.

"That's all to the good. But I wanted to bring you together, and then Esther and I would leave after dinner and allow you to have some solitude to talk to one another.'

"It was a good plan. Except—" Kerry wanted so much to race upstairs, throw herself on her knees next to Beth, and plead for her forgiveness. She sat with her hands between her knees and her back slightly hunched, thinking she might fall apart at any moment. Addison began to ask her more questions about the Palace and to urge her to eat. His efforts distracted her from her anxiety, but part of her mind was upstairs with Beth.

After an eternity, Esther returned. "The patient will live, it seems, but she must not try to eat any more. Did you or Mrs. Evans prepare any soup by any chance?"

Kerry scrutinized Esther, for what she wasn't sure, but Esther's mien betrayed nothing. "I have the broth from cooking the pheasant. It's clear. Will that help?"

"Admirably. Would you take it up to her, along with a little bread?"

Kerry climbed the stairs carrying a tray, and with each step she fought to replace her uneasiness with hope.

❖

Beth lay on her side with her head on her arm and stared at the brass knobs on the dresser. The entire room was exactly the same as it had been when she and Kerry had occupied it two years previously. The enamel washbasin was centered on the dresser, and behind it the window that overlooked the yard. It was a relief to lie still, and she wasn't sick to her stomach any longer. She heard a step on the stairs and tensed, wondering who it was, hoping it was Kerry. Then she sensed someone in the doorway. She turned over and there stood Kerry, smiling tentatively and holding a tray.

"Bethy? Are you all right?"

"I'm better now. Esther took care of me."

Kerry set the tray on the dresser, retrieved the old cane chair from the corner, and placed it right next to Beth. She picked up the bowl of soup and the spoon and sat down. Her nearness complicated Beth's already unsettled feelings. She stared at Kerry's hands as they held the soup bowl. They were so familiar and so dear, covered with innumerable burns and knife cuts, but they had always touched her with such care. Beth nearly burst into tears. Kerry seemed as shy and unsure as she'd been when they first met, which was curious.

"Do you want some soup?" Beth scooted herself upright and rested against the pillows. She accepted the bowl from Kerry and slowly sipped a spoonful. It tasted good. Kerry watched her closely for a few moments.

"Beth?"

"Hmm?" Beth's mouth was full so she couldn't actually manage any words. She found she wanted to hear what Kerry would have to say. She couldn't gauge the true level of her anger. Since their argument, then the talk with Marjorie, she was more confused and contrite than angry.

"I'm sorry you didn't realize I would be here. We were afraid if Addison told you, you wouldn't come."

Beth thought about that and decided she wasn't angry about the deception. "No. But that shock combined with what I've had to endure made me ill."

"I see that. I'm sorry for that and for...other things." They were silent for a moment. "I'm truly sorry for what I did. That comes directly from my heart. It was wrong to do it, and it was very wrong to lie to you about what I was up to."

Beth swallowed her soup and looked at Kerry for a long time. Her face was so drawn and so woebegone, she wanted to accept the apology right then and there, have no more discussion about it, and go on with their lives, but it wasn't that easy. They couldn't pick up their life together and go on as if nothing had happened. For one thing, her future was in jeopardy because she'd be forced to leave school if she couldn't pay for it. But more than that, they wouldn't be right with one another until they changed some old ways of doings things, both hers and Kerry's.

"So if you knew you were wrong, why did you go forward with your plan? Why did you deceive me, all the while knowing I would be very upset? I don't understand that. I thought I knew you, but it seems I don't." Beth didn't wish to sound harsh, but to her ears, her words sounded angry. So be it, she *was* angry. Still.

Kerry shifted in her chair and rocked a bit. She looked at the floor. It was terrible to see her suffer but it was necessary. A knock on the door startled them both. Kerry's eyes widened in terror but she didn't speak.

"Yes?" Beth said. The door opened a crack, and she heard Addison's voice.

"I'm sorry to disturb you, but may I come in for just a moment? Beth glanced at Kerry, who shrugged.

Beth answered. "Yes, of course."

He stepped into the room and looked from one to other, but all he said was, "If you're feeling better, Beth, Esther and I will depart to attend a concert downtown. You two are free to stay here and spend the night if you wish. We'll try not to disturb you when we return."

"I'm improving, thanks to some rest and food, and am content for you and Esther to leave. I don't believe we need you here." She looked at Kerry, who nodded.

"Excellent. Well, then. We'll likely see you in the morning." He gently closed the door.

When he'd gone, Beth asked Kerry, "Did you know I would be coming for supper?"

"Yes. I guess Addison wanted to put us together and see what would happen."

"And you saw what happened." Beth felt rather bitter about not being told the entire truth, despite her earlier attitude. Goodness, her mood was bouncing up and down. What a state to be in.

"Did my being here make you ill?" Kerry asked.

The naked pain and sincerity in her voice startled Beth. "No, Kerry, dearest. It was my own inner turmoil, along with too little sleep for too many days and too much anguish about my future, both about the near-term results of our examinations and my long-term prospects of completing medical school." It was an honest answer, if not a comforting one.

The use of their old endearment made Kerry smile, but sadly. She clearly was burdened by the weight of her remorse, as well she should be.

"Before we were interrupted, I asked you a question," Beth said.

"Yes, you did. I'm trying to formulate an answer that will be honest but also might help you find forgiveness for me."

"Well. Please proceed then." Beth tore off a piece of bread and chewed while she fixed her gaze on Kerry.

"That was somewhat of a surprise, Beth becoming ill, I mean," Addison said while the horses conveyed them down to the concert hall on Van Ness Avenue where a performance of Mozart was scheduled.

"Not especially, Addison. We created the situation hoping for the best, but one never knows how people will react."

"Do you think they can effect a reconciliation?"

"I'm not sure. I hope so. There are too many factors to consider, and I doubt if all will be resolved tonight."

"What a pity that all this has endangered Beth's career," Addison said. "I wish they'd come to me. I have some resources at my disposal."

"Well. That may be true. Sometimes it's too difficult to ask for help. I submit that for young women such as they, especially Kerry, asking for help would be a tremendous blow to her pride."

"How in the world? She was my ward! She knows she may come to me at any time."

"Addison, my love. It's not that simple. Though she is a young woman, she's casting herself in the role of protector and provider for Beth. That she went to such lengths to fulfill that role indicates how seriously she takes it and how seriously she takes herself."

"Eh. Well then, what am I to do?"

"Let's say nothing at present and allow them the time and opportunity to work things out. Then perhaps you could make an offer. I have some ideas." Her eyes glinted in the dark.

"I've no doubt you do, my love. You're scarcely ever without a plan to meet any eventuality."

"That is kind of you to say so. What would you say to me coming to share your house with you and to inviting Beth and Kerry to do the same?"

Addison was overjoyed. He wanted to ask Esther again to live with him but was afraid she would say no, that it would be too much of a crimp on her precious independence.

"I would welcome that indeed, my dear, if that would be your wish." He squeezed her hand and kissed her cheek. "I'm ecstatic."

"And Kerry and Beth? If they agree?"

"Why certainly. The house is certainly large enough to accommodate our numbers."

"We could all take part in household chores. I knew of several of Miss Goldman's circle in New York who lived in what they called communes. We could have our own. I suspect that if you put it to Kerry that way, she'd not object."

"And do you suppose I could persuade her and Beth to let me help Beth secure a loan to finance her tuition?"

"It would have to be done diplomatically. Let's proceed slowly."

"You're always right, Esther, my dear. In the meantime, we have Herr Mozart's lovely music to enjoy."

❖

"I want to try and explain myself to you, Bethy. I've got so many dreams for us. One of them is for us to have our own home and not have to share accommodations with other people."

"I'm aware of that dream. I share it with you but—"

"Please. Let me finish," Kerry said, not angry, but sad and pleading. Beth reined in her dismay and struggled to listen.

"I want you to have what you want to. When you said you wanted to be a doctor, I knew I would have to find some way to make that come true and also keep our other dream. How am I of any use to you if I can't give you what you want?" And that was precisely the problem, wasn't it?

Beth didn't hold back her frustration. "You're certainly willing to go to any lengths to give me what you think I want."

"I—" Kerry appeared dumbfounded.

"You told me you were done with the Barbary Coast forever. Do you remember saying that? Yet you went back to it just as fast as you could. Then you lied about it. Don't you see how horrifying that is for me?"

"I know, Bethy. I do, except—"

"No. There is no 'except'!"

Kerry flushed, and her shoulders moved up and down as she struggled to breathe, to fend off the onslaught of Beth's fury. Beth had surprised even herself with her vehemence.

"But that's the reason. You're the reason for everything I do," Kerry said.

"No, you can't make this because of me. It was your decision, which you didn't see fit to discuss with me." Beth had leaned forward, but she fell back on the pillows, feeling exhausted. They stared at one another, stuck in time and at a loss for words.

Beth inhaled deeply, trying to calm herself. She tried to focus on what she remembered from her talk with Marjorie about her part in this mess. She wasn't sure she was ready yet to take responsibility for her own actions until she'd heard more apology and less justification from Kerry.

Kerry's voice dropped to nearly a whisper. "Yes, it was my decision. I didn't want you to worry about me or about anything, really. I just wanted to make it possible for you to go to school and not to worry. I want you to be happy, and now you're unhappy because of me. I've ruined everything." Kerry started crying. She covered her face and sobbed, which melted Beth's heart and caused her rage to ebb.

"Will you be able to forgive me, Beth? How I can make this up to you?"

"Well. First of all, can you please let go of this idea that it's all your burden and none of mine?"

Kerry lowered her hands and raised her teary but questioning eyes at Beth. "But I am the one who must ensure our future. It's what I need to do. You're my love. I have to take care of you. Always."

"Always? You're certainly full of yourself. It's as though you're trying to be the strong one, the strong *man!*" Beth had no idea where she'd dredged up that idea; it had just come to her.

Kerry's jaw dropped. "I'm not, not—"

"Not what, Kerry, dearest? From our earliest acquaintance you've worn men's clothes. I'm not saying I dislike it, I don't. They suit you, and I've come to see that and appreciate it. I do *not* appreciate you, however, when you close me out of your thoughts, go off and do what you believe is right, and don't tell me because you don't want me to worry." Beth bit off the last few words so Kerry would understand just how devastating that was.

"I'm not some shrinking violet, some weak and pliable female after all, am I?"

"No, not at all." Kerry had stopped crying and was looking back at Beth with a considering expression as though she'd just realized something important.

"So will you apologize to me for doing that, as well as jeopardizing your life and liberty. Your health! Lying about your actions and generally throwing our lives into disarray?"

"I do. I apologize from the bottom of my heart. I would have never have done any of it if I'd known. I was wrong about everything. Truly. Very, very wrong, ill-advised, stupid, inconsiderate—"

She seemed prepared to go on forever, so Beth stopped her with a hand on her two clasped ones. "Kerry, dearest. I believe you."

Kerry kissed her hand. "Oh, thank God. Bethy, I'm so contrite, I love you so much. Whatever are we going to do though—"

Her expression was so woebegone, Beth almost started laughing. "Shhh. One thing at a time. Now you must promise me that you will never, ever, *ever* again keep anything from me."

"I promise! I swear, on my love for you. I'll never lie or do bad things, even if they're for you. I'll never treat you like you're not a strong and wise and resilient person, because you're all of those things. I'm not any of them. I just think I am."

"Kerry, dearest. Shhh. It's fine. You're many wonderful things. You meant well. Be still because I must tell you something very important."

Kerry nodded fervently and squeezed their four clasped hands.

"I was all too ready to believe you had all in order and organized. I let you mislead me. I didn't question you as I should have. And another thing, Kerry, you must be forthright about money. It's not enough to tell me all's well. I want to know the details. I've been remiss and that needs to stop. We're a partnership, are we not?"

"Oh, yes. We are. I see that." Kerry was nodding so vigorously, Beth feared that she'd hurt her neck. It was amusing in a way.

"We must share everything, for certain. I thought we did, but we most certainly did not. And that has led us to this painful place. We must promise one another that we will act differently going forward."

"What of your medical school, Beth?"

"I'm waiting to find out about a prize that will ensure my tuition next year, but after that. I don't know. I think you and I have some hard discussions ahead. I may have to stop for a time so we may financially regain our footing." She lowered her brows and glared a little at Kerry.

"I'm not sure, however. You will have to bring your bankbook and show me what's what. And then we can talk. Is it possible you could delay your home-owning dreams for a time? Or?"

Beth stopped speaking. There were far too many aspects to try to consider. The vomiting and the emotional firestorm had left her feeling weak and empty, in spite of her small meal of broth and bread.

Kerry was gazing at her fearfully. The poor girl was terrified she would do something wrong. They had done enough for one night. They weren't wholly healed, but they were much better than before.

Beth decided she wasn't upset at Addison and Esther's subterfuge. They, like Kerry, meant well. And it seemed to have worked.

"Kerry, my love. Would you please take your shoes and your trousers off and—" Beth started to say, but when she saw Kerry's expression, she laughed quite loudly.

"You're getting ahead of yourself. I want you to climb into this bed and hold me. Just hold me in your arms. Addison said we should stay the night. We shall, but we'll sleep. I'm worn out."

Kerry grinned and did as she was told.

❖

Beth fell asleep quickly. Kerry was happy and relieved. It was entirely normal to hold Beth while she slept. They were reconciled. That was all to the good. She was still wakeful because they hadn't resolved everything, but she had to agree with Beth that it was no good trying to do everything in one night. She needed to sleep, for the next day she was due back in the kitchen. Now that she'd regained her cook's job, she wouldn't do anything to disturb her good fortune.

She didn't need to worry about Beth for the time being anyhow. School was finished for the year. If she only could win that prize, it would be a small help. She thought long and hard and decided that what was important was Beth finishing her studies. They would buy a house later; they couldn't manage it now.

Kerry wasn't at all sure how they would manage *anything*, but she had to wait and trust and not simply act of her own accord anymore. She understood, finally, what had gone wrong. She was determined to never upset Beth so much that she would be banished from her sight. She had returned but she had to change.

She moved a bit and Beth sighed and, to her delight, snuggled closer, not waking up but instead seeking Kerry and the refuge of her embrace. The room around them was dark and cold and silent, but under the quilt, close together, they were warm. Most vital of all, they were together in spirit. Kerry started to fall asleep, worn out but relieved.

❖

They took up their routine as before, though Beth was at home all day long and, used to so much work and activity, was feeling restive. She waited for the mail every day, but for the next two weeks, nothing came. She spent some of her time looking through her textbooks, but mostly she tried to read or stared out the window, brooding.

She and Kerry were still estranged on some level. Kerry was waiting for her to give a sign that she was ready to renew their intimacy, but something held Beth back. She wasn't sure what it was. She was waiting to see how Kerry would be.

She was nervous and unsure about the future. In the back of her mind she was afraid Kerry would again do something to get herself let go from the restaurant or somehow change her mind about not pursuing criminal remedies to make money or something. Then there was the entire question of just where Beth would find herself come the fall term of 1902.

Things were still unsettled, and *that* added another layer to her anxiety. She had far too much time to think. They hadn't even discussed how they would celebrate Christmas, or where or if. Beth ruminated about all these matters until her head ached.

Scott came by for a short visit before he went back to Charleston to spend Christmas with his family. "This is a pleasant home, I should say." He sat in Mrs. Thompson's front parlor with Beth and looked around with such interest, Beth wondered if he was thinking of buying the place.

"My dear. This settee is too beautiful. Wherever did she find it?"

"Err. I'm not sure."

"Nonetheless, come sit by me and tell me everything."

So Beth described her reconciliation with Kerry.

Scott raised his eyebrows and sighed dramatically. "Mavis Warren, my mother's second cousin, nearly shot her lover Audrey with a shotgun when she found out Audrey had been spending their money on the horses. You're far too patient."

"Goodness, I don't want to shoot anyone, least of all Kerry. And how do you know your mother's second cousin nearly shot her lover? Or I mean how do you know she *was* her lover? Do people really talk about such things?"

"Oh, everyone knows, darling. We just *don't* talk about it. That's how Southerners are. It's easier on everyone that way. We say 'so and so is a little touched.' Or 'eccentric.' We're surprisingly quite tolerant of difference, except those tiresome bible thumpers who are always in everyone's business. No one likes them anyhow. My relatives just say, 'Scott, he's a nice boy. He's just artistic.' They *know* but they don't say anything. It would make everything unpleasant.." He waved the whole subject away with his hand. Gone, dismissed. Just like that. Beth admired his nonchalance.

"Oh, there's the mail carrier." Beth leaped up and sped to the front door when she heard the mail slot open and a stack of envelopes thump lightly on the hallway floor. She scooped them up and rifled through them. There it was: the envelope with the familiar university address. This time, she had someone with whom to share the news.

She sat down next to Scott and held up the letter.

"Well. Open it, for goodness sakes. Let's see."

"But what of you? Did you get a letter yet?"

"I did, indeed." He said no more, and Beth was frustrated.

"And?"

"The Carruthers Prize committee didn't see fit to confer the prize upon yours truly."

She tore the flap up and yanked out the envelope's contents and read rapidly.

Thank you for sitting for sitting for the exam for the Carruthurs Prize. We regret that we cannot award all deserving students. Thank you for participating and best of luck...

Beth was crestfallen.

"Whatever am I going to do? How am I going to attend class next year?" She started to sob.

"Come here, Beth."

His embrace wasn't Kerry's, but it was gentle and comforting. Beth let herself relax. It was truly a question of what she would do. What *could* she do? It seemed as though she would have to drop out of medical school and return to work as a nurse. The prospect held no joy for her now.

❖

"Kerry, dearest?" Beth shook her lover awake. "I'm so sorry you got home late last night, but we must talk."

Kerry rubbed her eyes and partially sat up. She yawned. "Sure, Bethy. Maybe you could get me some coffee and *then* we could talk?" She yawned again.

For some reason, the question, the yawns, and Kerry's general lack of urgency aggravated Beth. It wasn't fair. She was home thinking all day, and Kerry was at the Palace working very, very hard for twelve hours at a time. She went downstairs, made some coffee, and carried two cups upstairs. Kerry had arisen and splashed water on her face, put on some clothes, and seemed reasonably alert. She sat on the bed with her hands clasped and raised her eyebrows when Beth came back into the bedroom.

"Ah, this is the best. I'll be alive and ready for anything after a few sips." She took the cup and blew on it, sipping the hot liquid slowly. "What's on your mind, my love?" Her eyes crinkled at the corners, but at present, that failed to charm Beth.

"I'm not sure what to say and how to say it."

"Hmmm. Well. I'll just enjoy my coffee and keep silent."

"You act as though nothing's amiss and all is as usual!"

"Ehh?" Kerry was clearly confused, which made Beth want to shake her. "You know what I mean!"

"No, love. I don't know what you mean." Kerry was maddeningly calm and equable.

Beth could feel herself coming apart. "I'm going to be honest, as we promised one another we would be."

"Of course, my love."

"You've not yet told me how much money you have. I don't have any, and I don't know what I'm going to give you for Christmas. I don't have any money, and I don't know how I'll be able to continue at the Medical Department next year. Should I go back to nursing? Are you truly on the straight and narrow path?"

"Well…" Kerry blinked, looking overwhelmed. "I, uh. I'll show you the book from the bank. We can look at it together. You needn't give me anything for Christmas. Just your lovely self."

"That's the other thing. I'm, er. I would like but I'm not sure...
Oh, bother!" Beth, who was sitting on the bed next to Kerry, raised
her arms and slammed them into her lap in pure exasperation.

Kerry touched her arm. "Beth. I'm not doing anything you
wouldn't approve of. I never will again. I promised you. I meant it.
And I'm willing to wait until you're ready for—"

"I know, it's just..." Beth started to cry. "I'm worried. I don't
know what's going to happen—"

"We aren't in any money trouble until next fall. Am I right about
that?"

"Ye-yes. That's true. But I didn't win the Carruthers Prize, and
how in the world we'll pay for tuition and everything else and—"

Kerry put her arm around Beth and squeezed her. "Shhh. We'll
think of something together. Tomorrow, I have the day off. That's
another thing. I made an agreement with Fermel that I would get
Mondays off. That's the slowest day of the week. I promised him
I could help for a few hours if he really needed me, but he would
have to send someone up here to fetch me or tell me Sunday night.
He's amenable. The man is inordinately fond of flattery. I just tell him
every other day or so how grateful I am to be able to learn from him,
and he puffs up a little and doesn't say anything, but he doesn't abuse
me anymore. It's uncanny—"

"Kerry." Beth was reassured by the story but irritable at the
digression.

"Oh, sorry, love. I understand your worry, but look. It's eight
months until next year's tuition is due. We'll make a plan, I promise."

"Are we going to sit down together and review our financial
situation? You promised you would do that."

"Yes, love, of course. Now come kiss me. I must ready myself
to leave soon."

Beth complied, but she was still unsatisfied. Kerry had made a
lot of promises, but results, not promises, would make a difference.

CHAPTER TWENTY-THREE

Kerry thought about her talk with Beth all day long. She wanted to make Beth feel better, and she wanted to do everything Beth asked, but still she hesitated. When she was eighteen, Addison had had his name removed from her Bank of California savings account and she had sole control. She wanted to help Beth, but she wanted it to be only by her decision and on her terms. This was the only thing she'd ever had that belonged to her alone. She couldn't say what the harm would be if she shared with Beth, but she didn't want to. It was clear, however, that after this traumatic separation, Beth was adamant that they share everything, and that included knowing precisely how much money Kerry had.

The worst part about it was that Kerry knew she didn't have enough, not even for tuition, let alone a house. The cost of daily life alone had depleted her savings. That was what she didn't want to tell Beth: that she'd failed. The only person who could possibly help her with this was Addison. She didn't want to ask him for help, again. She didn't want to tell Beth they needed Addison's help. She didn't want to tell Addison the whole story.

She wanted it all to go away, but it wouldn't. If nothing else, though, when she confessed to Beth they didn't have enough money, she wanted to at least have an alternative plan, one that didn't involve selling moonshine. She was going to have to humble herself and do the right thing. That was the only way Beth would ever trust her and they could return to normal. And she still wondered about this mysterious Scott that Beth talked about all the time.

❖

"It would be easier if you would send me a note and then we could meet at home, but I suppose this is the way you choose and I'm going to have to be amenable." Addison wasn't angry exactly, but resigned. Kerry had arrived at the hospital mid-morning and practically threatened bodily harm if the desk nurse didn't locate him right away.

"I'm sorry, but I have to be at work at noon. This is the last time, I promise."

"I'm not sure you can keep that promise, but please, tell me what I can do to help." He thought he knew the answer, but he wished for Kerry to ask for what she wanted.

"I, uh, I need you to help me get a loan."

"For what, pray, do you need a loan?"

She shut her mouth and seemed ready to not say a thing. Addison was exasperated. His former ward was a stubborn, headstrong young woman. He admired that quality, but she would need to bend a little more and recognize that it wasn't always a weakness to ask for help.

"I can't say."

"Oh, Kerry. Please don't mistake my question as a preface to not agreeing to help you. Quite the contrary. I'll be happy to help you, but I want all the facts."

"Right. I need to find out how I may get a loan so I can pay for Beth's tuition."

"Yes. I imagined that might be the case. Why isn't Beth here with you to discuss this?"

"Because I'm the one who said I'd take care of her. You know what happened, and I have to be able to make good on my promises with Beth."

"What promises are those?" Addison asked, quietly.

Kerry's face fell. "I said I'd always take care of her, always give her what she wanted. She wouldn't have to worry—"

"Kerry. Those are good and generous and heartfelt promises, but they're unrealistic."

Her expression changed from dismay to anger.

"Hear me out, please," Addison asked. "You're not Beth's savior. She doesn't expect you to provide everything."

"No. *I* expect to. It's my duty."

Esther had been so astute. She had discerned precisely what was driving Kerry. He would have to be careful, but he must convince her that other paths existed.

"And so you can, to the best of your ability, and Beth will love you for it. But she doesn't expect miracles, and she certainly has no desire for you to put yourself in danger. That makes her worry. What she doesn't know is worse than what she knows. You're a very long way from the Barbary Coast and your father Jack's ways, aren't you?"

"I thought I was. I wanted to be, but it turned out not to be true." Kerry appeared crestfallen. "And it distressed Beth, and me. I hated myself for what I did."

"So. It's really time for you to consider just what you must do and what you're able to do. Allow me to help Beth secure a school loan."

"No!"

"Kerry. You said you would listen."

"I did, but—"

Addison held up his hand. "Please. Let me explain. "As a student of the Medical Department, Beth is eligible to secure a loan at a very favorable rate from the Bank of Italy. They are amenable to these loans because, as a physician, Beth will one day earn a good salary. She's a good risk, in other words. You're not a good risk, Kerry."

"No. I suppose I'm not."

"So then, I also propose that you and Beth move back to Fillmore Street with Esther and myself. Rent free. We'll all contribute to household expenses."

"With you and Esther?" Kerry's tone was one of wonderment.

"Yes. I'll let her explain all her theories to you next week when you join us for the day-after-Christmas dinner. I presume you'll be on duty for the Palace Hotel's gala banquet."

"Yes. But, Addison. Are you sure? Is this what Beth wants? What will she say?"

"I don't know. You should ask her and see what she says. I have reason to believe she'll agree. We three medical types will keep each other on our toes. You can continue to save your money for the future. This makes perfect sense if you think about it."

Kerry, for once, looked thoughtful rather than angry and nodded. "I'll talk to her as soon as I can."

"Please do. And in the future, you won't, I hope, come barging into the City and County Hospital demanding to see Dr. Grant. Unless it's a true medical emergency." He grinned to lessen the sting and Kerry finally smiled back.

❖

Beth tried to quell her curiosity, which was vexing her and causing her to be short-tempered, but Kerry was in one of her maddeningly uncommunicative moods. She'd only required Beth to accompany her to the park so they could go to the Conservatory of Flowers.

"Do you wish to relive our first real kiss? Is there some reason we're here?" Beth loved the conservatory for many reasons, but this Sunday a few days before Christmas, she was grumpy.

"I'll tell you everything, love. I wanted to be away from the house and in the park for this. Remember when you asked me to do the same?"

"I see." Beth didn't see, though. She'd not quite been in the doldrums she'd experienced prior to talking with Kerry at Addison's house, but she had been waiting, impatiently, for more evidence of either Kerry making good on her promise to be better or the opposite. Yet she'd seen nothing until today.

They walked inside the glass-enclosed building, and again the humid tropical atmosphere enveloped them. The winter sun gave the place an air of renewal as Kerry led Beth to the very back chamber, where "their" bench was located. They sat down and Kerry took Beth's hand.

"I brought you here because we need to be warm, or I would have planned a picnic."

"Are you going to kiss me again?" Beth asked, referring to two years before. She was sorry the question came out sounding irritable.

Kerry didn't react except to shake her head. "No. Not that I wouldn't like to, but that's not why we're here."

She drew a small booklet from her pocket, and Beth saw the title, BANK OF CALIFORNIA, on its red paper cover.

Kerry opened the book and pointed to the last line on the page, which read $320. Beth absorbed this information without comment.

"So now you see. That is the amount of our resources."

"It's not enough, is it?"

"No. Not nearly. You see why I didn't want to share this with you."

"Well, it's distressing but I'm not surprised." Beth was resigned to the cold reality of their predicament. She wouldn't finish school. She would go back to the Presidio to Marjorie and beg for her old posting back. She folded her hands and bowed her head. "Thank you for showing me. It's better that way."

"Yes. I am sorry for keeping silent before. But I have more to tell you."

Beth recoiled inwardly, wondering what crazy idea Kerry would present to her.

"I talked to Addison about our situation. He told me I can't get a loan because I'm a poor prospect. He said, though, that you can obtain one because you're a student. From the Bank of Italy."

"Mr. Giannini?" Beth asked, confused.

"I don't know that name. Sorry, love. Addison said he'd help if they were reluctant to loan money to a woman. But the loans are for students."

"Oh. I see. But we still have to live, and we still have to eat. I don't—"

"Beth. Wait. I'm not finished yet." Kerry took both of her hands in hers and caught her eye. "Addison said we should come back and live with him. And Esther. We needn't pay any rent."

"You're amenable to this?" Beth was suspicious because Kerry's sense of independence and duty would normally prevent her from agreeing to such a proposal. Either proposal, really. She'd been so adamant that she would be the one to take care of them.

"Yes. I have to be, Bethy. I didn't want to admit I couldn't take care of you. That led me to very dangerous decisions and actions, not to mention keeping all of it from you. And, well, you've seen the result."

"I have," Beth whispered. "I've never been so distressed in my life. I thought I should never trust you again, never believe you."

"I was afraid of that as well. And I hated myself so much for what I had to do, or thought I had to do. It was awful."

"It was more than awful. It was terrifying, devastating."

"Yes, it was all that. So I have a new outlook. I see that admitting I cannot do something or that I'm afraid isn't the end of the world. I can ask for help for your sake and for mine."

"Yes. It seems we're not alone in the world."

"No. Addison is our protector and our friend. I didn't want to see that I needed him anymore, but I do."

"So explain this to me in more detail, please." Kerry obliged, and when she stopped talking, Beth was beaming in relief and happiness, and so was Kerry.

"Esther is going to take up residence without Addison and her getting married. My word, she's a bold one. I'm beginning to understand just how unusual she is. Her story of her friend in New York!" Beth shook her head in wonder. "She fascinates me. If not for you, I'd be enamored of her myself."

"Be careful what you say, Bethy, or I may change my mind." Kerry's anger was feigned, because she was smiling, so Beth grinned too.

"Addison said Esther would explain what he called her 'theories' to us at dinner the day after Christmas. We're invited to join them for a late Christmas dinner because I'll be at the Palace on Christmas Day."

"That sounds marvelous. Then we can move in at the New Year? I have to tell Mrs. Thompson soon."

"We can move anytime. Our rent is paid so—" Kerry stopped and then said, "Beth? I don't want to distress you, but I want to know about Scott. You talk about him so much…"

"Are you jealous, Kerry, dearest? Of Scott?" This was ridiculous so Beth decided to have a little fun at her lover's expense.

"No. I'm just curious."

"Well, he's very handsome and intelligent and friendly." She raised her eyes to the ceiling with a dreamy expression.

"Beth…" Kerry was clearly becoming distressed, and Beth decided to stop before they quarreled again. She took Kerry's hand and caught her gaze, paused, then said, "Scott doesn't like women that way. He likes men." She let that information sink in.

Kerry's expression changed from dismay to confusion. "He's not—he's a—?" She couldn't find the word.

"Yes, love. We're best friends and comrades and classmates. It's not as you fear. He doesn't want to court me."

"Oh."

Beth wanted to laugh at Kerry's deflation. She was so endearing and so easy to read.

"Kerry, love. You're the one for me. There will never be anyone else. Never ever. Don't you see?" She squeezed her hand.

"Beth, let's leave and go somewhere private. I really want to kiss you now, and too many people are around here. She grabbed Beth's hand and pulled her off the bench and back through the many rooms of the conservatory until they reached the outside. Behind the building, they leaned against its wall and kissed for a long, long time. Beth couldn't remember the last time they'd kissed like this, over and over, tongues winding, their breaths coming faster.

Kerry finally broke off mid-kiss. "I want to go home right this minute, but I think Mrs. Thompson is about, isn't she?"

Beth couldn't wait another moment for them to get to their bedroom. She stared at Kerry and said, urgently, "She knows about us."

"She what?" Kerry looked alarmed.

"It's no matter anyhow. If she wanted to toss us out, we're going to leave anyhow."

"If you say so, Bethy. Then I'm with you. We must get home, and quickly, before something inside me bursts!"

They sprinted the seven blocks to Divisadero Street and caught the cable car north, where they sat as close together as they could. Beth wanted to climb into Kerry's lap and continue kissing, but she had to content herself with clandestine handholding, their palms warm and moist in spite of the December chill. Beth couldn't breathe. Her sense of Kerry's nearness and her anticipation of what they were about to do made her head swim. She'd kept her bodily needs tamped down in the months of their estrangement. With her happiness, they erupted with blinding force. She might literally come apart before they were able to make it home.

❖

As they removed their coats and scarves in the front hallway, Kerry thought, for some reason, of Laura lurking about Addison's home when they would come home, exhilarated from some outing but anxious to retire to their room and make love. It wouldn't always be so, Kerry thought. Someday, they'd have total privacy. At least, she realized, at Addison's they didn't have to hide their feelings. She no longer cared what Mrs. Thompson thought either.

She went to the kitchen to fetch some water and said a polite hello to Mrs. Thompson, who was preparing supper, but she didn't offer to help. Beth had gone upstairs, and she wanted to join her as quickly as possible. Kerry couldn't wait to feel their bodies press together. As she poured a pitcher of water, took two glasses from the cabinet, and left the kitchen without another word, she thought about her hands on Beth's lovely breasts. She'd help with cleanup later. At the moment, she had more pressing business to attend to.

When she arrived at their bedroom, dusk was starting to fall and Beth had lit the gas lamp on the dresser. She sat on the bed with her hair loosened, brushing it with long, methodical strokes. Kerry stopped in the doorway to admire her.

"You didn't wait for me." She crossed the room and put the water pitcher and glasses on the dresser next to the lamp. She splashed water on her face, hands, and neck.

"Whatever do you mean, Kerry, dearest? I've been waiting for you to come to your senses for months." Her voice was rough but soft, with an undercurrent of laughter.

Kerry dried her hands and sat down on the bed next to Beth. "I meant you didn't wait for me to take your hair down, like I like to do." She ran her hand through Beth's dark blond hair close to her scalp, and Beth shivered as she pulled gently on it.

"Oh. That. Yes. I've forgotten all our little tricks. I only thought to hurry and get ready for you."

Kerry moved her hand from Beth's hair to her cheek, turning her face. "And are you ready for me?" Her words had the effect she desired, as Beth inhaled sharply and kissed her hard.

Against Kerry's mouth, she whispered, "Yes. Please. I can't wait any longer or I may die."

They fought furiously to get out of their clothes. They were fumbling and clumsy but laughed and exchanged many more kisses as, at last, they removed all articles and tossed them aside. Under the quilt and the blanket, their bodies rapidly warmed the space with their combined heat.

Kerry buried her face in Beth's neck, kissing from her ear to her collarbone and reveling in her scent, which reminded her of a warm fall evening. To her surprise, Beth rolled them over until she lay on top of Kerry, her hair a heavy wave on Kerry's face and neck. Kerry pushed it aside to reach skin. Beth pinned her on her back, capturing her leg between her strong thighs, and thrust against her. She was immersed in Beth, her senses overwhelmed. She couldn't move, but she didn't want to. She would stay imprisoned there forever and die, euphoric and serene.

The first wave of their ardor subsided. Beth lay on her back, her arms at her sides, her eyes closed as Kerry touched her gently, almost idly from her throat, over her breasts, her stomach, finally letting her hand come to rest between Beth's thighs as she murmured wordlessly, helpless in her satisfaction. There was nothing else Kerry wanted, nothing she needed, nothing she missed.

After so long a time of being awash in miserable uncertainty and confusion, followed by fury and a sense of desolation, only in retrospect did Kerry understand how bad off she'd been. Those terrible and unsupportable fears were gone. She hadn't longed only for Beth's physical self, but the feeling of safety that Beth gave her. She had a sense of arriving home after an endless, unendurable journey. They were together again and all was as it should be. The universe no longer spun out of control but turned surely and predictably and agreeably, with them safe and serene at the center.

❖

"Kerry, it's a wonder you have the desire to cook anything after your day yesterday."

"Oh, it's no trouble. I'm glad to do it. As I said, after our labors for the banquet, it's easy and pleasurable to cook for merely four people at home."

Addison grinned and passed around the dishes of baked potatoes and roast goose and cranberry. "It's a home to be sure, not composed in the usual way, but a home nevertheless." He caught Esther's eye. She'd moved all her things over the previous week, and they'd had gentle discussions about the placement of some furniture.

He looked out over his table from Esther over to Kerry on his left, Beth on his right, and Esther directly across from him. He was paterfamilias, but not in the usual fashion. Esther and he were cohabiting without benefit of matrimony, and the idea bothered him less than he thought it would. As for Beth and Kerry, well, they were what they were. Esther's explanation sufficed. It didn't matter to him the reason for their love.

"Well, Beth, do you start clinical practice the middle of next term? That's how we did it at Bellevue. It's never too soon to get your feet wet with real patients. Laboratory work is all very well, but you can't learn to be a doctor by picking apart a dead body."

"Or by shocking a dead frog," Beth said, laughing merrily. Addison noted that Kerry once again couldn't stop looking at Beth. And she was visibly more relaxed. The worry lines were gone from her brow, and her expression was calm and contented.

"No, indeed," Addison said. "I was eager to begin practicing examination and diagnosis. But I have to say, it was a trial learning how to extract information from a patient."

"That's because male doctors cow their patients into submission with their superior knowledge," Esther said, causing three pairs of eyes to swing toward her.

Addison said, playfully, "So, Doctor Strauss, pray enlighten us on the correct way to interview a patient."

"To begin with, both men and women will trust a woman doctor more. Our approach is more benign and engaging. Women especially, who might be loath to discuss intimate matters with a male doctor, will willingly disclose crucial facts."

"Oh, that must be true," Beth said. "When I was nursing, the soldiers would tell us all sorts of things, private things. I would have to go and tell the surgeons sometimes. Their egos, bless them, wouldn't let them reveal weakness."

"Exactly!" Esther said. "Now you can use that ability in the service of reaching a diagnosis and planning treatment. It's the one thing that is different about women doctors, and it's helpful rather than the opposite."

"I'm anxious to begin seeing patients. That's the reason for all this education, after all, to serve them," Beth said. "Now I want to take a moment and make a little speech. Please indulge me."

Addison, Esther, and Kerry looked at her expectantly.

"I haven't had a chance to properly thank Addison and Esther for their help. Your support of my medical endeavors has made all the difference. Now that we're to be keeping house with you as well, that extends my debt of gratitude."

Addison and Esther said, at the same time, "Of course," and "It gives us pleasure."

Beth then turned to Kerry and took her hand across the table. "This year has had many difficulties, and it certainly has tested us." She smiled ruefully and Kerry squeezed her hand.

"But that's behind us. We've a new understanding and, with your help," she looked from Addison to Esther and back again to Kerry, "we're on a new path, a much smoother one, I hope. Thank you so very much."

"Hear, hear," Addison said. "Now. The food's getting cold. Let's enjoy what Kerry has prepared for us."

He watched Beth and Kerry hold one another's gaze for another moment. He looked across at Esther, who blew him a kiss. And they settled in to enjoy their delayed holiday feast.

The End

About the Author

Kathleen Knowles grew up in Pittsburgh, Pennsylvania, but has lived in San Francisco for more than thirty years. She finds the city's combination of history, natural beauty, and multicultural diversity inspiring and endlessly fascinating. Her first novel, *Awake Unto Me*, won the Golden Crown Literary Society award for best historical romance novel of 2012.

She lives with her spouse and their three pets atop one of San Francisco's many hills. When not writing, she works as a health and safety specialist at the University of California, San Francisco.

Books Available from Bold Strokes Books

Courtship by Carsen Taite. Love and justice—a lethal mix or a perfect match? (978-1-62639-210-6)

Against Doctor's Orders by Radclyffe. Corporate financier Presley Worth wants to shut down Argyle Community Hospital, but Dr. Harper Rivers will fight her every step of the way, if she can also fight their growing attraction. (978-1-62639-211-3)

A Spark of Heavenly Fire by Kathleen Knowles. Kerry and Beth are building their life together, but unexpected circumstances could destroy their happiness. (978-1-62639-212-0)

Never Too Late by Julie Blair. When Dr. Jamie Hammond is forced to hire a new office manager, she's shocked to come face to face with Carla Grant and memories from her past. (978-1-62639-213-7)

Widow by Martha Miller. Judge Bertha Brannon must solve the murder of her lover, a policewoman she thought she'd grow old with. As more bodies pile up, the murderer starts coming for her. (978-1-62639-214-4)

Twisted Echoes by Sheri Lewis Wohl. What's a woman to do when she realizes the voices in her head are real? (978-1-62639-215-1)

Criminal Gold by Ann Aptaker. Through a dangerous night in New York in 1949, Cantor Gold, dapper dyke-about-town, smuggler of fine art, is forced by a crime lord to be his instrument of vengeance. (978-1-62639-216-8)

The Melody of Light by M.L. Rice. After surviving abuse and loss, will Riley Gordon be able to navigate her first year of college and accept true love and family? (978-1-62639-219-9)

Because of You by Julie Cannon. What would you do for the woman you were forced to leave behind? (978-1-62639-199-4)

The Job by Jove Belle. Sera always dreamed that she would one day reunite with Tor. She just didn't think it would involve terrorists, firearms, and hostages. (978-1-62639-200-7)

Making Time by C.J. Harte. Two women going in different directions meet after fifteen years and struggle to reconnect in spite of the past that separated them. (978-1-62639-201-4)

Once The Clouds Have Gone by KE Payne. Overwhelmed by the dark clouds of her past, Tag Grainger is lost until the intriguing and spirited Freddie Metcalfe unexpectedly forces her to reevaluate her life. (978-1-62639-202-1)

The Acquittal by Anne Laughlin. Chicago private investigator Josie Harper searches for the real killer of a woman whose lover has been acquitted of the crime. (978-1-62639-203-8)

An American Queer: The Amazon Trail by Lee Lynch. Lee Lynch's heartening and heart-rending history of gay life from the turbulence of the late 1900s to the triumphs of the early 2000s are recorded in this selection of her columns. (978-1-62639-204-5)

Stick McLaughlin: The Prohibition Years by CF Frizzell. Corruption in 1918 cost Stick her lover, her freedom, and her identity, but a very special flapper and the family bond of her own gang could help win them back—even if it means outwitting the Boston Mob. (978-1-62639-205-2)

Edge of Awareness by C.A. Popovich. When Maria, a woman in the middle of her third divorce, meets Dana, an out lesbian, awareness of her feelings brings up reservations about the teachings of her church. (978-1-62639-188-8)

Taken by Storm by Kim Baldwin. Lives depend on two women when a train derails high in the remote Alps, but an unforgiving mountain, avalanches, crevasses, and other perils stand between them and safety. (978-1-62639-189-5)

The Common Thread by Jaime Maddox. Dr. Nicole Coussart's life is falling apart, but fortunately, DEA Attorney Rae Rhodes is there to pick up the pieces and help Nic put them back together. (978-1-62639-190-1)

Jolt by Kris Bryant. Mystery writer Bethany Lange wasn't prepared for the twisting emotions that left her breathless the moment she laid eyes on folk singer sensation Ali Hart. (978-1-62639-191-8)

Searching For Forever by Emily Smith. Dr. Natalie Jenner's life has always been about saving others, until young paramedic Charlie Thompson comes along and shows her maybe she's the one who needs saving. (978-1-62639-186-4)

A Queer Sort of Justice: Prison Tales Across Time by Rebecca S. Buck. When liberty is only a memory, and all seems lost, what freedoms and hopes can be found within us? (978-1-62639-195-6E)

Blue Water Dreams by Dena Hankins. Lania Marchiol keeps her wary sailor's gaze trained on the horizon until Oly Rassmussen, a wickedly handsome trans man, sends her trusty compass spinning off course. (978-1-62639-192-5)

Rest Home Runaways by Clifford Henderson. Baby boomer Morgan Ronzio's troubled marriage is the least of her worries when she gets the call that her addled, eighty-six-year-old, half-blind dad has escaped the rest home. (978-1-62639-169-7)

Charm City by Mason Dixon. Raq Overstreet's loyalty to her drug kingpin boss is put to the test when she begins to fall for Bathsheba Morris, the undercover cop assigned to bring him down. (978-1-62639-198-7)

Let the Lover Be by Sheree Greer. Kiana Lewis, a functional alcoholic on the verge of destruction, finally faces the demons of her past while finding love and earning redemption in New Orleans. (978-1-62639-077-5)

Blindsided by Karis Walsh. Blindsided by love, guide dog trainer Lenae McIntyre and media personality Cara Bradley learn to trust what they see with their hearts. (978-1-62639-078-2)

About Face by VK Powell. Forensic artist Macy Sheridan and Detective Leigh Monroe work on a case that has troubled them both for years, but they're hampered by the past and their unlikely yet undeniable attraction. (978-1-62639-079-9)

Blackstone by Shea Godfrey. For Darry and Jessa, their chance at a life of freedom is stolen by the arrival of war and an ancient prophecy that just might destroy their love. (978-1-62639-080-5)

Out of This World by Maggie Morton. Iris decided to cross an ocean to get over her ex. But instead, she ends up traveling much farther, all the way to another world. Once there, only a mysterious, sexy, and magical woman can help her return home. (978-1-62639-083-6)

Kiss The Girl by Melissa Brayden. Sleeping with the enemy has never been so complicated. Brooklyn Campbell and Jessica Lennox face off in love and advertising in fast-paced New York City. (978-1-62639-071-3)

Taking Fire: A First Responders Novel by Radclyffe. Hunted by extremists and under siege by nature's most virulent weapons, Navy medic Max de Milles and Red Cross worker Rachel Winslow join forces to survive and discover something far more lasting. (978-1-62639-072-0)

First Tango in Paris by Shelley Thrasher. When French law student Eva Laroche meets American call girl Brigitte Green in 1970s Paris, they have no idea how their pasts and futures will intersect. (978-1-62639-073-7)

The War Within by Yolanda Wallace. Army nurse Meredith Moser went to Vietnam in 1967 looking to help those in need; she didn't expect to meet the love of her life along the way. (978-1-62639-074-4)

Escapades by MJ Williamz. Two women, afraid to love again, must overcome their fears to find the happiness that awaits them. (978-1-62639-182-6)

Desire at Dawn by Fiona Zedde. For Kylie, love had always come armed with sharp teeth and claws. But with the human, Olivia, she bares her vampire heart for the very first time, sharing passion, lust, and a tenderness she'd never dared dream of before. (978-1-62639-064-5)

Visions by Larkin Rose. Sometimes the mysteries of love reveal themselves when you least expect it. Other times they hide behind a black satin mask. Can Paige unveil her masked stranger this time? (978-1-62639-065-2)

All In by Nell Stark. Internet poker champion Annie Navarro loses everything when the Feds shut down online gambling, and she turns to experienced casino host Vesper Blake for advice—but can Nova convince Vesper to take a gamble on romance? (978-1-62639-066-9)

Vermilion Justice by Sheri Lewis Wohl. What's a vampire to do when Dracula is no longer just a character in a novel? (978-1-62639-067-6)

Switchblade by Carsen Taite. Lines were meant to be crossed. Third in the Luca Bennett Bounty Hunter Series. (978-1-62639-058-4)

Nightingale by Andrea Bramhall. Culture, faith, and duty conspire to tear two young lovers apart, yet fate seems to have different plans for them both. (978-1-62639-059-1)

No Boundaries by Donna K. Ford. A chance meeting and a nightmare from the past threaten more than Andi Massey's solitude as she and Gwen Palmer struggle to understand the complexity of love without boundaries. (978-1-62639-060-7)